The Bell Deception

SHARY CAYA LAVOIE

DEDICATION

To Michele Vachon. A tiny match can light up a darkness, but over a great distance, a cell phone works a lot better.

To Jenny Bradley. How I want to mention the beautiful glow of a candle, the warm flicker of a campfire, the rich sparkle of the starlight. But anyone fortunate to have known and loved you like I did would understand that this description would never be complete without including the dynamic thrill of a firecracker.

To Jeffrey, Jacob, James and Kailyn. You know the light and joy you have given me is eternal.

DFTRM

CONTENTS

ACKNOWLEDGMENTS

I would like to acknowledge Officer James Lavoie of the Roanoke City, Virginia, Police Department for his guidance regarding usual police, courtroom, and jail and prison policies and procedures. I also appreciate his suggestions about various weapons and other criminal and police matters. Without his expertise, my search history would look like something off the FBI's Most Wanted List.

I would also like to acknowledge the State of Maine for putting their Prisoner Handbook online. Valuable information was retrieved from this source to make certain sections of this book as realistic as possible.

It is worth noting that some of the behaviors of members of law enforcement I have written about are purely functions of 'author imagination' and would not be tolerated by any of the law enforcement members I have encountered while writing this book.

Lastly, I would like to acknowledge Izabella Lavoie for her work on the front cover of this book, and Jessica Lavoie for her work on the back cover. It takes a village…

1

The alarm on her cellphone had been set to go off early but Kylie was awake long before she heard its obnoxious beeping. After all, this promised to be an incredibly special day. It was the last Friday in September and the weather forecast called for high temperatures and plenty of sun. It was also her last day of work before a week-long vacation. But mostly, it was her anniversary. On this very day, one year ago, she and Michael vowed to spend the rest of their lives together as husband and wife. Now, after a mere eight hours of work, they were going to celebrate this milestone, this marker of the happiest year of their life.

Michael was in charge of the arrangements. He was planning the odd years; she would do the even ones. She was glad he was taking care of this first year. She was sure he would arrange for the best of everything. That was his way. Tonight, their plans included a drive to

Kabascet to have dinner at Alexander's where they would feast on lobster and prime rib. Michael would order the best champagne; he knew about things like that. Then they would stroll hand-in-hand along the moonlit beach before retiring to the room Michael had reserved for them at the Ocean Harbor Inn. Knowing Michael, it would be the Presidential Suite. They would make love all night and sleep late into the morning. Kylie knew this would be a night they would never forget. Eventually, they would have to rise, but that would be okay because all they would have to do is enjoy breakfast, drive home, and begin their week of vacation. They were not going anywhere or doing anything special, but a week of having Michael all to herself sounded wonderful.

Before any of that could happen, though, she first had to put in her eight hours at Cayne Maine Medical Center. Looking regretfully at Michael as he slept peacefully on his side of the bed, Kylie threw the light blanket aside and stood up. It was time to get ready for work.

Kylie hummed quietly as she slipped into her freshly pressed white pants and tee shirt. She pulled a bright yellow smock over her top and added a matching yellow scrunchie to her long, auburn ponytail. She was so glad scrunchies were coming back in style. She just loved them. She put on her white Skechers and walked over to the bed where Michael slept. She admired his chestnut brown hair, so wavy it curled on the ends. Not being able to resist touching him, she let her fingertips gently push a curl away from his forehead. Then she leaned over and kissed his skin where the curl had been. "Goodbye, sweetheart. See you this afternoon."

Michael mumbled something that may have been, "Bye. Love you, too."

Kylie climbed into her Jeep and started the engine. Ah, what a good life, she thought to herself. She worked five 8-hour day shifts in the intensive care unit at Cayne Maine Medical, which required her to utilize every skill she learned in nursing school. After she and Michael were married, she had planned to switch to three 12-hour shifts, but Michael asked her not to. He said he could not bear being away from her for twelve hours at a time. He was so sincere when he asked her, rolling his big, chocolate-brown eyes, and fluttering his long, thick eyelashes, that she was happy to accommodate his wishes.

She parked in the employee parking lot and made the long walk into the hospital. Once inside, she joined the others who were herding themselves into the elevator. She pressed number five. The doors opened on a drab, olive-green hallway that staff and patients alike referred to as mucous green. Kylie stepped out and headed to the nurses' locker room. Once there she traded her purse and homemade lunch for her stethoscope and name badge. She closed her locker, spun the dial, and headed to the nurses' station for morning report.

The first few hours of her shift passed quickly. She had already suctioned her ventilator patient, Emma Gray, at least a half dozen times. She also bathed her, repositioned her, and restarted her IV, none of these being easy tasks as Emma Gray weighed close to 280 pounds. She grabbed a cup of coffee and sat down to begin her morning charting. It was already after 10:00 AM, surely Michael would be up and in his home office by now. She stared at the telephone, longing to call him, but instead, her attention turned to Carina, the charge nurse, who had suddenly appeared next to the row of beeping heart monitors that were situated just to the left of Kylie.

"Who's up for the next admission?" Carina's loud voice carried over all the other voices and sounds at the nurses' station.

Kylie sighed. "That would be me."

"Okay then, there's a head injury on the way. The E.D. should be here anytime with him. A 34-year-old male involved in a pedestrian versus motor vehicle accident. Apparently, the motor vehicle won. He is being admitted to Dr. Parker's service with a traumatic subdermal hematoma, fractured clavicle, fractured ribs, and the expected lacerations and contusions to the face and upper body. He's here until they decide whether or not he needs a craniotomy. Ellise has Room Ten ready. Are you all set?"

"All set. It's not like this is my first day here, Carina."

"As long as it's not your last."

Kylie laughed as she picked up her tablet and made her way down the brightly lit hall. She went to Room 10 to turn on the cardiac monitor and quickly check the equipment. The rooms were supposed to be in perfect working order, fully stocked, and ready for any type of admission, but experience taught her to verify this for herself.

Soon the E.D. nurse arrived pushing a stretcher with a Mr. Dick Garnet. Kylie spent the next two hours assessing him, cleaning and dressing his lacerations, and hooking up the various monitors and machines that are standard in an ICU. In between these tasks, she continued to run back and forth to suction Emma Gray. She completed Dick Garnet's admission chart and verified Dr. Parker's orders on her tablet. By the time she was done, or at least by the time she came to a possible breaking point, it was lunchtime.

"Marge, can you watch my two for a bit? I'm going to the break room to eat lunch."

"Lunch? You really think you are special, don't you?" Marge chuckled but agreed to watch Kylie's two patients.

Once in the break room, Kylie pulled out her sandwich and yogurt and started to eat. Boring peanut butter and jelly, but that was all she had time to make before heading out this morning. She could have asked Cassie, the housekeeper, to fix something for her, but even after a year of marriage, she just wasn't comfortable with having a daily house staff. She much preferred taking care of things on her own. Then she thought that now would be a good time to call Michael.

She grabbed her cellphone out of her pocket and punched in his number. After the fourth ring, it went to his voicemail. Hmph, for a self-employed, home-based biostatistician, he sure isn't great at answering his phone. Annoyed, she hit the end button and hurried through the rest of her lunch. She could almost hear Emma Gray's throat thicken with mucus as she tried to finish her yogurt. She was reasonably sure that Marge would avoid suctioning her, instead waiting until Kylie returned. Suctioning patients was often the least favorite task of the nursing staff.

The care of two high-acuity patients in an ICU is enough to keep even the best of nurses busy and the rest of the day passed quickly. As change-of-shift approached, Kylie had a tough time keeping her excitement in check. After all, this was the first wedding anniversary she had ever celebrated, and she looked forward to it more than she imagined possible. Nothing could be better than a romantic evening with Michael, especially when it was the start of an entire week with him. He was everything she ever hoped for in a husband and her love for him grew stronger every day.

A few short hours later, it was time to go home. Kylie had to apologize to Paige several times for trying to hurry through change-of-shift report. She rattled off patient vital signs and inputs and outputs so fast that Paige did not have time to grasp a word she was saying. "Again, I am so sorry for talking so fast. It's just that I'm anxious to get started on my romantic evening. Tonight, Michael and I are celebrating…"

"Your first wedding anniversary. Trust me, I got it the first ten times you mentioned it." Paige laughed and gave Kylie a quick hug, wishing her a great vacation. "Just be sure you show up here a week from Monday. We are understaffed, or haven't you heard?"

"I'll be here, although I can't make any promises that

I'll want to be here." With that, Kylie headed to her locker, gathered her belongings, and went to the parking lot. Finally, there was nothing standing in the way of her celebration with Michael except to shower and change into her new dress.

Kylie maneuvered her Jeep through traffic at a pace that was a bit faster than was prudent. She simply could not wait another minute to get home. Her overnight bag was all packed and ready to go, but she still had to shower, fix her hair, and do her makeup. Then she would slip into the low-cut, emerald-green dress that she bought for this special occasion. Michael loved her in green. He said it was the best color to go with her naturally auburn hair.

She pulled into the driveway and hit the button on the overhead console. The garage door slowly lifted. She peered inside and was surprised that Michael's black Lexus was not in its usual space. She wondered where he was. She pulled into her space, the one closest to the entrance of the house, and turned off the ignition. Tossing her keys into the cup holder, she exited the Jeep and went inside.

She started up the stairs to take a shower but came back down and went to Michael's office instead. His computer was off, his file cabinets were closed, and his trays of paperwork appeared not to have been touched today. That was odd, she thought. She clearly remembered Michael telling her he had tons of work to get through. It looked like he had not been in his office all day. She again wondered where he was.

Baffled and a little annoyed, she headed up the stairs for her shower. She walked down the hall and entered the big primary bedroom suite. This was Kylie's favorite room in the entire house, although she had to admit that many of the reasons she was so fond of this room had nothing to do with the décor. She looked around at the rich, creamy beige walls and instantly started to relax. Kicking off her shoes, she felt her toes sink into the plush carpet. She walked across the room to the overstuffed chair, put her feet on the ottoman in front of her, and melted into the rich fabric, enjoying its comfort. Then she thought better of it and sat back up. She didn't dare fall asleep when she had so much to do to get ready for tonight.

The small clock on her nightstand reminded her it was time to get up and head to the shower. The thought of their upcoming evening was the only thing that could convince her to leave the comfort of that chair right now. Once up, she pushed open the door to her dressing room and walked through to her bathroom. As she opened the door, her mouth fell in amazement. Oh Michael, escaped her lips as her hand came over her mouth and her eyes filled with tears. Across the ceramic tile floor, red and pink rose petals were strewn from the doorway where she now stood, just across from the white jetted tub on the other side of the room. The tub was filled with rose-scented water that was still hot enough for wisps of steam to fill the room. On the edge of the tub, Kylie noticed a glass of wine sitting in a crystal bowl of partially melted ice chips. Next to the wine was one perfect, ripe, red strawberry, dipped in rich, brown chocolate. An elegantly wrapped gift was sitting on the granite counter between the two porcelain sinks. On top of the gift was a folded sheet of paper.

Kylie walked to the sink, enjoying the feel of the rose petals as they brushed between her toes. She gently lifted the notepaper and read what Michael had written.

To my beautiful wife of one year,

I know how hard you must have worked today, and I didn't want you to feel rushed as you got ready for our celebration tonight. Please enjoy the treats, linger in the bath, and relax with the wine. As long as you are downstairs by 7:00 PM, we will have plenty of time to make our dinner reservations. I will be patiently waiting in the living room.

Love you,

Michael

Kylie folded the paper and laid it on the counter. Then she picked up the package that was wrapped in shiny, metallic silver paper. She removed the bow and slid her manicured nail under the tape, carefully sliding it along the seam of the wrapping paper. Soon a small, silver box appeared.

Not realizing she was holding her breath, Kylie opened the box. Inside was an exquisite solitaire emerald necklace lost in a sea of diamond accents. The pendant was dangling from a delicate chain of gold in exactly the right length to work perfectly with the dress she was planning to wear that evening. Michael was utterly amazing. He always knew exactly what to do to make her life the best it could be.

With trembling hands, she put the necklace back in the box and set it down on the counter. She stripped out of her work uniform and slid into the warm, steamy bath water. Every muscle in her body relaxed as she soaked in the scented water. She knew she was the luckiest woman in the world.

With ten minutes to spare, Kylie made her entrance into the couple's large living room. Her auburn hair was pulled away from her face and hung in long, smooth waves down her back, held in place with a sparkling clip at the back of her head. Her green eyes shined under long, dark lashes. Her cheeks were rosy above her perfectly symmetrical dimples. She was small in stature, so she wore high heels to bring herself closer to Michael's 6-foot 2-inch frame. Her emerald-green dress was simple, cut low in the front, and fitted snugly against her petite frame. The only embellishment to her outfit was the new necklace that Michael had bought as her anniversary gift. It was the perfect accessory for such a simple dress. When she walked into the living room, she felt pretty. When she saw the look on Michael's face, she felt beautiful.

"You look absolutely divine, my darling. Happy anniversary."

Eyeing Michael in his navy suit and crisp white shirt, a

bright red tie bringing out just the right amount of pizazz, Kylie replied, "Happy anniversary to you, too. You look very handsome tonight. All the other wives celebrating their anniversaries will be so jealous of me. I will be with the most attractive man in the room."

He smiled. "Do you like the necklace?"

"Oh, Michael, it's beautiful. It seems like you always know just what to get. I love it. Thank you. And I love you."

"I love you, too, and I plan to show you just how much tonight. But right now, we must get going so we don't lose our reservation." Michael escorted Kylie to his Lexus to make the 45-minute drive to the restaurant, assuring they would arrive in plenty of time for their 8:30 PM reservation.

The ride was pleasant. The sky was clear, and the weather was unseasonably warm for an evening in September by the coast of Maine. Kylie sat dreamily looking out the window when the romantic tunes they had been listening to on the radio were interrupted by the jangle of Michael's cellphone.

"I'll get it."

Kylie reached for Michael's phone, but Michael gently placed his hand over hers and said, "No, let it go to voicemail. This is our night."

"Michael, what if it's something important? What if it's a new client?" Let me at least read the number off to you." She pulled the phone out of the console and read the number off the screen. It only showed 'private caller.' "Do you recognize the number? Do you know who it is?"

Michael seemed agitated as he responded. "No, I don't know who it is. Don't answer it. Just stick it back in the console where I had it. Or better yet, turn the damn thing off. This is our night. I don't need to talk to a client, new or otherwise."

In silence, Kylie hit the off button on the side of the phone and placed it back in the console. She stared out the window into the darkness, pretending she was admiring Maine's beautiful coastal scenery. Michael tried to appear focused on his driving. To Kylie, this only made him seem preoccupied and distant. She thought about the phone number on his cellphone.

They arrived at the restaurant and waited quietly until their name was called for their reservation. Alexander's was a popular spot with tourists, even this late in the season, and every table was filled. Still, it didn't take long before the maître d' escorted them to one of the small, round tables lining the glass wall overlooking the Atlantic Ocean. Wherever they dined, Michael always managed to get the best table in the restaurant.

Michael ordered a bottle of 1990 Krug Brut Champagne. As they were waiting for it to arrive at their table, he started to seem more relaxed, back to his old self. He admired her eyes, her hair, the sound of her laughter. She gazed into his warm, brown eyes. So lost were they in pledging their undying love for each other, they forgot about time and space and everything except each other.

Eventually, Michael noticed the champagne sitting in

a silver bucket next to their table. Their server quickly appeared and poured a flute for each of them. Michael took Kylie's hand into his, smiled at his wife, and toasted their first year of marriage. "Here's to us," he began. "May our next year be as happy as the first."

Kylie raised her glass and smiled. "To our sacred vows."

For the next two hours, Kylie and Michael waded through several courses of delicious food. They gorged themselves on hot bread, soup, salad, lobster thermidor, prime rib au jus, and finally, chocolate rennet with raspberry sauce. Kylie felt like she could barely move after eating so much, yet she insisted it was well worth the extra miles she would have to log on the treadmill. Michael assured her that just to be with her made everything worthwhile.

Feeling full, relaxed, and content, they walked to the front of the restaurant. Michael thanked both the server and the maître d'. Kylie had to use the ladies' room, so Michael insisted that she wait for him in the restaurant while he retrieved the car from its distant parking space in the city garage. Very few businesses in the downtown area had their own parking lot and Alexander's was no exception. With a quick kiss, Michael stepped outside into the night.

Just 15 minutes later, as Kylie watched from the entrance of the restaurant, Michael pulled up and opened her car door. She climbed into the vehicle and they made the short drive to the oceanfront for a moonlit stroll along the beach. Michael drove cautiously through the still-busy downtown area, his eyes darting left and right as he guarded against both vehicular and pedestrian traffic venturing out in front of him. He frequently checked his rear-view mirror.

"You seem a little on edge, honey. Is there something wrong?"

"No, I'm fine. Just watching out for these damn tourists. They're everywhere this time of year. I swear, the leaf-peepers are worse than the summer crowd."

"Well, okay. I just want to make sure you are enjoying our anniversary as much as I am."

Michael reached for Kylie's hand and squeezed it tightly. "You know I am, babe. I'm just trying to keep us safe."

Kylie leaned back in her seat and smiled. "I know you are. And you know there is nothing I wouldn't do for you, either."

The next few blocks passed in silence, each lost in their own thoughts. They both had a dreamy look of wonder on their faces. Finally, Michael pulled into a space in the lot next to the public beach and parked the Lexus. Kylie quickly switched from her heels to a more sensible pair of flats and Michael helped her out of the vehicle. She grabbed her purse and a light wrap. Now that the sun was down, the night was not as warm as it had been.

Michael casually put his arm around her shoulder and pulled her close to him. He looked admiringly at his wife of one year. At 28, Kylie could easily pass as a college coed, so petite and fresh-faced, it was hard to believe she had been working as a nurse for the past six years. Her green eyes shined in the moonlight under her dark, sweeping lashes. Her skin was clear and creamy, her nose thin and upturned. Her lips, outlined tonight in a coppery-red lipstick, were full and voluptuous. As Michael well knew, they were also soft and sensual. To a stranger, Kylie would appear happy and confident, but to Michael, she looked like a lost, young girl, still trying to break free of a troubled past.

Kylie noticed him staring at her. She smiled coyly, but still, he stared. Finally, she asked, "What are you thinking about?"

"I'm thinking about how beautiful you look tonight."

Kylie stopped walking and faced Michael. She reached her arms inside his coat jacket and wrapped them tightly around his waist, pulling his body to hers. She could feel the taut, lean muscles of his back. She pressed against him and grinned. "Are you sure that's all you're thinking about?"

Michael laughed. "Alas, you know me so well." He put his hands on each side of her face, tilting her head until she was looking up at him. Slowly he leaned toward her, lips parted. She tipped her head upwards to accept his kiss. His kiss was gentle at first, tasting of sea salt and sweet desire. His lips pressed into hers, his tongue persuading her mouth to open further. He rubbed his body against hers. She could feel his warm breath as his breathing quickened and his kiss became harder, more demanding. His fingers splayed outward and slid into the nape of her hair. She felt the passion in each fingertip as he stroked the back of her head and neck. A gentle moan escaped her lips when his hand brushed against her bare back. His mouth moved from hers, sweeping over her cheek and neck. "Do you know what I want to do now?" he murmured breathlessly in her ear.

She sighed and opened her eyes. "What do you want to do now? I would love to hear the details."

"I want to throw you down on the sand right here, right now. But seeing as there are people around, especially a rather irate mother with two adolescent boys who cannot stop staring at us, we better start walking instead."

"Okay but tell me one thing. What kind of mother has kids that age on the beach this late at night?" Kylie laughed. Then she added, "You know, stopping in the middle of this is going to be hard."

"It's a lot harder than you know," Michael added with a wink.

They finally broke apart and started walking along the shore, shoes in hand and water lapping at their feet. They didn't talk much. They didn't need to. The feelings they shared were expressed so much more with their silence than their words could ever convey.

They strolled through the sand and water, unaware of anything but each other. As the hour became late, the beach became deserted. Michael stopped and looked around. It was completely dark outside, the only light coming from the faint sliver of a silver moon. They could see the pier directly in front of them. Michael took Kylie's hand and led her away from the water and across the still-warm sand. They plotted a path through the seaweed and driftwood, finally approaching the worn steps of the pier. Kylie clutched Michael with one hand, her purse with the other, and they made their way up the stairs to the top of the pier.

"Oh, Michael, it's beautiful up here." Kylie looked around as she walked along the deserted pier. The ocean water extended as far to the east as the eye could see, finally merging with the black, star-filled sky. The crescent moon cast a thin, silver sheen across the water. Kylie continued walking toward the end of the pier making slow, twirling movements so she could appreciate the view from all sides. Michael watched her in amusement, finally joining her by the rail at the far end of the pier.

He came up behind her, wanting to touch her, afraid if he did, he might not be able to stop. She leaned back against his chest and he ran his hands up and down the length of her bare arms. "You're cold."

"Mmm, a bit. I should have brought something a little heavier than this wrap. I always forget how chilly it can be by the ocean."

"Typical woman," Michael laughed. "You forget to bring something practical, like a warm sweater, but you have your purse."

A smile played across Kylie's mouth. "Chauvinist," she mumbled as she turned and faced Michael, again sliding her hands around his waist. "I know what I need."

"I take it this means you need the warmth of my suit

jacket?" He removed his coat and laid it over Kylie's shoulders.

The two of them made their way to the very end of the pier. They were alone with only the moon to light their way. Kylie looked over the rail of the pier. From here the ocean water looked almost black, deep and swirling, as it hit against the posts. Kylie turned to Michael and looked into his eyes, so dark against the night backdrop. She ran a finger across his cheek, her thumb resting on his full lower lip. He moved towards her and their mouths met. Their kiss was slow and tender.

As they kissed, Kylie unwrapped her arms from Michael and pulled his coat tightly around her. Then she fiddled with her purse so it wouldn't slip from her shoulder. With one hand clutching her bag, she reached her other around his waist, again pulling him closer. She could feel the warmth of his body against hers.

Suddenly a loud splash came from the inky, swirling water below. "What was that?" Michael broke the kiss to look over the rail.

"Be careful, Michael." Kylie pulled on his arm to hold him back. "Don't hang over the rail so far. You're going to fall right in."

Michael gently shook her off and continued to scan the water below. "Did you hear that splash?"

Kylie also peered over the rail but could see nothing but the water as it lapped the legs of the pier. "Could it have been a fish?"

"Well, it must have been a big one to make a noise

like that. It sounded like it bounced right off one of the posts."

"Maybe a stupid fish? Maybe a fish not in a school?" Kylie laughed. "Get it, a fish not in a school? School of fish?"

Michael groaned. "I hope that was the champagne talking and you don't really think that was funny." He stopped searching the water with his eyes and glanced at Kylie. As always, the grin on her face warmed his heart. "You're still cold. Let's get going."

"Okay but tell me one thing. Do you want to leave because I'm cold, or because you're hot?"

"Well, you've got me there." He took her hand in his and they headed down the pier, stopping only long enough to slip their shoes on. Then they went back to their vehicle. It was dark and late, and the champagne was having an effect on Kylie. She dozed during the ride to the inn.

After checking in, Kylie and Michael took the elevator to the fourth floor, which was the highest floor of this quaint, seaside inn. They stepped off the elevator and walked across the hall. Michael unlocked the door and stood back for Kylie to enter the room first.

She looked around the suite in awe. As always, Michael had outdone himself. The room was exquisite. It wasn't a modern room; this inn had made its stand by the ocean long before either Kylie or Michael had been born. Yet it offered a charm and elegance that the new high-rise hotels just couldn't provide. The walls were the palest of blue, which complemented the polished oak floors that may have been original to when the inn was built. The king-size bed on the far left had a white, shiplap headboard and a thick, down comforter. The comforter was plain white but looked warm and inviting. On either side of the bed was a nightstand, and over each nightstand was a brass wall light, giving a hint of a nautical theme without being obvious. Across from the bed was a small sitting area with a worn blue couch and two wooden rocking chairs. There were a dozen yellow tulips in a white vase sitting on the coffee table. Leave it to Michael to find yellow tulips, her favorite, in September. One entire wall of the room was glass. The blue striped curtains were pulled to one side revealing the dark ocean lit with a ribbon of silver by the crescent moon. Kylie could hear the waves as they rushed, never-ending, to the shore. Overall, the room was quintessential New England.

She opened one of the French doors and stepped out on the balcony. The balcony held two white Adirondack chairs topped with thick, blue-and-white striped cushions. Between the chairs was a small, white table with a clay pot filled with bright red geraniums. Kylie could easily picture herself enjoying lazy afternoons sitting in one of those chairs watching the people below as they frolicked along the shore. But now she could feel the ocean breeze going right through her, so she stepped back inside and closed the door.

Michael was stretched on the bed, shoes off and shirt unbuttoned. He had been watching her with a grin on his face and eyes full of passion. She walked to his side of the bed but as soon as she was within arms' reach, he pulled her onto his lap. Twisting sideways to face him, Kylie looked deeply into his eyes. How could she be so lucky as to be able to call this man her husband? Her love for him was so complete, so overpowering, that she no longer felt in control of herself. She leaned over and kissed him.

At some point, their time together ended, and they both fell asleep on top of the thick white comforter. The room was dark except for a hint of light coming from the window. Kylie awoke suddenly, her heart racing. Someone was banging on their door. She glanced at the clock; it was just after 3:00 AM. Who would be banging on their door at this hour? "Michael, Michael, wake up."

Her command was unnecessary. Michael was already pulling himself upright. He searched the floor for his pants. The banging continued, this time followed by, "Police, open the door."

"The police? Oh my God, what is going on? Michael! Do they have the wrong room?"

"I don't know, but I'd like for us to have some clothes on before I open the door to find out."

Michael finally snapped on the bedside lamp and found his pants on the floor near the foot of the bed. He pulled them on and looked over at Kylie, still naked, struggling to unzip her leather overnight bag.

"Police. Open the door now or we're coming in."

"Uh, just a minute, officer." Michael turned to Kylie, amazed that even while the police were threatening to barge into their room for reasons unknown to either one of them, the sight of her naked body still caused his breath to quicken. "Kylie, no time. Just get back in bed and cover yourself up. I'll see what they want."

"Michael, I'm not dressed. I need my clothes."

"I said there's no time. They're going to walk in here any second. Please, get under the covers."

The logic of Michael's words registered and Kylie ran back to the bed, quickly pushing aside the decorative pillows and sliding under the blankets. Michael walked toward the door, still zipping his pants. He glanced over his shoulder to make sure Kylie was safely tucked under the covers and reached for the door. Before his hand even made contact with the doorknob, however, the door slammed inward. Three officers wearing khaki pants and navy-blue tee shirts, all with olive green vests stamped with the words US MARSHALL, entered the room. They were followed by one man wearing a dark gray suit, clearly a plainclothes law enforcement officer.

"What's going on? Who are you looking for?" Michael looked from one officer to another trying to find answers. Kylie shivered as she clutched the blankets over her chest.

"Michael? Michael Clifford Bell?" The older, gray-haired man in the suit approached Michael.

"Yes, that's me. But what is this all about? What do you want with me?"

"Turn around, please. I am Detective Jennings of the Kabascet Police Department." The detective said this in a steady and methodical monotone, however, he made no attempt to explain why they had entered the room.

Instead, he reached under his gray sport coat and pulled out a pair of silver handcuffs. Slightly rougher than was necessary, he clamped the handcuffs around Michael's wrists.

Michael looked dazed. From the bed, Kylie yelled, "What are you doing? Why are you arresting my husband?"

The detective ignored Kylie and continued with Michael. Handcuffs in place, he began reading him his rights.

Kylie was frightened. She had no idea what to do. Neither the officers nor the detective were telling them anything. She started to panic as they led Michael toward the door. "Michael, don't go. Michael, what do I do?" She felt a scream fight its way out from the pit of her stomach. Forgetting that her nearest item of clothing was strewn somewhere across the floor of the room, she started to get out of bed, desperately wanting to keep Michael in her sight.

Michael looked back at his wife. He noticed, at the same time one of the Marshalls noticed, that her blanket had slipped down from her shoulder, exposing the soft, pink tissue of her breast. "Why you…" Michael shook loose of the detective and tried to force his way to the uniformed officer. Before he succeeded in taking even one step toward him, the detective grabbed the handcuffs that were securely fastened around his wrists and yanked upwards. Pain shot through Michael's upper arms. "Want to add resisting arrest, buddy?"

Crying hysterically now, Kylie readjusted the blankets

and started to follow Michael as he was hauled out of the room. Just as they passed through the door, she heard the detective say to Michael, "Michael Clifford Bell, you are under arrest for the murder of Louis Joyce."

Then Michael was gone. The detective was gone. The three Marshalls were making their way out of the room. The more lecherous of the three Marshalls paused to pick something up off the floor. Smiling, he turned back toward Kylie and threw her black lace panties on the bed. "Have a good evening, ma'am." Then he walked out of the room and pulled the door shut behind him.

Kylie was alone.

2

The handcuffs had finally been removed and Michael rubbed his wrists. He was alone now, but he had no doubt that he was being watched from the other side of the glass. He had been searched, fingerprinted, photographed, and swabbed; each procedure more humiliating than the last. Now he was sitting in a small, gray room, barefoot, wearing only a pair of navy pants. His belt and wallet had been confiscated. He had a worn blanket loosely draped across his shoulders. The only furnishings were the metal table bolted to the floor in the center of the room and the two chairs on either side of it. The air was hot and heavy, but still, Michael shuddered as he sat in the harsh light. They couldn't question him while he was sitting here waiting for his attorney, but they sure as hell could have provided him with a shirt and some shoes. Michael started to raise the now cold coffee to his lips, but then he remembered the numerous times he had asked to use the men's room with no response. He set the coffee down without taking a drink.

Elbows on the table, he rested his head in his hands. He was being accused of murdering Louis Joyce. How could this be happening? How did anyone know he even knew Louis Joyce? And where the hell was Phil? With all the money he paid that legal leech, he would have expected him to show up within seconds of hanging up the telephone.

Michael tried to figure out the mess he was in. He went over it and over it, but as always, his mind drifted back to Kylie. He kept thinking about her, stuck in that bed, looking so lost and vulnerable, while they hauled him away. She wasn't any more successful at keeping it together than she was at keeping the blanket wrapped around her body. And that cop who stared at her. As soon as Phil got here, he wanted that little prick dealt with. He was out for blood with that one.

The minutes turned into hours. Michael sat there shivering from either cold or nerves, he wasn't sure which. He tried to figure out his situation, but no matter how hard he concentrated, his thoughts continuously went to Kylie. He was sick with worry. Would she know what to do? Was there someone she could call for help? She had no family to speak of, and while she had many acquaintances, she didn't have any real friends. He was always the one she turned to for support. How he wished he could be there for her now.

He sat there lost in his thoughts, nauseous with worry, when he heard voices just outside the door. He tried to focus on what was being said, but the sounds were muffled and distant. Finally, the door opened and Phil Ackervale walked in. Phil was the same age as Michael, but with his balding head, thick, black-framed glasses, and the extra 15 pounds he carried around his middle, he appeared to be several years older.

"Phil, it's about friggin time. What took so long?"

Phil stood there, the only time since college that Michael had ever seen him with a rumpled shirt, jeans, and tennis shoes instead of his usual Brooks Brothers suit and Ferragamo Oxfords. "In case you weren't aware, Michael, you called me out of a sound sleep at 5:00 on a Saturday morning. I got here as quickly as I could. Now, tell me, what is going on? What kind of a mess have you gotten yourself into? They tell me that they've got you dead to rights for murder. Detective Jennings says it doesn't look good. It's only been a few hours, and they have an overwhelming amount of evidence."

"I, I don't know." Michael stared straight ahead as he spoke, rubbing his hands together. "I was out with Kylie. It was our anniversary and we wanted to celebrate. We planned a special night and everything was fine. We had dinner. We walked on the beach. Then we went back to our room. But somehow the police got this ridiculous notion that I murdered some guy. Louis Joyce. And here I am."

Michael slumped in his chair. Tired, actually exhausted, and physically sick with worry and fear. Nothing made sense to him anymore. This was supposed to be a time of celebration. Instead, he was sitting here trying to convince his lawyer that he wasn't a murderer. This couldn't be real. How could any of this be real?

"Michael, don't lose it now. Pull yourself together. We've got a lot to get through if there's any hope of getting you out of here."

"Out? You can get me out?"

"I think we can arrange to get you out on bail. But it will cost you."

Michael stared at his lawyer, his friend for over 15 years. Like Michael, Phil was 38 years old, but unlike Michael, he didn't worry about healthy eating, going to the gym, or getting any more exercise than walking from the parking lot to the courthouse. Where Michael would only indulge in red meat and dessert on rare occasions, Phil believed that steaks and ice cream should be a daily event. The two always joked that with the way justice in the world worked, Michael would be the one to have a heart attack at 50, while Phil would live to be 90. To a stranger, a first glance at Phil might lead one to think he was a bit confused, or perhaps even dimwitted. But Michael knew better. Phil was one of the smartest people Michael had ever met, and certainly the sharpest attorney around. After all, Michael was not used to settling for anything less than the best. "Just get me out of here, Phil. And get them to let me see Kylie. I don't care what it costs. Money is no object."

****

Kylie lay alone in the king-size bed, crying and

despondent. What was she going to do? Their celebration wasn't supposed to turn out this way. This wasn't the way it was planned. She curled her fists into tight balls and slammed them into the pillow. She kicked her legs. Loud moans escaped her lips. Yet none of it made any difference. Michael was gone and she had no idea what to do about it.

She lay there for a long time but finally came to the realization that any action on her part, right or wrong, would be better than just lying there. She pulled herself away from the bed, grabbed her overnight bag, and went into the bathroom. She was startled to see the reflection that stared back at her from the mirror. Her long hair hung in tangles around her drawn face. Her eyes were red and swollen with lines of eye shadow thick in the creases below her brow. Black streaks of mascara covered her cheeks.

Splashing water on her face proved fruitless so Kylie turned on the shower and let the warm, soothing water pour over her. She finished quickly and dressed in black denim capris and a rose tank top. She tied her hair back in a loose bun and pulled black Nike slides from the bottom of her overnight bag. It was early and the air would still be cool, so she unpacked a front zip sweatshirt and threw it on the bed.

She packed the rest of their belongings and looked around the room to make sure she wasn't missing anything. This room was supposed to be the highlight of their anniversary celebration. Everything had been perfect. Now she could only see the horror that was encompassed by these four walls. How could it go from so right to so wrong? Michael had been arrested. Hauled out like a common criminal. That image played over and over in her mind. But this wasn't a case of repetition breeds affection. It was insanity. They were wrong. Michael was a good man. He wouldn't hurt anyone, let alone kill someone. She had to straighten this out. She took a final look around and gathered their belongings. Then she left the room, slamming the door behind her.

The clerk at the inn had been helpful, even discreet, providing Kylie directions to the police station. Kylie wondered if that had been the same clerk who gave the police a key to their room just a few short hours before. She shook that thought from her mind. It didn't matter. It's not like the clerk would have a choice in the matter. She would have cooperated in the same way if the police had shown up on her nursing floor.

She started Michael's Lexus and drove carefully, afraid that the uniformed police officer from last night would be watching her and would try to find some excuse to stop her. She didn't need to worry, the U.S. Marshalls didn't pull people over for speeding, but Kylie's mind was not operating with that much logic. She was running on pure emotion. Luckily, she didn't have to drive far.

She parked the Lexus across the street from the small brick building with Kabascet Police Department engraved in the white cement over the front doors. She didn't notice the blue sky or the golden leaves on the maple trees in front of the building as she crossed the street. She felt nothing but trepidation as she entered through the front door. Although this was a small police department in a historic section of the town, once inside the building, it had a very modern feel to it. The waiting room was rectangular with chairs lined in neat rows across the room, not quite the wooden benches she had been expecting. There were no windows and only one door other than the entrance. There was a large reception window made of thick layers of glass, so thick that Kylie assumed it was bulletproof. Behind the glass sat a woman of about 40. She had dark eyes and dark hair. She did not wear a uniform, but she did have a badge that indicated her last name was Myers. When Kylie approached the window, the receptionist held up her index finger indicating that Kylie should wait. Kylie stood there, unknowingly tapping her fingers against the sides of her legs, for what felt like an eternity. Finally, the receptionist hung up the telephone and pushed a button activating a speaker in the waiting room.

"Can I help you?"

Kylie gave her name and explained who she was. She asked if she could see her husband. Myers, the receptionist, pointed to the chairs and told her to have a seat, someone would be out to get her in a few minutes.

Kylie sat on a blue vinyl chair closest to the reception window and folded her arms across her chest. The room was warm, but she was shivering. She was tired and scared and felt utterly alone. She didn't understand why she hadn't heard from anyone. Didn't Michael get at least one telephone call? And what about his lawyer? Did Phil know what happened? She wished she knew what was going on.

Then she started thinking about last night. Everything had been going so well. The dinner, the beach, the inn. It couldn't have been planned any better. It was perfect. She could taste the champagne they shared. She could see the warmth in Michael's brown eyes as he smiled down at her just before he kissed her. She could feel his arms around her, pulling her close. They shared so much. How could it have all gone so wrong, she asked herself for the 100th time that morning.

She heard a phone ring from somewhere on the other side of the glass and looked up. No one was paying any attention to her. She wiped a tear away with her finger and tried to escape from the present again with thoughts of last night, but the moment had passed. Instead, she looked around the bleak waiting room of the police station. Gray walls, blue chairs, polished concrete floor, a few scattered end tables with nothing but dust on them. The room did nothing to calm her insides. With every sound she jerked her head up, sure someone was coming through the door to take her to see Michael. Every time she was proven wrong.

She sat there for a very long time. She looked around the room trying to find something even remotely interesting to stare at, but there was nothing. The walls were bare. Finally, the door opened and a tall, blond police officer by the name of Kent Dumas appeared before her. "Mrs. Bell? Would you follow me, please?"

Kylie jumped up and followed Officer Dumas through the thick metal door. She heard a distinct click as the door closed and automatically locked behind her. "Mrs. Bell, if you would come in here. We're going to do a quick security check before bringing you back to the holding cell. If you could please pass me your purse."

Kylie handed the officer her purse to search while a female officer joined them in the small room. First, the officer used a hand-held wand to check Kylie for weapons. Then she patted her down, a bit more thoroughly than she ever had done while passing through airport security. Kylie tolerated the humiliation without expression; she would do whatever was necessary to see Michael. Once they decided she was clean, Officer Dumas again asked her to follow him.

They crossed the hallway and went down a flight of stairs. The heavy door opened onto another hall that led to two sets of double doors. Kylie noticed that the first set of doors closed and locked before the second set opened. Once they passed through both sets of doors, the hallway widened enough to accommodate a curved desk in the corner of the room. Two additional police officers were seated behind the desk. Across from them was another short hallway, this one with three jail cells lining its interior.

"Before we go down there, ma'am, you must understand that this is not the usual procedure. Visitors are generally not allowed back here in the actual holding cell area."

"But I'll get to see Michael, won't I?"

"Yes, ma'am, just for a minute. Now, there are a few rules I need to tell you. If you break any of the rules, you will be immediately escorted out of the cell area."

"Yes?" Kylie tried not to show her impatience while listening to the officer explain what she was and was not allowed to do. Her mind kept jumping to Michael. She only wanted to see him.

"First, you will not be allowed to enter the cell and your husband will not be allowed to come out. You may approach him, but you will not be left alone. Please do not ask me to excuse you while you talk because I will be within hearing distance at all times. Second, you may not hand any item to your husband, or accept any item from him. Third, when I say your time is up, I expect you to exit the cell area quietly and immediately. There will be no long goodbyes. Do you understand each of these rules?"

"Yes, yes, I understand," Kylie said while twisting her wedding ring around her finger. "How long will I have with him?"

"Just a few minutes, ma'am. As I previously stated, this is not standard procedure. Now, before we go any further, are you willing to follow each of the rules as I have outlined them to you?"

Desperately needing to see Michael, Kylie eagerly shook her head. "Yes, I agree. I will follow your rules. Now can I see Michael?"

Officer Dumas proceeded down the hall with Kylie close at his side. Her short legs were almost in a run to keep up with his brisk stride. Then, right before her, sitting on a dirty cot in the only occupied cell, was Michael.

"Michael, oh Michael, are you alright?" Kylie rushed to the cell, trying to reach her hands between the black iron bars.

"Kylie!" Michael jumped from his cot and raced to the cell closest to where she stood. "I am so happy to see you. I didn't know they would let you come down here. They told me I wouldn't see you until the arraignment on Monday." His strong hands reached for hers and he held her, tight. Frustrated that he couldn't take her in his arms like he longed to, but relieved just to let his fingers brush against hers, he moved closer to the bars.

"Michael, what is going on? Why do the police think you murdered someone? Who? When?" Kylie fired question after question rapidly at Michael, appearing anxious as she was trying to understand the mess he was in.

"They say I killed this guy, Louis Joyce. He was shot last night in an alley right near the restaurant where we had dinner."

"Louis Joyce?" Who is he? Do you even know him? Why do they think you did it?"

"Ya, I know him, and I guess it is pretty obvious to the police that I wasn't too fond of him. But I didn't kill him, Kylie. I would never do that. You have to believe me. No one here does, but I need to know that you believe me."

"Of course, I believe you. How can anybody think you would kill anyone? That's not who you are. But how could they think you did this last night? You were with me the entire time."

"I tried to explain that to them, but nobody would listen. Plus, Phil told me that my wife as an alibi isn't very convincing. And after we left the restaurant, we were on the beach, alone, for a very long time. Oh, God, Kylie, I don't know what to do. I just want to hold you, to touch you. I love you so much. I can't stand being separated from you like this."

Tears freely poured down Kylie's cheeks as she tried to lose her hand further into Michael's. "I love you, too, and somehow this will all work out. It has to. Innocent men are not sent to jail. They'll realize that you didn't kill anyone. That you couldn't kill anyone."

Officer Dumas took a step closer to them and announced that she would have to leave in one minute, so they needed to say goodbye. Kylie stared into Michael's brown eyes. "What do I do? Where do I go from here?"

"I saw Phil this morning. He knows everything that is going on. I asked him to talk to you, to fill you in, so we can figure out how this horrible mistake happened."

Officer Dumas stepped close to Kylie. "Time is up. Let's go."

She started to shake her head no. "I don't want to leave. I need more time. Michael?"

"You have to go, Kylie. There's nothing you can do here. Meet with Phil, and do what he tells you. I trust him. He is our only hope at making them understand what a terrible mistake they are making."

Officer Dumas placed his hand gently on Kylie's shoulder. "It's time to go, ma'am. Now."

As Officer Dumas led her away, Kylie turned and looked back at Michael. He was just standing there in his orange pants and shirt, not moving, watching her go. She cringed seeing him locked in that filthy cell like a caged animal. Not even trying to stop the tears from running down her face she cried out, "I love you, Michael. I love you."

Michael stared after her, trying to smile. He was trying to appear strong for her sake, but inside he felt the pain of his situation seep into his heart. He had never felt so alone and so afraid in his entire life. "I love you too, babe," he mouthed to her as she walked away from him.

After she left Michael, Officer Dumas brought her back upstairs to one of the interrogation rooms. He left and within just a few minutes she was joined by Detective Lee Jennings of the Homicide Squad. Detective Jennings asked her if she was comfortable. Then he brought her a cup of hot coffee. His attempt at kindness was wasted on her. He was the same man who put handcuffs on her husband the night before. She already hated him. He started questioning her about the events of last night. He had her start with what happened from the time they left the house until the time Michael was arrested. At first, she went over everything fairly quickly. He was putting together a timeline of events, trying to get times and places in order. Then he started repeating his questions, asking for more details.

For the next several hours they reviewed every move she and Michael made last night, from the time they left the house until the police showed up at the inn.

Detective Jennings taped their interview. He took notes. He asked her the same questions repeatedly. Sometimes he would change the form of the question, but it was still the same question. He had her start at the beginning of the evening. A few times he would have her start in the middle. Twice he had her go over the evening from end to beginning. No matter how many questions he asked her, or how many ways he asked, her story never wavered. Yes, they were together all night at the restaurant. No, they didn't talk to anybody at the beach. They went directly from the beach to the inn. They did not make any stops along the way. Kylie found the questioning frustrating. Detective Jennings was never going to trip her up. Her story was not going to change no matter how many times she told it.

Suddenly there was a loud knock at the door. Before Detective Jennings even finished saying 'Come in' the door burst open. A uniformed police officer, closely followed by Phil Ackervale, entered the room.

"What the hell you doing, Lee? You know you shouldn't be questioning my client's wife without notifying me first. I know you're a big fan of bending the rules, but this? Stooping a bit low even for you, don't you think?"

"Why Phil, how nice to see you. Coffee?"

"Knock it off, Lee. No, I don't want coffee. I've come to collect my client's wife. You know, the one with spousal privilege. The one you had no right to be interrogating."

"Interrogating? Now Phil, don't be silly. Mrs. Bell and

I were just having a conversation. She was in here of her own accord. She was free to leave at any time. No one was forcing her to stay here." Detective Jennings looked directly at Kylie. "No one told you that you had to stay here, right, Mrs. Bell? We weren't holding you here by force, were we, Mrs. Bell?"

Kylie shook her head and started to respond but Phil cut her off. "Not another word, Kylie. He has no right to be questioning you. Just gather up your things, and let's go back to your house."

Unsure what was happening, Kylie picked up her purse and without a word to anyone stood up and walked out of the small room. Once she was in the hallway, she was joined by Phil. Phil took her by the elbow and briskly led her down the hall toward the main entrance. He didn't say a word to her until they had exited the building. Once outside in the warm September air, he released his grip on her arm and turned to face her.

"Kylie, from now on, please do not speak to anyone without my being present. As Michael's wife, they have no right to talk to you."

"They were just asking what we did last night. We have nothing to hide, Phil. Michael didn't do anything wrong."

"That may be, but we don't want them to have the ability to twist your words. Telling the truth isn't always enough. You and Michael are going to be paying me a great deal of money to defend him, and quite honestly, I'm exceptionally good at what I do. So please, listen to what I tell you."

Kylie was at her breaking point. Michael was in jail. She didn't know what she could say or not say. Phil was upset with her. She was alone and didn't know what to do. She started to cry. "I'm sorry, Phil. They didn't tell me I could leave. They just started asking me questions."

"It's all right, Kylie. We'll figure it out. Just don't talk to them without me again. No matter what they say. Also, don't talk to any reporters. Don't trust anyone, okay? Only me. I'm the only one looking out for Michael's best interest."

"Okay, Phil, but what do I do now?"

"For right now, go home. Go home, pull your shades, lock your doors, and stay put. Don't answer the phone and don't open the door. Unless it's me. I'll come over soon and we can start going over the details of the case. Nothing is going to happen until Monday, so you have the weekend to get yourself together. I'll be over and explain to you what to expect on Monday. Okay? Just take care of yourself until then. Michael is going to need you."

Kylie nodded. Then she turned away and made her way back to Michael's Lexus. The drive home was long and lonely. Kylie couldn't shake the feeling that she was deserting Michael by leaving him behind. On more than one occasion she had to pull to the side of the road to calm down and wipe the tears from her eyes.

Finally, she made the left-hand turn onto Willow Brook Lane. She drove the three miles to the very end of the cul-de-sac where their spacious, four-bedroom colonial sat on its secluded, two-acre lot. As Kylie approached the house, she noticed a small group of people standing near the drive of her home. Did the usually distant neighbors decide to have an outside social gathering? As she got closer, a cold chill flooded her entire body. They weren't the neighbors, they were reporters. How could they have found out about Michael's arrest already? It hadn't even been 24 hours since it happened. An image of the uniformed police officer grinning at her as he tossed her panties on the bed came to mind. She wondered if he tipped the reporters off.

Without signaling, Kylie made a quick right turn and pulled into her driveway. She ignored the reporters who ran toward her car yelling questions at her. "Mrs. Bell, were you with your husband when he killed Louis Joyce? Does your husband's family know about this? Did they really handcuff him and take him out of your hotel suite naked? Mrs. Bell…"

Kylie increased her speed to get away from the vulture-like reporters, thankful that Michael had convinced her to buy a house that sat far from the road. She hit the button on the overhead console to raise the door to the middle bay of the three-car garage. She barely slowed as she drove in, quickly lowering the door behind her. Even after it was closed and she could no longer hear the reporters yelling at her, she sat motionless with her hands on the steering wheel, shaking with an unexplainable fear. It took her a good five minutes and several slow, deep breaths, before she could force herself to open the car door and leave the safety of the vehicle.

Once inside the sanctuary of her home, Kylie relaxed. She first went to the windows of every room in the house and pulled the drapes shut. She realized she was being foolish. The reporters wouldn't come on her property, and they couldn't see in from where they stood. The house sat several hundred feet from the street. Still, it would at least stop her from imagining them peering inside.

Next, she pulled out her cellphone to check the messages. There was only one. She listened to Phil Ackervale's voice telling her that he would be at her house promptly at 6:00 PM and don't go to any trouble. He would bring dinner. She wondered how she would face this long day alone.

Most of the day Kylie spent wandering around the big house in a stupor. She walked from room to room, not knowing what to do. Currently she was in the large living room in the front of the house. It was a pleasant room with warm beige walls, beamed, twelve-foot ceilings, and oak hardwood floors. A huge stone fireplace dominated the far end of the room. It was surrounded by light maple cabinetry that housed a 70-inch flatscreen television and sound system. In the center of the room was a plush, beige sectional couch and two oversized recliners. An array of pillows in greens and browns covered both ends of the couch. In the middle of the floor was an oval carpet that had all the colors of fall. The room was saved from being bland by the unique artwork that decorated the walls. The shelves of the cabinetry held books and sculptures and brightly colored jars and vases. The overall effect was one of warmth and comfort. Kylie sat in the chair closest to the fireplace and covered herself with a rust-colored blanket. Again, she wondered what to do. It was times like this when she turned to Michael, but she couldn't do that now. She had no one. It would have been nice to have family, a mother to call, or a father to get advice from, but sadly, this was not an option. Kylie drew her legs up under her and rested her head on a pillow. She closed her eyes and thought back to her childhood.

Kylie grew up in Dublin Falls, a small town in central Maine. Her mother worked as a server at a small diner in the center of town. Her father, when he was sober enough to go to work, would find employment as a mill worker at one of the many local shoe factories. Even when both of her parents managed to put in a full week of work, money was sparse and there was seldom enough to make ends meet.

When Kylie was very young, the shortage of money didn't seem to matter. She may not have had as many toys as the children she went to school with, and their home was small and run down, but it was surrounded by fields and woods and even a small creek that would swell to the size of a river with the spring melt. She didn't have any siblings and seldom did a classmate from school drop over to play, but she knew where to find the prettiest butterflies and which trees had nests in them and there was always Maisey, the yellow cat that hung around long enough to finally become hers. She was alone, but she learned not to be lonely.

Even as a child, Kylie knew being poor wasn't the problem. The problem was her parents. Her mother claimed to be too tired to do much of anything because she worked so much, but Kylie knew that her mother being gone all day and most evenings wasn't because she was at the restaurant. That job ended at 5:00 PM. She wasn't sure where her mother went every night, but it sure wasn't home. Since her mother wasn't there to make dinner, and her father was too drunk to cook, most nights Kylie would cook the family meal herself. She would make macaroni with butter or macaroni with ketchup or on special occasions, macaroni with hamburger. She would eat by herself and leave two bowls on the kitchen table for her parents. At some point, her father would get up off the couch and make his way to the refrigerator for another beer. He would stop to eat along the way. Her mother would get home late, usually long after Kylie went to bed, and eat her dinner. Sometimes she would even wash the dishes, but more often than not, Kylie would have to do them in the morning, before she left for school.

After dinner, Kylie would stay in her room which had nothing other than a twin bed with a faded blue blanket and a small table with a lamp next to her bed. There she would do her homework, or read the books she borrowed from the school library, until she fell asleep.

Once or twice when she was young, the people from Child Protective Services stopped by, but her parents never beat her and there was food on the table, so when her father told them to get off his property, they had to oblige. Kylie often wondered what it would be like if they took her away. She dreamed of being put in a house with a mother and a father who loved her and took care of her. The mother would cook her meals and buy her pretty dresses and when the father came home from work, he would play games and take the family for ice cream. There would be brothers and sisters and maybe even a dog. Those thoughts made her happy, but they never lasted for long.

Her teenage years were even more difficult. She was tiny and thin, more from her constant habit of running around outside than from the meager portions of food she was provided. Her clothing, always several seasons behind the times, was usually too long and loose. Other kids made fun of her, and while she longed for the high school football captain to notice her for the beauty she carried on the inside and not the $200 fashions she could never wear on the outside, it never happened. She was simply not meant to be Cinderella.

Being poor and alone might have been tolerable if her parents had been the kind, loving, church-going parents that other poor kids in her community had. They weren't. Her father opted for alcohol and her mother opted for anyone who wasn't her father, so even the upstanding do-gooders of the town shunned Lance and Donna Dixon, right along with their petite, unkept daughter, Kylie Ann.

The one bright spot Kylie liked to remember was her schoolwork. School was easy for her, and she always scored high grades in all of her classes. Even her more advanced classes did not cause her to struggle. Because of her excellent grades, high aptitude scores, and low-income family, Kylie was accepted into the University of Maine on a full, 4-year scholarship. She chose nursing as her major because she wanted to be in a position where she could help people who needed her. Maybe she could provide people with the help that she never received.

A beeping cellphone brought Kylie away from the memories of her childhood and back to reality. As was the case with the last three calls, only the words 'private caller' showed up on the illuminated screen. She hesitated before answering, it was probably just another reporter calling. But it could be Michael and she couldn't take the chance of missing a call from him, so for that reason she picked up her phone.

"Hello."

"Mrs. Bell, this is Iona James. I'm calling from the Portland Press Herald."

"Stop, I have nothing to say. Don't call me again." Kylie hit the end button and slammed her cellphone on the chair next to her, her entire body shaking in anger. Why couldn't they just leave her alone? Wasn't she suffering enough?

Still trembling with a combination of fear and anger, Kylie pushed the blanket aside and stood up, resuming her pacing from room to room. The house where she once found so much comfort now felt cold and empty. She went into the kitchen to make a cup of tea. She hoped the warm drink would soothe her.

The spacious kitchen was usually bright and cheerful with its large, stainless-steel appliances surrounded by light maple cabinets and clean, white granite countertops. There were cabinets with glass doors filled with bright white dishes with yellow sunflowers painted on them, a perfect complement to the white and yellow subway tile backsplash. On the far end of the counter was a bright yellow stoneware canister set. There were two big windows over the kitchen sink. The windows had yellow and white gingham curtains tied back on either side. The floor was the same wide-planked oak that extended throughout the entire downstairs.

To the right of the kitchen was the round breakfast nook. The nook had five windows with a built-in bench so people could sit all around the table. In the center of the white wooden table was a vase filled with twelve yellow tulips. Kylie looked at the flowers and felt a tear slide down her cheek.

Eventually, Kylie managed to make herself a cup of tea. She sat at the end of the island on one of four white, high-backed stools with yellow cushions. She ran her finger around the top of the green stoneware mug, waiting for the tea to cool enough to take a sip. She stared out the window into the wooded backyard. No matter what she looked at or what she did, her mind was always on Michael.

The afternoon dragged on. By the time the doorbell rang at exactly 6:00 PM, Kylie's eyes were again red, and her face bloated from hours of crying. She wanted to see Michael on the doorstep more than she wanted anything, but since that could not be, she was glad to see Phil standing there instead.

Phil was still dressed casually in navy Dockers and a beige dress shirt, but his hair was combed and his shoes were polished. He had the well-finished look that Kylie expected from him. "Please, Phil, come in. I'm so thankful that you could come over. I just don't know what to do."

Phil stepped into the oversized foyer. He took Kylie's two hands in his own in an unusual display of affection and looked directly into her eyes. "How are you holding up? Are you doing alright?"

"Alright? Alright? No, I'm not doing alright. I'm losing my friggin mind. Phil, what am I going to do? My husband is in jail on these insane charges. They say he killed someone. He wouldn't kill anyone. He couldn't. He was with me all night. I can't believe this nightmare is happening to us. Everything was perfect, and now, it's all falling apart. I don't know what to do. So no, I'm not alright. I'm not even close to alright."

"We'll get through this, Kylie. It won't be easy, but we won't give up. We'll take it one step at a time. Now, how about we go into the kitchen and have dinner? I feel quite confident assuming that you haven't had a bite to eat all day."

Phil let go of Kylie's hands and picked up the brown bag he had placed on the floor next to his briefcase. Then he led the way into the kitchen. He walked to the table and unpacked several boxes of his favorite Chinese foods, Lo Mein, General Tso's chicken, vegetable-fried rice, egg rolls, and steamed broccoli. Kylie pulled out plates and glasses and sat down for her first meal since her dinner with Michael the night before.

While they ate, Phil explained Michael's situation. "The police have an amazing amount of evidence against him considering the murder took place less than 24 hours ago. Apparently, Michael was seen outside the restaurant arguing with this Louis Joyce fellow. An eyewitness was startled by the intensity of the argument and took notes. He was able to provide the police with a detailed description of Michael. When the police canvassed the area to look for him, they came across a garage attendant who said that a suspicious man had walked into the garage at about the same time as the murder. He said he was suspicious of Michael because Michael looked angry when he walked into the garage, shaking his head and muttering to himself. Then the attendant noticed him as he pulled out in a black crossover vehicle at what the lot attendant referred to as an excessive rate of speed. Cameras in the garage easily identified Michael as the driver of the vehicle. He was also a perfect fit for the description of the man who was seen arguing with Joyce."

"Michael never mentioned arguing with someone. He never even mentioned talking to someone."

"Which brings me to my next question. How could he have been seen arguing outside of the restaurant, alone, when you both said in your sworn statements that you were together all evening? Not one person recalls seeing you standing there with him."

"We were together. We drove to the restaurant together, ate dinner, went to the beach, the inn. It was our anniversary. Of course, we were together."

"Then how could Michael have been seen on the garage camera getting into the Lexus by himself? Where were you?"

"Oh, wait, I didn't go with him to get the vehicle. I went to the ladies' room. Surely, they can't think…"

"Ah, but they can. Now they can easily place him at the scene of the crime, arguing with the victim, and both he and his alibi were caught lying about their whereabouts. And this is what they've learned before even beginning their investigation." Phil shook his head and used his napkin to wipe away the sweat from the back of his neck. Then he stared intently at Kylie. "Kylie, why did you talk to the police today without me? Why didn't you wait for me to join you at the police station? I'm Michael's lawyer."

Kylie used her fork to push the rice around her plate, trying to hold back tears. "I don't know. They said I could see Michael. They let me see him. Afterward, they just brought me to a room and asked me a bunch of questions. I didn't really think about it."

"Well, they tricked you, Kylie. They used Michael as bait and tricked you into talking to them without me. And there's not a thing I can do about it. You're not under arrest. I'm not your lawyer. You went there on your own."

"I'm sorry, Phil. I didn't know."

Phil looked at her and tried to be a bit more

compassionate. She was young and scared. She really didn't know what she was doing. He reached out and patted her hand. "It's alright. We'll figure it out. But please, do not, under any circumstances, talk to the police again unless I'm there with you. Understood?"

"I understand."

Phil returned to his dinner, but Kylie simply sat there with her fork in her hand. The weight of what Phil was explaining to her was quickly sinking in. She lied to the police. Maybe it wasn't intentional. It seemed reasonable that going to the bathroom wasn't a reportable event. At least, it had seemed reasonable to her. A good prosecutor and twelve small-town jurors who would enjoy seeing someone of Michael's status being forced to rot in jail might not be as understanding. After all, Michael was a Bell of the infamous Bell Computers and Commodities. The handsome family who had it all, money, looks, talent. Didn't that automatically mean he was spoiled and self-centered, with too much money to understand what it was like to be an average Joe?

"You see, Kylie, the Bell family is already subject to gossip. With something as exciting and juicy as a murder, well, there's no telling what people will believe. With the evidence they already have, and anything else they find that they can twist and tie into the crime, along with the public's love-hate feelings toward those who live the life they can only dream of, well, it isn't going to be easy."

Kylie's head was spinning as she tried to sort through everything Phil was saying to her. This just couldn't be happening. Michael was kind and gentle. He wasn't like his family. He surely wasn't a killer. How could they portray him that way? It just wasn't right."

Kylie thought of Michael sitting in his cramped, dirty cell. It was barely fit for a human, with only a mineral-stained sink and the toilet located three feet from the cot. The cot with a thin mattress where he had to sit, eat, and sleep. She could clearly see his haggard face covered in dark stubble and the fluorescent orange shirt and trousers he was forced to wear. Hell, even the sneakers with no ties were fluorescent orange. She pictured him being served hash in a plastic bowl and drinking water out of a tin cup. This was not the life Michael was used to. He lived a life of comfort and luxury. A life filled with housekeepers and cooks and tailors who provided him with custom-fit clothing. How would he ever be able to survive this ordeal? How would she? Then another thought came to her. "Phil, does this mean Michael will have to stay in jail until his trial?"

"No, I don't think so. While the Bell name may inspire envy, it also provides a solid, community-minded reputation. Of course, it doesn't hurt that there are sufficient resources available for the judge to impose a ridiculously high bail. That should keep the prosecutor, and perhaps the public, satisfied for a while."

"So, he will be able to come home? When?"

Phil wiped his mouth off and placed his napkin back on his lap. Then he turned toward Kylie and looked intently into her green eyes. "I am not making any promises. This isn't going to be an easy road. There is a bail hearing on Monday. Hopefully, that will go well.

Assuming the judge agrees to bail, you will need to come up with whatever amount he sets. Keep in mind that the prosecutor will fight this. She will want him to remain in jail until the trial. Anyway, if the judge agrees to bail, he will likely set an amount of at least one million dollars. Maybe as high as two mil, but not likely any higher than that. I don't imagine that will be a problem. Once that is done, Michael will be released. He could be home as soon as Monday night."

Once Phil had said Michael could be back home, Kylie heard little else. She talked to him about how the bail hearing could go, but she was only half listening. Phil seemed to sense that. He abruptly rose from his seat and said he had to leave. It had already been a long day and he had a lot of work ahead of him to be fully prepared for the hearing. He gave Kylie a few instructions and told her what documents she would need to provide. He then planned to meet her at the courthouse about an hour before the bail hearing. It was scheduled for the first thing Monday morning.

Kylie walked Phil to the front door and extended her hand to him. "Thank you, Phil, for everything. Just let me know what I have to do. I love Michael, and I would do anything to have him back home with me. So don't hesitate to call, okay?"

Phil grasped her hand warmly. "I know you do. Now, try not to worry. I know that won't be easy, but you have to take care of yourself through all of this. Michael has enough to worry about. Let's not have him worry about you, too. And you know he's in good hands, right? I promise you, Kylie, we're going to do our best for him." Phil put on his most fatherly image and smiled at Kylie. Then he added, "Oh, and Kylie, there's no point in your going to the jail to see him tomorrow. I know they let you in today, but that was an exception, and they won't be willing to break that rule again. Especially since they know they can no longer talk to you without my being present. So, keep a low profile. Better to just stay home and keep to yourself. Don't answer the door. Don't answer the phone. Don't answer any questions from reporters. I know they are just doing their job, but anything you say can and will be twisted until it comes out nothing at all like you meant it. Media sensationalism is a real thing. Right now, no publicity is better than bad publicity. Okay?"

She smiled. He didn't have to tell her that twice. The last thing she wanted to deal with was a story-hungry reporter. "Okay, Phil, and thank you again. Make sure you call me if anything comes up. Anything, no matter how minor."

"I will. Now you get some sleep."

"Oh, Phil, one more thing. Please, when you see Michael tomorrow, tell him I love him."

"I will. He already knows it, but I will. Good night." With a final wave of his hand, Phil pulled the heavy oak door closed behind him and made his way to his car.

Kylie watched the BMW until she could no longer see the red taillights at the end of the driveway. She turned off the outside lights and actually remembered to set the security alarm. Michael would be pleased, she thought.

She wandered back into the kitchen. Cassie, the housekeeper, was not scheduled to work weekends. Michael liked to have weekends home alone with Kylie, so no staff members worked from Friday night until Monday morning. Kylie scraped the two plates from dinner and loaded them into the dishwasher. She added the glasses and the silverware and closed the door. Then she folded the remaining cartons of food and stuck them into the refrigerator. She wiped off the table, turned off the kitchen light, and went upstairs.

Although she didn't work today, Kylie was completely exhausted. She took a hot, steamy shower and pulled one of Michael's worn tee shirts over her head. The shirt had been laundered, but she imagined his scent was still ingrained in the fabric and it comforted her. She climbed into bed, sad with the realization that she had never before slept alone in it. Thoughts of Michael seeped into her mind, and she cried herself to sleep.

3

The night was long and restless, but Kylie managed to stay in bed until morning. How would she ever get through this day? It was impossible to believe that Michael would not be home, that she wouldn't even see him until tomorrow. She climbed out of bed without her usual morning optimism.

She put on a pair of worn jeans and one of Michael's tee shirts and fastened her hair into a loose bun. She didn't plan to leave the house today and she wasn't expecting any visitors, so it really didn't matter what she looked like. Next, she went downstairs into the kitchen for a light breakfast. She wasn't hungry, but Phil's words of taking care of herself so she didn't worry Michael, played through her mind. Despite her good intentions, after rambling through the pantry and finding nothing appealing, she settled for a cup of black coffee.

She took her cup into Michael's office and sat behind

the massive cherry desk. She slid her hand along the highly polished surface, liking the way it felt beneath her fingertips. She stared at the telephone and wished she had somebody she could call. Anybody. But she was alone. Her mother had died several years ago in a car crash on the Maine Turnpike. Donna Dixon had been taking a drive with one of her favorite customers from the diner when something caused him to swerve. The pickup truck with the oversized tires flipped over the guardrail and rolled seven or eight times down a steep embankment. Both her mother and the driver were killed instantly. Donna had only been 46 years old when she died.

After the accident, Kylie's father started drinking even more heavily than before. No one in town recalled seeing him at the gas station or in the grocery store or even at the local bar. Eventually, he quit showing up for work. Finally, the mail carrier noticed he hadn't been getting his mail out of the mailbox and his beat-up pickup truck was parked in the same spot in the yard. It hadn't moved in weeks. This was unusual for him, so the mail carrier called the police for a wellness check. They found him on the couch surrounded by not only empty racks of beer bottles, but also empty whiskey bottles. They didn't even bother with an ambulance; they said it was at least a week too late. It could have been his heart or his kidneys or cancer, it didn't really matter. He was gone. The state and the bank were left to fight over who got to repossess the house. Lance Dixon hadn't been paying his mortgage or his taxes. He didn't leave behind a stash of money, or a bank account, or anything else of value. There were no family heirlooms, no treasures. He didn't even leave any happy memories. There was nothing Kylie wanted from this time in her life. She left everything to the creditors to dispose of and simply walked away. She never looked back.

Not only did Kylie not have warm memories of her family life, but she also never developed close relationships with other children from that time in her childhood. When she was younger the kids at school either taunted her or avoided her. They never befriended her. Even in college, she didn't develop any lasting friendships. There were a few girls she studied with, but they were never close enough to call them friends. Even at work she seldom had more than a coworker bond with the other nurses. She was friendly and got along well with everyone, but that was usually as far as it went. The one exception to that was Hannah Martin. She and Hannah started their nursing careers at the same time, and both worked the night shift on the medical-surgical floor for about a year. Then Kylie transferred to days and Hannah accepted a position in Vermont. They stayed in touch and even now exchanged Christmas cards, but over the past year, their friendship had dwindled. Kylie had lunch with other nurses that she worked with. They swapped shifts and shared stories about their lives, but as far as hanging out after work or having a girls' night on the town, that just didn't happen. The only person she ever felt close to was Michael, and now he was locked up like a common criminal. It didn't matter what the police said. It didn't matter what anyone said. She knew that Michael did not kill that man.

Not knowing what to do with herself, Kylie got up from Michael's desk and walked around his office. She rifled through the papers on his desk, opened and closed his filing cabinet drawers, and even rummaged through the trash can. She wasn't sure what, if anything, she was looking for. Maybe just a way to feel closer to him by seeing what he was doing on his last day at home. She sighed. It didn't work. He still wasn't here. He was locked up in a dingy jail cell for a crime he didn't commit. She left the office and went back into the kitchen. She heated her coffee in the microwave and brought it to the kitchen table. The curtains were drawn in case there were reporters, but she did risk a peek through the crack in the middle. The sun was bright against the blue sky and the maple trees in the back were in full autumn glory—reds, yellows, and oranges. The movement of their leaves indicated there was the gentlest of a breeze. This was always her favorite season, but this year it meant nothing. She got no joy from the view. She let the curtain fall shut.

She wasn't sure how long she sat there sipping her coffee. The big house now felt so lonely. She even toyed with the idea of calling Michael's parents. It didn't take her long to dismiss that idea. She had only met Michael's father, C. C. Bell, a few times, and he wasn't exactly the warm and fuzzy type. Michael's mother, Cynthia, was polite but very standoffish. Actually, she was the coldest person Kylie had ever met in her entire life, and that included her own distant, self-centered parents. Cynthia had led a sheltered, pampered life and probably wouldn't be able to deal with the scandal that Michael's incarceration would bring to her family. The only thing that female icicle ever cared about was the image she portrayed. The more Kylie sat there thinking about Michael's parents, the more she realized that it was quite possible that Michael's upbringing was even stranger than her own.

Michael grew up in a family that was as rich as Kylie's family was poor. Both of his parents came from old money, and lots of it. Michael's father, Clifford C. Bell, had the foresight to invest in a promising young computer company back in the early 1970s. He had a knack for buying just the right company at just the right time. Overnight, he practically tripled the already substantial family fortune. Everything the man touched turned to gold. Everything financial, that is.

Michael's mother, Cynthia, was an only child, and therefore, the only heir to the fortune of Randolph and Vivian Drake of Drake Enterprises, a worldwide import-export company. Her youth was filled with cotillions, trips abroad, and Miss Lucinda's Finishing School for Girls. She was taught everything there was to know about good manners and running a house staff. She was meticulously dressed and well poised, and she always said the right thing at the right time. Her manners were impeccable. Her parents spent thousands of dollars to make sure she was a lady, with the hope that someday she would marry well and carry on the family ancestry in an appropriate fashion.

For the most part, they were successful. Randolph and Vivian were delighted when C. C. Bell, as they were advised to call him, asked for their daughter's hand in marriage. Two years later, after a lavish wedding and reception, and an even more lavish honeymoon, C. C. had assumed the role of taking care of Cynthia.

C. C. moved her into his mansion on the coast of Maine, where he filled her closets and jewelry boxes with the best of everything. She had tailored dresses and designer shoes and diamonds and emeralds and rubies for every occasion. There was a fleet of vehicles, complete with a driver at her disposal. For longer trips, there was a yacht and a private jet. In return, Cynthia managed the staff with an iron hand. She was the perfect hostess and acted as the perfect wife at any event where she accompanied C. C. This lifestyle worked for both of them, as neither of them wanted or expected her to ever have an original thought or desire. Her role was to please C. C. and she was rewarded handsomely for performing this role with excellence.

While their marriage may not have been warm and passionate, it was mutually beneficial for all parties concerned. C. C. could continue with his quest to add millions to his fortune, and Cynthia was renowned for the most glamorous parties in all of New England. They were both happy, or at least satisfied, in their own way. Things were going splendidly until the day that C. C. came home and announced he wished to sire an heir.

"What do you mean? You want a baby? You expect

me to become pregnant?"

"Yes, Cynthia, I believe that is the way it is usually done. Surely you must have known this day would come. A day to think toward posterity."

"C. C., we never discussed having children. I do not recall signing up for having to suffer through backaches and morning sickness and gaining fifty pounds just to satisfy your ego." Cynthia was furious, although this fact would have been lost to an average bystander. Her tone was controlled and dignified, but C. C. understood her anger. It was the first time in their ten years of marriage that she had ever spoken out against any decision he had made.

C. C. looked at his wife, a petite blond woman with the best haircut and makeup that money could buy. Her nails were manicured, her jewelry was expensive, and her impeccable clothing would never dare to be anything above a size two. Ah, why does she have to make this difficult? We both know what the end result will be. "Yes, of course, Cynthia. If you do not wish for me to impregnate you so that I may have an heir, I understand. With all the staff we employ in this house, I'm sure it won't be difficult to find someone who will bear my child. And, of course, share in my fortune."

The smile that played upon Cynthia's lips vanished. She glared at her husband with intense blue eyes. C. C. was momentarily attracted to the fire he saw burning in them, quite different from their usual shade of appeasing blue. But the raw emotion that had clearly shown on her face passed. Three months later, C. C. and Cynthia Bell were announcing the arrival of the Bell family heir.

Michael Clifford Bell was born in March of the following year. He was a healthy, well-behaved child with his father's dark, chiseled good looks and his mother's innate sense of style. His father didn't want him to be too spoiled, and his mother didn't want him to be too troublesome, so they agreed to pay the nanny a generous salary to ensure that their wants were reality.

Clara, the nanny, spent Michael's early years entertaining him with walks in the garden, swims in the pool, and going on paddle boat rides on the pond that sat just north of the stables. In the winter they went sledding and they built snowmen, although such frivolity was never allowed within sight of the main house.

When Michael was old enough for school, Cynthia declared that no child of hers would be allowed to rub shoulders with the common people of this God-forsaken village her husband insisted they live in. Her son would receive his education by having tutors come to the house. Michael cried and begged to be allowed to attend regular school. He longed for friends. He wanted to play tag and toss around a football and do all the things he would see the boys who lived in town do, but Cynthia would hear nothing of it. Clara tried to compensate for Michael's loneliness by sneaking footballs and Nintendo games into the house and playing with him, but somehow a 50-year-old nanny with a gray dress and white apron could not compare to a group of active 6-year-olds.

As Michael grew older, the distance he felt between his parents and himself grew. His father's choice to become a parent had more to do with parading his well-mannered, handsome young son in front of groups of socialites so they could be appropriately impressed with his offspring than it did with any actual desire to raise a son. His mother didn't even pretend that she had more than a passing interest in him. This became evident over his fourteenth summer. That was when they announced they were sending him abroad for the remainder of his education. Again, despite loud protests and a tearful goodbye with Clara, which ultimately cost her the position of the nanny, Michael was sent first to Scotland, then to England, to pursue his education. He wasn't allowed to come home until his high school diploma was in hand.

After four years abroad, Michael returned to Maine as a grown man. The years of living away from his parents had changed him and he felt like a stranger in their home. He tolerated them for one short summer, but then he left to pursue his college education. After completing six years of school at Yale, Michael returned home with two things. He had a master's degree in Bio-statistical Mathematics that had been awarded with honors, as his father would not have it any other way, and he had a wife.

"Mother, Father, I would like to introduce you to Melanie. Melanie Bell. My wife."

Cynthia's face turned ashen gray and a cold, stern look of detest settled onto C. C.'s face. "Michael, may I have a word with you in the study? I'm sure your mother won't mind entertaining your, eh, Melanie, in the front parlor while we talk."

"Certainly, Father. Whatever you say." Sarcasm rolled off Michael's tongue effortlessly.

Cynthia flashed her husband an evil look as she instructed the housekeeper where to deliver refreshments. Choosing to forego the most basic lessons she had learned in finishing school, she barely glanced at her guest as she escorted her into the parlor.

"Michael," C. C. said to his son, "what the hell do you think you are doing? What were you thinking, going off and marrying that, that money-sucking little hussy? We never even had a chance to meet her, let alone vet her and her family, and you go off and marry her? Didn't all that money I spent on your Yale education teach you anything about common sense?"

"Gee, Father, are you trying to tell me you don't approve of Melanie?"

"Approve of her? I don't even know her. Not that it would matter. One look at her and a total idiot could tell she is not suitable for you."

"Apparently that's true, Father. You and Mother seemed to sense that right away."

C. C. turned his cold, hard stare at Michael. His dark brown eyes looked almost black. He was seething. "Watch your mouth, son, or I will cut you off so fast you won't know what hit you. No heir of mine is going to bring the likes of someone like that, that Melanie, into my house and expect to show her off as his wife. Not while I'm alive. Now, how long have you been married?"

"Only three days, Father, but I can assure you, it is all

nice and legal."

"Three days. Good. Then it should be a relatively easy matter to get an annulment. As for Melanie, do you think $30,000 will take care of her? That's $10,000 a day, probably more than she'll earn in a year. Hell, from the look of her, that's probably more than she'll earn in a lifetime."

"With all due respect, Father, I am not going to allow you to annul my marriage. Did it ever occur to you that perhaps I love Melanie? That I want to be married to her?"

"Love. What do you know about love? You are a child, Michael. And apparently, not a very bright one. I don't believe your interest in Melanie has one thing to do with love. From the way she's dressed, I would say your interest in her is something else entirely."

"First, Father, I don't believe you should be noticing the way my wife is dressed. She's a bit young for you to be looking at her that way. Second, are you saying I married her for sex, Father? That would be foolish. I didn't have to marry her for that. Does that make you feel better?"

"Well, if it wasn't for that, then I would say you are trying to punish your mother and me. Not that I can understand why. We have given you everything, absolutely everything since the day you were born. Still, I sense you are using that girl to get back at us for some unknown injustice you think you have suffered. Well, I won't have it. I didn't spend the last 24 years raising you so you could throw it all away on that, that ridiculous blond bimbo. The annulment papers will be here tomorrow and either she is gone, or you both are."

The next morning when C. C. and Cynthia Bell came downstairs to breakfast, they were not accompanied by their son. Two days later, at a party at the Bell Manor honoring Senator Greenwood, C. C. Bell announced that his son, Michael, would not be joining them for the festivities, as he had decided to travel abroad.

Michael told Kylie very little about his life after he and Melanie left his parents' home. She knew they had moved to Boston. She knew he was only married for a few years before he returned home, but he always changed the subject whenever she tried to question him about that part of his life. She sensed it was a very unhappy time for him. She wanted to know more, but clearly, he did not want to talk about it. He always responded, with, 'What difference does it make what I did then? It's now that matters, and now I'm with you.'

Kylie sat in Michael's office most of the morning thinking about the night Michael told her the story of when he brought Melanie home to meet his parents. He didn't show any expression when he told her about his marriage and his parents' cold reaction to it, but when he had finished, she hugged him just the same. They did talk about it again, but for today, she had lingered in the past long enough. It was time to think about the problems of the present.

Her first thought was the money they would need to post bail on Monday. She thought about turning on Michael's computer and trying to go through his financial records. She didn't usually concern herself with that, Michael and his team of accountants took care of the finances. Then she decided against it. It didn't matter if the judge set bail at a million dollars. Hell, it didn't matter if the judge set bail at ten million dollars. There would be enough to cover it. Anyway, by now Michael would have discussed this with his attorney. Phil would have a much better understanding of their money than she would.

She got up from Michael's desk, went to the front windows, and peeked through a crack in the curtain. From her limited vantage point, she could not see any reporters flocking near the front of her house. She didn't believe it, but she hoped that they had moved on to other stories.

Next Kylie retreated to the breakfast nook and pulled out her cellphone. She looked up the headlines for her local news. There, the first headline in bold, black type for all the world to see was:

Michael Clifford Bell, Son of Bell Fortune Heir and Industry Tycoon C. C. Bell and his wife Cynthia Bell, Arrested and Charged with MURDER

Kylie gasped. She started to shake. At that precise moment when her cellphone rang, she didn't think to check to see who was calling. She simply answered the phone.

"Hello."

"Just what the hell has that fool son of mine done this time?"

Kylie cringed. "Mr. Bell."

"Tell me, what is going on? After all these years, what inspired him to kill Louis Joyce?"

"He didn't. He couldn't. Michael wouldn't kill anyone. You must know that."

"I don't give a damn whether he killed that no good bum or not. I care that he got caught. That boy seems determined to drag down the Bell family name. Well, I won't have it. Now, who's he got working for him? What attorney did he choose?"

"Phil. Phil Ackervale."

"Phil. Yes, he's a good man. But he'll need a team of attorneys working for him. I'll take care of that. Has Michael been indicted? Phil must have scheduled a bail hearing by now. Do you know when? I will need to adjust my schedule. And ensure he has adequate counsel. Wouldn't do to have a son of mine not receiving the best legal counsel available."

Kylie was overwhelmed by his stark manner as he fired off question after question. He had never called her before. She didn't think he even had her phone number. Her mind raced as she tried to figure out how to respond to his controlling manner. "All I know is that the bail hearing is scheduled for the first thing Monday morning. Phil told me to be there, but I won't be able to see Michael before then."

C. C. Bell sighed audibly over the phone. "I'll take care of it, although perhaps I should let that boy sit in jail for a while. Maybe then he'll learn something about respect. We told him not to get involved with her, but no, he wouldn't listen. Damn stubborn mule. Now look where it's gotten him. And look what it's doing to the family name."

Without so much as a goodbye, the phone went dead. Oh, I'm fine, Mr. Bell. Father. Thank you for asking. Holding up quite well under the circumstances. Kylie stood there glaring at the phone she still held in her hand. What a cold-hearted bastard, she thought. She didn't expect him to ask how she was, but at the very least he could have asked about Michael. After all, Michael was still his son, or better yet, the latest Bell heir.

Still angry, Kylie started pacing the big, empty house. She walked for what felt like hours, not knowing what to do. Finally, she settled in the oversized recliner in the family room and thought about Michael. She wondered if he was thinking about her, too.

4

Michael was uncomfortable as he lay on the small cot in his cell. A lump in the thin mattress was digging into his back, but so far, he resisted the urge to see exactly what was causing the lump. He was trying to concentrate on the information he had exchanged all morning with Phil, but his mind kept wandering to thoughts of Kylie. How was she holding up? Would she still love him when this was over? Would she believe, with absolute certainty, that he did not kill Louis Joyce?

He wished he had told her more about his life back when Joyce was a part of it. He had talked to her about his childhood, or rather the lack of it, and he did tell her about being married to Melanie. But he never discussed what happened after he took Melanie by the hand and left his parents' house. At least not everything. As he sat in the small cell on the lumpy mattress, he thought about that time in his life.

After he showed up at his parent's house and his father had pulled him into the study and given him an ultimatum, either to leave his new wife or leave his father, he chose the latter. He left the study and joined Melanie and his mother. Without explanation, he took Melanie by the hand and led her to the front door. His only words until they got into their vehicle were, 'Time to go.'

"Gee, Michael, your mom's about as warm and friendly as an ice cube. I don't think she liked me very much." Melanie's innocent blue eyes were focused on him as he headed south down the turnpike.

"Don't worry about it, Love. She doesn't like me very much, either."

Michael drove in silence trying to control the rage that was simmering deep within his gut. He knew his parents would not be happy with his choice of a bride. After all, Melanie was about the furthest thing from a rising socialite as she could be. With her wild blond hair and free-spirited nature, she was more like a hippie from the 1960s than the wealthy, aristocrat type his parents would choose for his wife.

Still, his father had a lot of nerve, accusing him of marrying her simply to get back at him. Why would his father think that he and his mother were important enough for him to take any action against them whatsoever? He didn't care enough about them to try to get back at them, regardless of whether or not they deserved it.

He glanced at Melanie and smiled. Her bleached-blond hair hung in a wild array of waves down her back with no particular style. She wore blue eye shadow and thick, black mascara. Her skin-tight shorts exposed significantly more leg than should be legal, and as always, she was braless underneath her lightweight halter top. Melanie was a free spirit in every sense of the word. As he drove, she sang along with the music that was blaring from the radio, absentmindedly playing with the small necklace she always wore. She had told him once that it was her good luck charm. Her grandmother had given it to her when she was a little girl, and she liked the way the tiny silver bell felt in her hand. She laughed when she said it was destiny that someday she would become a Bell herself. She was sweet, a mere child, and she would never be capable of marrying him simply for his money. Melanie just didn't think that way. Perhaps that was one of the reasons he was attracted to her.

One thing Michael did know, he did not marry Melanie to annoy his parents. That was simply an added benefit. He didn't even marry her because she had a body that kept on giving and a sex drive to match. No, he married her for one and only one reason. She was carrying his child.

"Michael, where are we going? I thought we were going to live with your family until our baby arrived."

"Change of plans, Love. But don't worry. Everything will work out just fine. My father may talk about cutting me off from the Bell money, but that won't happen. My grandfather will never allow it. So, what I'm thinking now is, well, what do you think of living in Boston? I have a good job offer there, and a few of my friends from school live there now. We could get a nice townhouse on the square. Maybe there will even be enough room for you to have a small studio. Then you can sculpt and paint all day without interruption. Would you like that?"

"That sounds wonderful. Boston's a cool city. Lots of young artists are there. And my own studio? I would love that. But we need a nursery first. In just over six months our little addition will be here." She patted her belly, which had not yet begun to swell with their child, as she grinned at Michael. She was so naïve that sometimes it scared Michael. He felt like she was a child that needed to be taken care of, too.

Michael stood up and walked around the small cell, truly appearing like the caged animal he felt himself to be. He liked to pace when he was upset, and this simply wasn't the place to do it. He had to get out of here soon. Surely Phil would be able to get him out on bail tomorrow. As he walked, he let his memories of Melanie flow. He hadn't thought about her in such a long time. She was so young when they met. Even now, after so many years had passed, he remembered her more like a child than a full-grown woman.

His mind again drifted back in time. Six months had passed since they leased a small brownstone in one of the more art-inspired areas of Boston. Apparently, his father was more interested in keeping him away from the family estate than cutting him off from the funds, because so far Michael noticed no decrease in his spending allowance.

Or more likely, his father did try to cut him off, but his grandfather had refused to allow it. His grandfather always did have a bit of a soft spot for me, Michael thought with a smile.

It was just after Christmas, which Michael and Melanie had spent alone when their daughter was born. Molly Destiny Bell weighed in at just six pounds, two ounces, and was, without a doubt, the most beautiful baby ever created. She had pale skin, wispy blond hair, dainty features, and the biggest blue eyes Michael had ever seen. He could stare at his infant daughter for hours, utterly amazed at her every feature, her every movement. He had never known such love as the day she was born, and he knew from the first moment he saw her that there was nothing he wouldn't do for her. He never minded getting up at night when she cried, warming her bottle when she was hungry, or even changing her soiled diaper, regardless of how odiferous it was. He loved his daughter with all his heart and soul.

Melanie loved Molly, too, and she tried her best to be a good mother. Michael worried continuously, though. Melanie just didn't seem to have a knack for taking care of a baby.

One day Michael came home from work to find Molly strapped in her carriage alone on the front walkway while Melanie was inside restocking the diaper bag. Melanie was sure no one would ever bother such a tiny baby. And when Molly was about eight months old, Melanie thought it was cute the way Molly liked to play in her paint cans in the studio. She laughed as Molly covered herself with the more vibrant colors of paints. An artist in the making, she said. It never occurred to her that the paint could be dangerous if ingested by a baby.

As the years went by, Michael couldn't even count the times he would come home to find incense burning on tables low enough for Molly to reach, or large, heavy sculptures precariously balanced on small, triangular stands. One time, when Molly was about two, Michael walked into his home to find three homeless men sitting at the table having dinner alone with Molly, while Melanie was in the kitchen preparing more dessert. They weren't harmful, just hungry, Melanie insisted.

Michael understood that Melanie wasn't a bad mother. She loved their daughter as much as he did. She was just completely naïve to the dangers that existed in the world. He warned her over and over that something bad could happen and that she had to be more careful. She just laughed and told him to stop being such a pessimist.

In January, just after Molly's third birthday, Michael was busy at work when he suddenly felt an urge to go home. For no apparent reason he became restless, agitated. He thought he would crawl right out of his skin. Without explanation, he left his office and drove through the increasingly heavy snow that fell in huge flakes, covering the city in a blanket of white. He was surprised to find the house empty. Melanie seldom left her studio in the afternoon other than to look after Molly, and to venture out in such foul weather was rare.

He walked through the rooms looking for a clue as to

where she could be. At first, he was angry that she hadn't left a note, but then he realized that she probably thought she would be home long before he returned from work.

He walked into the small galley kitchen, thinking perhaps she had started with a recipe for dinner and needed an ingredient. Melanie was rather adventurous with her cooking. There was no sign that she had been in the kitchen all day. As he turned to walk back to the living room, the red blinking light on the answering machine caught his eye. He walked over to retrieve the message.

"This call is for Mr. Michael Bell. Mr. Bell, this is Officer Jason Jefferson of the Boston Police Department. If you could please call me as soon as you receive this message." Officer Jefferson then left his telephone number but no explanation as to why he wanted Michael to call him.

With unsteady hands and a heavy heart, Michael dialed the phone. "Officer Jefferson, please."

"Hello, this is Jason Jefferson."

"This is Michael Bell. You left a message for me to call you." The silence that ensued from the other end of the telephone caused the sweat on Michael's hands to increase as he gripped the receiver. The sick feeling that was in his stomach was quickly spreading to the rest of his trembling body.

"Mr. Bell, I'm sorry to have to tell you this, but there has been an accident."

"An accident? Oh God. Molly? Melanie? Are they okay?"

"Your wife and daughter have been brought to Boston General and you need to go to the hospital as soon as possible. That is all I can tell you at this time."

"You need to tell me. Please. Are they okay? Are they alive?"

"Mr. Bell, I have no information to share with you over the telephone. I do have a car on the way to your home now to take you to the hospital. Please watch and Officer Renita Donaldson will arrive shortly. She will bring you to the hospital."

Michael slammed the phone down and ran out the door. He had no intention of waiting for some officer to show up to bring him. Lord knows how long that could take. He jumped into his Volvo and practically flew to the hospital. He didn't care if there was traffic or if it was snowing or if he was driving recklessly enough to get himself killed. Nothing mattered except Molly. And Melanie.

Luckily, the snow was keeping most people off the streets as Michael slid through more than one red light, but he did manage to arrive safely at the hospital. He parked in the first empty space he saw and ran to the emergency department. As soon as he gave his name, a young doctor with brown eyes and a kind face walked over to him. "Mr. Bell, I'm Dr. Bradley. Please come with me."

"Molly. Melanie. Are they okay? I need to know. Are they okay? Please, tell me."

Dr. Bradley led Michael into a small room at the end of a hallway where they were joined by a nurse and another man who appeared to be a member of the clergy. Dr. Bradley suggested that Michael sit down, but Michael was agitated. He wanted answers. With his hands clenched into fists by his sides, he stood very close to Dr. Bradley, their faces only inches apart. Michael's voice was raised and he enunciated each word loudly and clearly, ensuring Dr. Bradley fully understood his request. "Will you please tell me about my wife and daughter? Now!"

Dr. Bradley lowered his eyes and cleared his throat. Then he looked at Michael. "Your wife and daughter were struck head-on by another vehicle. Your daughter suffered multiple injuries, the most severe of these to her head and chest. She is stable right now, but she is going to require surgery. We won't know the full extent of her injuries until we run additional tests. She is not conscious, but she is breathing on her own. We will do our best. We have a pediatric neurologist on his way in and the pediatric surgical team is on standby. We are doing everything we can."

"Oh, God. Is she going to live?"

"It is too early to know anything definite, but right now she is holding her own. We have a team of specialists doing everything they can for her. You have to know that she hit the windshield hard, the injuries to her head are extensive. We are giving her a 70% chance of survival."

"That's good, right? Seventy percent is good."

"Yes, her chance of survival is good. But you have to understand, if she does regain consciousness, we're not sure what her mental state will be. With the injuries she suffered, it's too early to know if she can ever return to a normal life like she had before."

Michael was hearing the words and at some level he was understanding. His Molly, his beautiful, smiling, impish, happy little Molly may never regain consciousness. And if she did, she may never be the same. He understood, but it was too much right now. He couldn't deal with it. Instead, he was focusing only on the part where she had a 70% chance of living. It was the best he could do. His mind was spinning, but he knew he had to pull himself together and ask the next question. "And my wife? Is Melanie okay?"

Dr. Bradley wiped his forehead with the palm of his hand and again looked Michael in the eye. "I'm sorry to tell you, Mr. Bell, Michael. We did everything we could, but your wife's injuries were too many. Too severe. We weren't able to save her. I'm so sorry. She didn't make it."

Michael felt a cold chill pass through him. Melanie. Dead. How could this be? She was so young, so full of life. In his mind he could see her laughing, her blue eyes sparkling, not a care in the world. That was her nature, happy and carefree. She couldn't be dead. She still had pictures to paint and statues to sculpt. She had a daughter to raise. She couldn't be dead. She was practically a child herself. But Michael looked at Dr. Bradley, and at the nurse standing quietly at his side, and at the clergy waiting to offer comfort, and he knew it was true. Melanie was gone and Molly was severely injured, and his life was never going to be the same. It took all he had but he pulled himself together and fought back the panic and the tears.

"Can I see Molly? I need to see my daughter. Please."

Dr. Bradley led Michael into one of the brightly lit emergency rooms. "Just for a moment, Mr. Bell. Michael. Then we'll need you to sign some documents so we can take her to surgery."

Molly looked so small lying on the stretcher surrounded by tubes and wires and machines that beeped and buzzed. Michael walked to her bedside and took her small, limp hand into his own. Nothing he had ever felt could compare to the pain he was feeling at that moment. Even knowing Melanie was dead didn't touch him the way seeing his daughter lying there so pale, so helpless, did. He stood there, broken, and watched as they whisked his baby girl away to run scans of her head before surgery. Once they finally brought her to the operating room and Michael was alone in the waiting room, he did something he hadn't done in almost four years. He called his parents.

"Hello, Father."

"Michael?"

"There's been an accident. Melanie is dead."

"I'm sorry, Michael. I know you seemed to care for her."

"She was my wife. Of course, I cared for her. But there's more."

"The baby? How is the baby?"

"Not good. She's in surgery. She has a skull fracture. And bleeding on the brain. She could die. Or she could live but not wake up. She's only three-years-old. My baby's only three-years-old and she may never wake up again."

Michael could no longer control his emotions and the tears spilled out of his eyes. He walked to the far corner of the waiting room and cried in a way he had never cried in his life. He dropped his phone as the tears poured out and moans of anguish escaped his lips. He put his hands over his face but that couldn't stop the pain. Nothing could.

He wasn't sure how long he carried on this way. He didn't care. He didn't care about anything but Molly. He prayed. He begged. He bargained. But mostly, he cried.

After a while, the tears stopped and he wiped his eyes. He picked up his phone and sat in one of the chairs. He was still alone. He looked at his phone and was surprised to see the connection to his father was still active. For a minute he just stared. He wasn't sure why he chose to call his parents, he just needed to talk to someone like family. As of now, they were the closest thing to family he had. Then he put the phone to his ear. "Father?" In a gesture that seemed uncharacteristic of C. C. Bell at the time, and that shocked Michael in later years as he looked back on it, his father made the most humane gesture he had made in Michael's entire life.

"I'll be right there, son. Holmes is bringing the car around as we speak, and it shouldn't take more than a few hours to arrive."

During the next several hours, Michael spent his time in what the nursing staff referred to as a quiet room where he could be alone. He learned that Melanie had been killed instantly when her car was hit head-on by a Chevy Silverado that lost control on one of Boston's icy streets. He cried for her, he felt sorry for her, he knew he would even miss her. He also found he resented her when the E. D. physician told him that Molly was not buckled securely in her car seat when the accident occurred.

As promised, C. C. Bell arrived at the hospital within hours of his son's telephone call. Studded tires on the Hummer, Michael figured. Legalities were of no consequence when his father wanted something. Tall with steely gray hair, dressed in dark clothing with a long, black overcoat and rich, leather gloves, he made a formidable impression. While most fathers would have made their first priority to comfort their grief-stricken son, C. C. Bell was not like most fathers. He practically ignored Michael, who was pacing back and forth across the small waiting room. Instead, he immediately demanded an update on his granddaughter's condition. The news was not good.

Molly had suffered a severe traumatic brain injury and the chances of her waking up were slim. Dr. Bradley advised she could remain in a coma or possibly a vegetative state for months or even years. If she did awaken, which may or may not happen, the chances of her being the normal, healthy child she was previously were minimal. Of course, it was far too early to know, but they did want the family to be prepared for the worst. Michael was lost in his grief, unable to decide what to do next. He couldn't think straight. He just kept picturing his active, happy, baby girl lying on that hospital bed with the bandages and tubes and instruments.

C. C. was never at a loss, however, and he quickly took charge. He realized that Molly would need highly skilled medical care, possibly for the rest of her life. What she wouldn't need was her picture flashed across every television set or popping up on every computer so people could gawk at the poor little rich girl. Her bruised and beaten face would end up in every newspaper and on every magazine cover. She was only three. She didn't need to be hounded for the rest of her life by reporters looking for a story on how sad her life was. Michael would never be able to deal with that. And honestly, C. C. would rather the Bells be known for their wealth, their glamour, their charity work, than be pitied for their injured heir. C. C. had dealt with the press his entire life and he knew how harsh and unfeeling they could be. He also knew how determined and bloodthirsty they could be. So, out of actual concern for his granddaughter, and only limited concern for the Bell family name, C. C. quickly formulated a plan to protect her from the rest of the world. The next day, the family publicist released a statement about the tragic deaths of Melanie and Molly Bell, wife and daughter of Michael Bell, daughter-in-law and beloved granddaughter of multi-millionaire C. C. Bell.

While Michael paced, lost in his private world of despair, C. C. realized the full extent of the tragedy. He also knew that Michael would be completely unable to deal with it. Molly Bell was never going to recover. Her chance of growing into a healthy, active young woman was gone. At best, she would lie in a hospital bed while someone came in to exercise her arms and legs and feed her through a tube. She would be oblivious to the world for the rest of her life. She would require nursing care around the clock. Michael would attempt to take care of her by himself, but what kind of life would that be for him? He was still a young man and while this was tragic, Michael would need to find a way to go on.

Also, C. C. realized that they would have to deal with the press. The press would have a field day with Molly. Pictures of her tiny body would be flashed across every television screen, and found on every magazine cover. There would be headlines about the tragic life she would now have to live. Reporters would stalk them just for pictures of the girl's broken body. For his granddaughter's sake, he had to find a way to prevent this from happening. He may have gone wrong with Michael, but he would do the right thing by Molly. He owed her this. He would not allow her to be the subject of such humility. Not now, at age three. Not ever. For as long as she lived, her dignity would be preserved. She would be well taken care of, the best care that money could buy.

C. C. made the arrangements quickly. He met with the Chief of Staff of Boston General, along with the Head of Pediatric Neurology, the Head of Pediatrics, and the physician leading Molly's surgical team. As soon as the storm cleared and Molly was strong enough to make the journey, a fully staffed medical helicopter would be enroute to a small, private hospital in Latchy Harbor on the coast of Maine. The Head of Pediatric Neurology and Molly's surgeon, along with their most trusted critical care nurse, would be on board. Naturally, arrangements had been made for both the current hospital and the receiving hospital to receive rather sizeable donations that would facilitate private rooms with round-the-clock care for the young 'Jane Doe' for as long as necessary.

Already C. C. had his people searching for a property near Latchy Harbor to purchase to turn into a small medical facility where Molly could be transferred once she was well enough. There would be a specialized staff to take care of her, a staff that not only excelled with their medical expertise but could also be trusted to keep the fact that Molly was still alive a secret. Obviously, the staff would be small. It was amazing how quickly things could be accomplished if one was willing to pay for them.

While this was occurring in Latchy Harbor, back in Boston, other provisions were being made. Michael would return with his father to the Bell Manor. There they would hold a respectable funeral for Melanie and Molly, and no one else would ever need to know that Molly was alive. Thanks to the arrangements made by C. C., Molly would receive the best care possible. Michael would be able to spend as much time with his daughter as he wanted. Discreetly, of course. The granddaughter of C. C. Bell would not be subjected to the travesty of publicity. Perhaps then, the son of C. C. Bell could find some peace. If by some miracle she made a full recovery, so be it. The Bell family would be caught in a non-truth. But C. C. was a realist. He understood what the doctors were trying so hard not to say. She was not going to have a full recovery. It would be a miracle if she was going to recover at all.

Under the circumstances, it was a good plan. It may have been the best possible plan for all involved. Michael, for the first time in years, was in full agreement with his father. But neither one of them could foresee the one flaw in their plan. The one flaw that would haunt them in years to come. That flaw was Louis Joyce.

5

It was Monday morning, the day that Michael would be formally charged with murder. Hopefully, he would also be released on bail. It didn't matter what amount the judge set, they would pay it. They would do anything if it would bring Michael home.

Kylie dressed in the outfit she had selected last night before bed. Phil instructed her to look modest but not dowdy, conservative but not business-like, virtuous but not obvious. She should appear put together, but not wealthy. Unsure of what to wear, she finally decided on a black pencil skirt and a pale pink keyhole blouse. She braided her hair and wore just a hint of makeup. Her only jewelry was a watch and her wedding band. Nothing flashy. Just an average American woman going to bail her husband out of jail.

She gathered up the items Phil told her to bring and stuffed them into her purse. She wished her purse didn't have the Coach brand on it, but it was better than the Louis Vuitton she had originally selected for today. She understood why she was bringing the financial documentation Phil had requested, but she wished he had taken a few minutes to explain why he needed Michael's passport.

Kylie went to the garage and climbed into her Jeep. Not the Lexus and absolutely not Michael's toy, the lava orange Porsche 911 convertible. Phil had been very specific about which vehicle to drive. It seemed silly to Kylie, it's not like people didn't already know Michael was wealthy, but she followed Phil's instructions. She would have taken a taxi if he had thought that was best.

The October sun was surprisingly warm and Kylie would have liked to take the top off the Jeep, but a realistic fear of hovering reporters made her use the air conditioner instead. She drove in silence without even the radio to break the solitude. As she passed down tree-lined streets, she wondered what it would be like at the courthouse today. How would Michael look? Was he holding up alright? Would he have to wear that horrible fluorescent orange outfit to the hearing? Would he be handcuffed? The humiliation he was being forced to suffer was so unfair. So much for being innocent until proven guilty.

She pulled into the courthouse's small parking lot, glad she chose to arrive early. Looking around as she headed toward the front door, she couldn't help but notice a familiar vehicle parked near the entrance. The black BMW x7 with windows almost as dark as the paint was a sure sign that C. C. Bell must be here. She looked around for Holmes, but she didn't see him anywhere. Odd, he never lurked too far from whatever vehicle he was driving.

Kylie entered the courthouse and walked down a long, narrow hall. Doors jutted off both sides every few feet and she had no idea where to go. She looked around for someone to ask when a voice called out to her.

"Mrs. Bell, ma'am, perhaps I could be of service."

She turned around to find a thin, blond man standing only a few feet away from her. "Holmes, I didn't see you. I didn't realize you would be here."

"I am Mr. Bell's driver, ma'am. Surely you expected Mr. Bell to attend his son's court hearing."

"Actually, no. They have not exactly been on friendly terms over the last few years."

"The last few years? More like the last 38 years. But perhaps I overstep. Anyway, that makes no difference now. He is here today for his son."

"Yes, I suppose you're right. So where is he?"

"He wanted to arrive early to see Michael, er, Mr. Bell, before the court hearing."

"But I was told that no one was allowed to see Michael except his attorney. They wouldn't even let me in to see him."

"Please take no offense, ma'am, but you are not C. C. Bell."

****

Michael had just changed into the suit that Phil had brought him. He wasn't too impressed with the material or the cut, but Phil wanted him to look like an average man and average men didn't go to court wearing custom, $5,000 suits. Phil had just finished explaining today's procedure to Michael when the door of the small interview room they were seated in burst open. Michael expected to see a uniformed guard, or maybe more of the attorneys his father sent over, step into the room. He was shocked to see his father enter instead.

"Michael, I have come to, holy hell, you look awful. What is that rag you are wearing? Couldn't that wife of yours provide you with something decent to wear?"

"Hello, Father. Have you given up the comfort of the mansion just to provide me with fashion advice?"

"Don't be smart with me. It just seems like a man of your means could find something a bit better to wear than a second-hand Wal-Mart reject. I'm guessing that it's something that your wife selected?"

Phil leaned forward, not the least bit intimidated, and stared directly into C. C. Bell's eyes. "I selected it. Leave Kylie out of this. Michael doesn't need to flaunt his wealth in front of the judge or the public. It's one of those things they teach us in law school."

"Ah, Phil Ackervale, always nice to see you. I assume you've made use of the team of attorneys I sent over to you."

"Sure did. Put them right to work. They should be busy until next Christmas doing the research I requested."

"Don't tell me you're going to try this case without their assistance."

"No, C. C., of course not. We both know I will do everything in my power to provide Michael with the best legal defense possible. But please, don't tell me how to try this case. Nobody is looking out for Michael's interest any more than I am."

"Well, we shall see about that. Nonetheless, make use of the added legal support, Phil. They're a bright group of experienced lawyers."

Michael heard enough. He stood to level the playing field, refusing to allow his father to tower over him any longer. "Father, if you're not here as a fashion expert, and I assume you and Phil haven't made some type of business arrangement to work together, then tell me, why are you here?"

"I came to show my support for you. You are my son. The Bell name is at stake here, Michael."

"Ah, yes, the Bell name. That explains your presence. But really, Father, you shouldn't have. Phil has everything under control, and I expect things to go smoothly. And on the off chance you are curious, I am innocent, you know. I didn't kill Joyce."

"Yes, yes, of course you are. But this isn't about guilt or innocence. It is about which side can afford the better counsel."

"Only you, Father, could make a statement that going to court isn't about guilt or innocence, and truly believe it."

C. C. turned to Phil. "Just get him out of here. He

doesn't need to be locked away like a criminal. I don't want to see a picture of my son in an orange jumpsuit popping up on my television or my computer, and I sure as hell don't want to see his mugshot show up again. The Bell name has never been disgraced like this before, and it needs to stop. Now. The only pictures I want to see are pictures of Michael and that wife of his acting like the happy couple they claim to be. So, make sure the bail hearing goes his way. Do I make myself clear?"

Phil nodded his head in the affirmative. Anything to get C. C. off his back. He had more important things to do than deal with the arrogant, self-absorbed father of his number one client. He started to tell Michael it was time to go, but Michael cut him off before he had a chance to speak.

"Phil, is Kylie here? Is she in the courtroom?" Sparks flew from Michael's brown eyes.

"Of course she's here, Michael. She's your wife. She has to be here to show her support. Plus, wild horses wouldn't have been able to keep her away."

"How is she? How is she managing the pressure? Is she okay? Have the reporters left her alone?"

"She's holding up. She's stronger than you would expect. Now, straighten your tie. It's time to go."

The courthouse was filled with people from all walks of life. Kylie sat on the first bench behind the defendant's chair, exactly where Phil told her to sit. Next to her was her father-in-law. The pale salmon shirt he wore did nothing to distract from the expensive cut of his black Armani suit. With his elegantly styled salt-and-pepper hair and exaggerated good looks, he attracted more attention from both the curious townspeople and the press in a way that Kylie never could.

Kylie's fingers nervously played with the hem of her skirt as she waited for the hearing to begin. She looked so small, so fragile, seated next to C. C. She didn't speak to him. He offered no support to her, no kind words, no warm pat on the back, no comforting smile. Instead, they both stared straight ahead. All she could think about was seeing Michael. She couldn't touch him or talk to him, but just to sit within ten feet of him sounded wonderful.

She anxiously watched the double doors on the far right of the courtroom, willing Michael to enter. She desperately needed to see him and if she stared at the door, she wouldn't miss a single second when he walked through. Finally, the doors opened and Michael was escorted into the courtroom by an armed guard dressed in a brown uniform. The guard led Michael to the chair next to Phil and another attorney whom Kylie was not familiar with. Michael kept his head down as he walked the short distance to his seat, but his eyes were frantically searching the crowd. Surprise registered on his face when he saw his father sitting on the hard wooden bench in the front, but they quickly skirted by him and rested on Kylie.

God, she looked beautiful. She sat at a slight angle with her skirt pulled demurely over her knees, her ankles crossed, and her hands clasped tightly on her lap. Everything about her portrayed a natural elegance that all the money in the world could not buy.

For just a second, Kylie's eyes met Michael's. She let a smile play across her lips. She envisioned touching his face in her hands, running her fingers through his thick, brown curls. But that was only a vision. She remained firmly planted on the hard, wooden bench and watched as he was seated, facing the judge, his back toward her.

"All rise. The Honorable Evan R. Appleton presiding."

A surprisingly young man of small stature with short brown hair and a dark robe entered the room. He took his place on the bench and struck a small, square pad with his gavel, calling the court to order. Kylie found herself whispering a quiet prayer as she focused her attention on the judge who held her husband's future in his hands.

The room became eerily still and the proceedings began. Kylie was surprised at how full the courtroom was with attorneys, town officials, members of the media, and curious onlookers. With such a large crowd, she expected the room to be noisy, but a chilling quiet prevailed throughout the arraignment. She fought to hold back tears as she watched while her husband was officially charged with the murder of Louis Joyce. How could anyone believe that Michael was guilty of murder? It was ludicrous. He wasn't capable of such a horrendous crime. He was a kind man with a good heart, and he had been hurt enough in his life to avoid hurting anyone else. As Kylie watched Michael stand before the judge, she knew, beyond a shadow of a doubt, that he did not kill Louis Joyce.

Kylie wiped her eyes and focused on the hearing. The attorneys were now arguing about whether or not bail was appropriate in this case. The prosecutor, Meredith Tyson, rose from her seat on the opposite side of the room from where Michael was sitting, her heels clicking as she walked across the wooden floor. She was a tall, thin woman with gray hair and dark eyes. She wore a black tailored suit and a crisp, white blouse. A small silver watch fit snugly on her left wrist. She was the epitome of efficiency and professionalism. She removed her glasses and let them hang by a beaded chain from her neck. When she spoke, her voice was clear and commanding. "Your honor, the people request the defendant be held without bail. He has access to unlimited funds and is well accustomed to travel abroad. Additionally, the defendant has limited ties to the states."

Phil quickly jumped from his seat. "Your honor, I'm surprised to hear that Miss Tyson considers a wife, parents, employment, and a secure standing in the community as limited."

"Certainly your honor can see the possibility of Mr. Bell's wife joining him on his travels."

"Mrs. Bell is not on trial here."

Judge Appleton thumped his gavel, bringing the two attorneys to an immediate silence. The judge looked from one attorney to the other. He then glanced at Michael, Kylie, and finally, C. C., who sat erectly and didn't so much as blink while returning the stare of the judge. "Bail is set at one million dollars, cash or bond. The defendant will surrender his passport. Additionally, the defendant will be remanded to a local radius, let's say 50 miles, of the courthouse."

"Your honor." Both attorneys simultaneously jumped to their feet to object to the judge's ruling.

Judge Appleton addressed them both. "Miss Tyson, I have specified a 50-mile radius. The Portland Jetport is over 60 miles away. You should be comfortable with this ruling. Mr. Ackervale, would you like me to reconsider the amount of bail? Perhaps you would prefer two million dollars?"

Both attorneys returned to their chairs and mumbled something that sounded like they were withdrawing their objections.

Kylie's heart leaped in her chest, causing her to unknowingly raise her hand to her heart. At first, the thought of trying to raise a million dollars for bail startled her, but then she came to her senses and realized that this sum would not be a hardship for the almighty Bell family. Honestly, it wouldn't even be a hardship for her and Michael. Although she had been married for a year, she still hadn't adjusted to the vast wealth of the family she married into. She turned to look at C. C., but he had already stood to exit the courtroom.

Michael was taken back through the double doors, closely followed by Phil. The other attorney who had been sitting at Michael's table, a nervous little man with dark, thinning hair and wire-rimmed glasses, approached Kylie. "Mrs. Bell?"

"Yes, I'm Kylie Bell."

"I'm Tim Stone, one of your husband's attorneys. Do

you have the documents Mr. Ackervale requested?"

"Yes, right here." She withdrew a manila envelope from her leather handbag and handed it to the attorney. "When will I see Michael? Can he come home now?"

"It will take a couple of hours to process him. Why don't you get yourself some breakfast and come back here around noon? There's a coffee shop right across the street."

Kylie was disappointed, she wanted to see Michael right away, but she had no choice. She walked down the hall Tim Stone had pointed her toward and went out the side door of the courthouse.

The Daily Grind was directly across the street from the courthouse. It was a small coffee shop with tables and booths crammed in every possible space. It had dingy yellow walls and mismatched wooden tables and chairs. The booths had white Formica tables and torn green vinyl benches. It didn't try to be inviting. It didn't have to. Its location, sandwiched between the courthouse, the police station, and the start of the busy downtown area, assured its success. Kylie squeezed between various lawyers talking with their clients and anxious family members, and the occasional police officer, to a small booth near the back. She wasn't hungry and only wanted black coffee, but her stomach had been upset all morning, so she ordered coffee and a bagel. She knew she had to make an attempt at keeping up her strength.

The server had just put her order on the table when an attractive young woman came and sat on the bench directly across from her. Kylie looked at her, both curious and confused as to why this woman she didn't know joined her. A brief glance around the restaurant indicated there were still a few empty tables available.

"Mrs. Bell? Hi. I'm Virginia Jones. I wonder if you wouldn't mind answering a few questions for me about your husband's case. How do you feel about the bail hearing this morning? Is Clifford Bell involved? Is he going to post bail? Are you at all nervous about Michael going home with you?"

Kylie dropped the bagel back on her plate and stared at this woman. She wasn't sure if she was more shocked or furious with the nerve of this reporter. "Excuse me, please. I am having my breakfast. I do not wish to answer any questions, so please…"

"Oh, I understand. You go right ahead and eat. We don't need to discuss the bail hearing." Kylie picked up her bagel and raised it to her lips. "But if you could just tell me about the murder. Were you with Michael when he killed Louis Joyce?"

Shock rippled through Kylie's entire body and she glared at the woman sitting across from her, no longer hearing her questions. She longed to pick up her cup of coffee and fling it at her. Wouldn't that create an interesting headline in tomorrow morning's news? Instead, she pushed away from the table and hastily cleared a path through the busy shop to the exit door.

"There she is. Mrs. Bell. Mrs. Bell. Have you posted bail yet? Kylie, over here. Mrs. Bell, were you sitting with Clifford Bell this morning? Does that mean he is involved with the murder?"

Kylie experienced a panic swell inside of her. Why were all these reporters bothering her? Didn't they realize she didn't want to talk to any of them? Clutching her purse to her chest, she ran blindly from the coffee shop door onto the sidewalk. The overzealous reporters surrounded her and shoved their microphones in her face as she ran. She stumbled while stepping off the curb, but quickly collected herself and ran into the street. More than one horn blared but she didn't care. She dodged vehicles as she made her way through the traffic, seeking the sanctuary of the courthouse. She would rather sit on a hard, wooden bench in the hallway and wait for Michael than deal with even one person from the media. She was shocked at how rude and overbearing they were. She would be even more shocked the following morning when she looked at her phone and saw the news headline:

Wife of Suspected Murderer Michael Bell, Son of Bell Fortune Heir and Industry Tycoon C. C. Bell, Flees Local Coffee Shop to Avoid Paying Check

Time passed slowly for Kylie. She sat in the drab hallway alone, lost in her thoughts. When she closed her eyes, she could almost feel Michael holding her, brushing his lips across hers. She missed him. He was truly the husband she always wanted. Ever since she was a little girl playing alone in the fields behind her house, she would imagine being rescued by a handsome prince.

Michael was her prince.

She met Michael at the hospital when she was still working in the Emergency Department. It had been a slow night and the other nurses were gathered around the main nurses' station drinking coffee and gossiping. Kylie wasn't comfortable with that. She preferred to stay busy with work instead of sharing details of her life. While they chatted, she volunteered to cover the small triage room that separated the actual emergency rooms from the entrance. She sat there, neatly arranging the Band-Aids in their plastic bin from largest to smallest, when she heard someone approach.

"Hello, is this where I come to see a doctor?"

Kylie looked up, at first annoyed at being disrupted from her sorting. Standing there, smiling down at her was, without a doubt, the most handsome man she had ever seen. Tall and muscular, he had thick, curly hair and brown eyes highlighted with golden specks. His high cheekbones and square, angular chin gave him a rugged, masculine impression, while the dimples that flanked both sides of his face when he flashed a bright, easy smile made him seem boyish. She thought he must be a dream. In reality, no one looked that good.

"Miss? Excuse me. Can you help me, please?"

Kylie jumped, partly because his deep, baritone voice caused her toes to curl, and partly because she was sure he was aware that she was gawking at him. She could tell by his grin that he was clearly pouring on the charm. She tried to act like she dealt with Adonis every day, but when she stood up to help him, the entire bin of Band-

Aids flew from her lap and disbursed themselves across the floor of the entire room. For the first time in her life, Kylie looked around at the mess she created and didn't care. She did, however, care that her face had turned a deep shade of red and her usual confident nursing attitude had been replaced with babbling incompetence. Finally, she managed to say, "Yes, of course. Please, come right in and sit down. What seems to be the problem?"

"You mean other than the fact that there are about a million Band-Aids on the floor?"

Regaining her composure, Kylie smoothed her uniform and said, "Oh, yes. Sorry about that. You startled me. What brings you to our little emergency room tonight? I mean, what brings you to the emergency room tonight, uh, the emergency department? What brings you to the emergency department tonight?" God, could she sound any more pathetic?

A sheepish grin crept onto Michael's face. It was obvious this wasn't the first time a woman had behaved this way in his presence. "Let's just say that I've learned it's not a good idea to remove one's dart from a dartboard when a large, drunk, truck driver announces it is his turn to shoot." At this, Michael pulled up his left hand for Kylie to examine. Inserted right through the center of his hand, and almost coming through his palm, was a yellow and black feathered dart. Blood was oozing around the hole from the dart onto the white handkerchief that was wrapped around it.

"I tried to pull the dart out, but when I did it started

to bleed heavily, so my mates at the bar told me to leave it in."

"Yes, wise choice." Kylie examined his hand carefully. The dart had punctured one of the larger veins in the hand, so she secured it in place with white tape. She quickly entered the necessary information into the computer and took his vital signs, commenting that his low heart rate was probably due to his excellent physical condition. Brilliant, she thought to herself. That's the kind of comment one could think of but not say aloud. Then she took him back to one of the Emergency Department bays.

As Dr. Hernandez examined Michael's hand, Kylie set up both a surgical suture kit and a wound dressing kit on a silver stand next to the stretcher. She made sure the necessary syringes, sutures, silk, sponges, numbing medication, dressings, tape, antiseptic and antibiotic creams were present along with scissors, clamps, gloves, drapes, and gauze pads. Then she watched as Dr. Hernandez quickly and efficiently removed the dart and stitched Michael's hand. Once she was done, Kylie pulled on purple gloves and dressed the wound.

Kylie had treated many injuries as a nurse in the emergency department, but never before had she been so intrigued with a patient's hands. Michael's hands were soft and well-manicured, yet still strong and masculine. She could almost imagine them stroking her cheek and she had to make a conscious effort not to close her eyes and indulge in the feeling while she worked. She gently cleaned his wound and applied the antibiotic ointment to the stitched area before covering it with a clean, white dressing. She taped the dressing in place with white tape. "All done. You're as good as new."

"Oh, I'm not sure I was as good as new even when I was new." He flashed her a bright, slightly crooked smile, and she tingled all the way down to her toes. She had never met a man who had this effect on her.

"I have some discharge instructions here for you. Shall we review them?"

"Anything you say. I never turn down the request of a pretty lady."

A slow blush crept over Kylie's face and she became flustered trying to review the instructions. By now he must really be wondering about my competency as a nurse, she thought. How could she possibly concentrate on the signs of infection when he was causing every inch of her skin to tingle just by sitting close to her? "If you notice any wound coming from your drainage, uh, no, any drainage coming from your wound, well, not any drainage, only if it's green or dark yellow. Not clear, clear is okay, but not green. Green is bad. Well, green's not bad. I like green. I mean, as a color, green's a good color. But drainage green, er, I mean green drainage, not so good."

Michael laughed as Kylie tried to review the instructions without success. He was confident that at any other time, she could have rattled those instructions off without needing to look at the discharge sheet, but apparently, he was having the same effect on her that she was having on him. Suddenly, he was glad he let his friends talk him into coming to the Emergency Department to have the dart removed. "So, let me see if I understand this. Green drainage is bad. Green the color is good. Clear is okay. Is that clear the color or clear the drainage?"

"Clear the drainage. Clear the color is, actually, is clear even a color?"

"Apparently, I'm not a very good student. I think I need some remedial work. How about I hang around until you get off work and then I take you out for a coffee? That way I'll be sure to understand what you're telling me."

"Coffee?"

"Yes, I'm sure you're familiar with it. Dark, hot, good for the brain. Essential for life."

"I'm familiar."

"Great. So, you'll allow me the pleasure of taking you out for some?"

Warning signs were going off in Kylie's mind. She had always learned that it wasn't safe to go off with perfect strangers. And from what she could tell, he was about as perfect as they came. Anyway, he wasn't really a stranger. She was as familiar with the Bell name as everyone else in town. The Bells were quite a legacy. And it's not like no one would know where she was. She would mention it to Morgan and Jenny before she left. "Sure, Mr. Bell, coffee sounds great. But I don't get off for another twenty minutes."

"That's okay. I'll wait." He laid back on the gurney and stretched his long legs out in front of him. From the defiant look he had on his face, it was clear he planned to wait for her right there on the stretcher. She hurried back to the desk to complete her charting. Luckily, she had no active patients, so she didn't have to hang around to give report to the next shift of nurses. The second her shift was over, she punched out and joined Michael.

"I'm sorry our first date couldn't be something a bit more romantic than the hospital cafeteria. I'm usually much more creative than this, but not much is open at this hour. And I wasn't sure if you would be comfortable going off with me to places unknown."

"Oh, so this is a first date? I thought this was remedial discharge instructions."

"Please, I'm trying to save face. Let's just call it a date, okay?"

Kylie laughed. It was a sweet, melodic sound that pleased Michael. He liked the curve of her mouth when she was happy. He liked the shape of her lips. He found himself wondering what those lips would taste like and how soft they would feel under his. Would her kiss be soft and gentle or hard and full of passion? What would she do if he leaned across their table right now and pushed his mouth onto her full lips? He shook his head and rested his forehead on his outstretched hand. He had to stop this line of thinking. For all he knew, she was married with six kids at home.

He lifted his head to find Kylie staring at him with a questioning look in her eyes. He realized she had been speaking but he had no idea what she just said. He looked at her blankly.

"Are you okay? You look a little out of it."

"I'm fine. Really. Must be all the blood I lost during my little incident." He put on his best grin, hoping it would allow him to worm his way out of any further questions. It had always worked in the past.

"Okay, it's a date. I won't even offer to reimburse you for the coffee."

The date continued for another two hours before Michael walked Kylie to her car. Kylie usually dreaded the walk to the distant parking lot, but tonight it felt like she was floating on clouds. Michael was perfect. She was completely infatuated with him, and she sensed that he was attracted to her, too.

She did everything but cross her fingers for luck as they approached her car. Would he ask her on a second date?

"Thank you, Kylie, for agreeing to have coffee with me tonight. I enjoyed it."

"It was my pleasure."

She turned to face him as she slipped the keys out of her purse and pressed the button on her key fob, causing the lights to blink as the door unlocked. He was standing quite close to her now. He was looking into her eyes and she thought she noticed a subtle movement of his head as she raised her face to look into his. She thought he was going to move in and kiss her, but he stopped. Instead, he took her hand firmly in his and gave it a gentle squeeze. "May I call you?"

With a surprised look on her face, Kylie fully opened her eyes. "Oh, yes. Of course. I would like that."

He helped her into her car and reached across her to pull the seatbelt snugly around her. With a click of the belt and a slam of the door, he left her to drive herself home. He made the brief walk back to his car in a happier state of mind than he had experienced in years.

Their second date proved much more romantic than their first. Michael called her three days later and invited her out for dinner. He said to dress casually and more importantly, warmly, and to expect a beautiful view of the shore.

Eager with anticipation, Kylie pulled on black pants and a royal blue shirt. She put her hair in a twist in case it was windy at the shore, holding it in place with a silver rhinestone clip. She tried not to peer out the window every couple of seconds to see if he had arrived yet. By the time he got there, she had pulled the curtain back at least a dozen times.

Finally, his car pulled into the drive. Kylie felt a ripple of desire rush through her body when she opened the door and saw him standing there. Large, muscular body, lopsided, boyish grin, a small bouquet of yellow tulips. As they walked to his car, he put his hand gently on the small of her back. Just that simple act stirred up a passion that burned deep inside of her. Never before had a man affected her this strongly.

Kylie had expected him to drive to one of the restaurants that lined the beach. She was taken aback when he instead headed for the pier. Seeing the surprised look on her face, Michael said, "Oh, did I forget to mention that we would be enjoying the beautiful ocean view from the water, not the shore?"

He took her hand and led her down a narrow wharf. Docked at the very end was a gleaming white yacht, the C. C. Carillon, being attended to by a small, uniformed staff. He helped her climb aboard and soon they were cruising over a moonlit ocean.

"Michael, you were right. The view is incredible."

"I totally agree," he added as he gazed across the small, covered table directly at Kylie.

The engines slowed and one of the staff members, a weathered-looking man named Van, served an exquisitely prepared Beef Wellington in a rich, red cabernet sauce. Kylie wanted to appear ladylike, but the meal was so enjoyable that she ate every bite before placing her fork across her clean plate. "That was delicious. Thank you so much, Michael."

"My pleasure. I'm glad you enjoyed it. I think everything tastes better in the sea air." He leaned across the table and tucked a piece of wind-whipped hair behind her ear, his fingers lingering just behind her earlobe. Kylie felt her body burn with desire.

"I'm having a wonderful evening. How about you?"

"This is amazing. I've never been out on a boat at night before. It's incredible."

Michael stood up and pulled Kylie to her feet. They walked to the rear of the yacht and Michael put his arm around her to steady her as the engines picked up speed. Kylie thought she would melt with yearning.

"Do you see that light over there?" he asked as he pointed to a small beam on an island off the rocky shore.

That's the lighthouse on Seal Island. Submerged just below the water are rows of jagged black rocks. It's been said that more than one captain has gone down with his ship on those rocks, at least before the lighthouse was built."

"How tragic. To be close enough to home to see the lights burning and then not make it. We're not going anywhere near them, are we?"

"No, no need to worry. Captain Hoffmeister has been navigating this harbor since before you were born."

Suddenly, Michael took Kylie's face into his hands and kissed her. The intensity of his kiss startled Kylie and she took a step back, but he reached his arm around her and pulled her close to him. Overcome with longing and the realization that he wanted her as much as she wanted him, Kylie put her arms around his broad back and returned his kiss. She could feel her lips tingle as he pushed his mouth hard against hers. His hands caressed her shoulders and the back of her neck. She felt a moan escape when he parted her lips with his probing tongue, his breath hot against her mouth. Her body burned with a hunger that pulsated throughout every vein, every muscle in her body.

Ready to give in to her desire, Kylie looked deeply into Michael's eyes. They were sincere. She wanted to trust that he was not trying to hurt her.

Michael pulled away and smiled, his breath quick. "I don't know what to say. I'm sorry. I don't usually force myself on a woman like this."

"Oh, you force yourself on a woman in a different

way?" Good Lord, Kylie, she thought to herself. Why did you have to say something so stupid? Michael looked at her questioningly and she wondered if she should tell him about her habit of making really stupid jokes when she was nervous. No. No point in scaring him off so early in their relationship. Instead, she gave him a lame smile and rested her head against his chest.

He held her against him as the boat made its way toward the dock. When they turned to go back to the table to sit down, Kylie was surprised to see the dishes had been cleared and all that remained was a single red rose lying in stark contrast to the white tablecloth. Could this night be any more perfect?

"Mrs. Bell, you can come in now."

Kylie was startled and opened her eyes. So lost in remembering her second date with Michael, she forgot she was sitting on a bench in the hallway of the courthouse. It took her mind more than a few seconds to reorient to the present time, saddened at having to leave the joyous memory of that beautiful night behind. Attorney Tim Stone was staring at her through his thick glasses. "Mrs. Bell? Did you hear me?"

She reached her hand up and ran it through her hair. "Yes, yes I heard." She pulled herself to her feet and smoothed out her skirt with the palms of her hands. At only 5'3" she was on the shorter side, but with her 3-inch heels, she was the same height as the lawyer who was now holding open one of the many identical doors that lined the long gray hallway. She walked through the door and there, standing close enough to touch, was Michael.

"Kylie."

She ran into his waiting arms and pushed up against his broad chest. Immediately his arms were around her, his hands running up and down her back as if he couldn't touch enough of her at once. Her eyes glistened with tears as she squeezed him back. It felt like it had been forever since he held her, not just the two days it had really been.

Phil gave them a moment, but then he was back to business. "Okay you two, let's finish up at the courthouse, and then you can go home to do that." Michael brought Kylie to his side but kept his arm firmly clenched around her. They both tried to focus their attention on Phil.

"Michael, you understand that you cannot leave this area for any reason. It's expected that you can't leave the country or the state, and thanks to the judge's last comment, you can't leave Cayne. Let's not make anyone nervous and talk about putting you back in jail. This is going to be a very public case and people won't like it if they think you are wandering around free because of your money."

"Do you think they'll be okay to find out that I'm wandering around free because I'm innocent?"

"They won't see it that way. Trust me. Do what I tell you and we'll get through this."

"I understand. But what about Latchy Harbor? I do need to travel that far."

"We've discussed this, Michael. That is further than the 50-mile limit imposed by the judge. You can't do it.

And let's not forget the press. They may be hot on your heels for a while. Do you really want them to follow you there?"

"But Phil," Michael glanced nervously at Kylie and then back at Phil, "I have to. You know that. How can I not go?"

Kylie cast a questioning look at the two men but said nothing. "Stay close to home, Michael, unless you want to trade Kylie for a roommate named Bubba. Don't leave town."

"Please listen to him, Michael," Kylie cried. "How would I ever face the public again if you cast me aside for a 350-pound man with a tattoo of his mother across his chest? I'd be scorned."

Kylie's comment lightened the tension in the room, slightly, and slowly the team of attorneys, Michael and Kylie, filed through the gray metal door. "Have you made the arrangements, Tim?" Phil asked the attorney who appeared to be next in command.

"I did, sir. If Mr. and Mrs. Bell will follow me, we will exit the building this way." Tim stood and made a general sweeping motion toward a long hallway near the back of the building.

Phil shook hands with Michael and reassuringly patted Kylie on the shoulder. "You two go with Tim and he will try to keep you clear of the press. We will stall by the front doors to give you a running start. Oh, and don't worry about the Jeep. I'll have it delivered to your home later on today. It's not like you'll need it to go anywhere any time soon." His last comment was directed toward

Michael with a firm look. "I won't bother you today, but we'll get together soon."

After their goodbyes, Tim brought them across a short hallway and down a flight of stairs that led to a dark, smelly alley in the rear of the courthouse. He handed Michael an envelope containing his license and the paperwork from the court along with a set of car keys. Once they stepped into the trash-filled alley, Tim pointed to a small Toyota Prius parked next to a dirty recycling bin. "That's your transportation home, sir."

"That tiny little car is supposed to get me home? Tell me, Tim, does the key go in the ignition or do I wind it up from the back?"

"Oh no, sir. It's a very fuel-efficient model and it is actually quite comfortable." Tim rambled on another minute before he saw the playful smile that had perched on Michael's face. "Oh, sorry sir. It's just that, well, that's my car. I will be by with your Jeep later on today to switch back."

"Don't trouble yourself, Tim. Why don't you keep it until morning? I'm pretty sure we'll be rather occupied for the rest of today." Michael winked at Kylie and walked her to the inconspicuous silver vehicle. Suddenly he couldn't wait to go home.

6

The house was exactly as it was when he and Kylie left to celebrate their anniversary, yet somehow it felt warmer and more welcoming as they walked in now than it did when they left. He was home. Kylie continued to the other side of the room but stopped and turned toward Michael. She laughed at the look of wonder that was on his face. "Are you going to drop and kiss the floor, or what?"

"Well, I'd like to, but I think I'll settle for you, instead."

"Be still my heart." She tried to express a pouting, dejected look, but instead walked back to Michael and pulled his arms around her. He was her husband and she wanted to be as close to him as possible.

"I've missed you so much, Kylie. I feel like I've been away for months; it's hard to believe it's only been a few days."

"Me too, Michael. Me too." She held him tightly, her arms wrapped around his waist, enjoying the feeling of his hot, muscular back against her palms. She kept her face close to his chest. She could feel his body heat penetrating the thin material of his shirt as she savored the smell of his very essence. It was so good to have him home where he belonged, and she didn't want to ever let him go.

Michael pulled away first. He took a small step back, but like a man hungering for oxygen, he couldn't keep his hands off of her. As much as he wanted her, he knew they had other issues to address. Issues that he should have dealt with a year ago. He reached over and tucked a long, stray curl behind her ear. "I guess we have to talk."

"I think so. Are you hungry? Do you want me to make an early dinner while we talk?"

"No, let's get this taken care of first. After you hear what I have to say, you may not want to make me dinner. You may not want me at all."

"That could never happen." She reached up and rested her hands on his shoulders, looking directly into his eyes. "I love you, Michael Bell, and there is nothing you can say or do that will ever change that. Nothing. We were meant to be together forever, and we will be. Do you understand what I'm saying?"

"Do you think I killed him? Louis Joyce? Are you telling me you will stand by me even if I did?"

"I don't think you killed him, Michael. I'm sure of it. You are not that kind of man. I know you better than anyone. I know your heart. Your soul. You are not a

116

killer. I also want you to know that our love is eternal. It transcends anything that man can create on this earth. Don't you see that? We were meant for each other. Our love is forever."

"I love you, Kylie. I am so grateful you are my wife. And I am sorry that you are being dragged into this horrible mess, this nightmare." Once again, he pulled her close and nuzzled his mouth along the top of her head, breathing in the fresh kiwi scent of her shampoo. They clung to each other, both making silent promises to love each other forever, no matter what.

"C'mon, let's go into the family room and sit down. We might as well be comfortable. This discussion isn't going to be fun."

They walked down the short hall, Michael stopping in the kitchen just long enough to pull two beers from the refrigerator to bring with him into the family room. A brick fireplace sat beneath a glossy maple mantle. Above the mantle, the focus of the room was their wedding picture. Kylie stared at that picture as they sat next to each other on the oversized couch. Michael followed her gaze and for a moment; neither of them spoke. He opened the beers and passed one to Kylie. She leaned up against him, continuing to look at their wedding picture. It was hard to believe a year had passed since that day, the day she married the love of her life.

Their wedding was on the last Friday night in September. It was an elaborate affair with 275 guests. At first, Kylie was upset that Cynthia Bell was insisting on this type of extravaganza for her wedding, but after a while, even she was caught up in the planning and prepping. At least she was caught up in the minimal number of decisions that Cynthia allowed her to make. "After all, dear," Cynthia would say in her most condescending tone, "it's not like you have any experience planning an event of this magnitude. Just leave the details to me and things will go smoothly. It will be the perfect wedding. You'll see."

Initially, Kylie was angered, if not hurt, by Cynthia's comments. Michael assured her that he would be more than happy to put an end to it. He didn't care if they had an elaborate wedding or if they got married at city hall. He just wanted them to be married. He also explained that Cynthia was going overboard with this wedding because she hadn't been invited to his previous wedding. This would be her only chance to upstage the weddings of every daughter of every friend in her social circle. This made Kylie think about things from Cynthia's perspective, and while she didn't care about being used to impress Cynthia's friends, she tried to be understanding. Why not let her put on the wedding of all weddings? Might as well start the marriage off with a happy mother-in-law. Anyway, if this massive, elaborate wedding appealed to Cynthia, then so be it. She turned the wedding plans over to Cynthia and found that things did go much smoother when she wasn't involved.

Of course, there were a few details that did annoy Kylie. Cynthia's superiority could be troublesome, especially when she made Kylie feel unworthy of marrying into such a distinguished family. She referred to

Kylie as Kylie Dixon of the Northeastern Textiles Dixons instead of Kylie Dixon whose alcoholic father occasionally worked for shoe manufacturing companies. When Kylie wanted to have Hannah Martin, the closest thing she ever had to a best friend, serve as her maid of honor, Cynthia nixed the idea. "No, dear, that won't do at all. She just won't fit in with the image we need for your maid of honor." Instead, Cynthia chose a family acquaintance named Olivia Pembroke to serve in that role. Olivia was tall and graceful and looked like a New York fashion model. She was everything Kylie was not, and Kylie hated her from the moment she laid eyes on her size two frame and her mile-long legs. To this day she wondered if Cynthia really chose her to honor a family friend or as a dig because Kylie possessed none of the qualities that came so naturally to Olivia.

Then there was the battle that almost ended Cynthia's wedding planning. Kylie had her heart set on a strapless white wedding gown. She had dreamed about it since she was a child. It would be a soft, satin dress with a cinched waist and a long, flowing skirt. The bust would be outlined with tiny pearls and crystal sparkles and the train would fasten in a bustle in back of her when she danced.

Cynthia told her that was not acceptable. It would contrast with the style she had chosen for the attendants, and she discreetly lowered her voice and pointed out that Kylie didn't have the shoulders for that elegant of a look. Kylie put her foot down, however, and refused to relinquish her choice of dress. She would not wear the gaudy ivory lace dress that Cynthia selected. It was her

119

wedding, and she would only wear the white satin dress. Deep inside, though, Cynthia had done damage. Kylie was having doubts about how the dress would look. What if she really did have bad shoulders? What if the dress didn't fit in with the rest of the wedding? She cried to Michael about it because she didn't know what to do. Should she give in to Cynthia or was Cynthia playing on her insecurities to get her own way? In the end, Michael became involved and told his mother to back off. Kylie wore the dress she wanted, the dress of her dreams.

What Cynthia couldn't have in a bride, she decided to have in bridesmaids. She selected six of the most beautiful and stylish young women she could find. They were all daughters of distinguished family friends, and they were all happy to be in Cynthia's only son's wedding. Each bridesmaid, dressed in an elegant gown of emerald green, royal blue, or magenta, looked lovelier than the one before. They were perfection, and when paired with the wealthy young men wearing black tuxedos and crisp, white shirts who ushered them down the aisle, the image rivaled any picture out of the finest bridal magazines. Kylie could have easily felt dowdy and inferior if it wasn't for Michael, but the look on his face was clear. He thought she looked beautiful. To Kylie, nothing else mattered.

The wedding was a candlelight service held on the grounds of the Old Rollins Inn, a historic landmark situated high on the Maine coast. Prior to marrying Michael, Kylie couldn't have afforded to set foot on the grounds of this resort as a housekeeper, let alone the guest of honor. The magnificent green lawns were surrounded by thousands of white candles, all kept burning with the assistance of an entire team of workers that Cynthia employed. White netting and bold flowers were expertly arranged throughout the wedding area. A five-piece orchestra filled the air with waves of classical music, and the large staff ensured that every glass was filled with the finest champagne. The tables were stocked with caviar, canapes, and other delicacies. With subtle hints of lighting adding to the natural glow of the full moon, the wedding was basked with an enchanted white light that was as unusual as it was beautiful. The wedding was a success, and while Michael Bell may have been marrying a woman of minimal heritage, at least he did so in style.

Kylie was smiling with these memories when Michael adjusted his arm. His slight stirring brought her back to the present. "Oh, sorry. I guess I was lost there for a bit. Whenever I look at our wedding picture, I can't help but think of our wedding and how I am truly the luckiest girl in the world."

"I'm glad you remember it so fondly. As I recall, there was a time when city hall sounded mighty good."

"True, but I'm glad we did it the way we did. It really was beautiful, and if Cynthia got her jollies off by making it the social event of the year, so be it. I still came out on top."

"Mmm, and sometimes on the bottom," Michael added with a playful gleam in his eye.

Kylie readjusted her position and turned to face

Michael. He smiled at her and said, "I guess this means it's time to talk."

"I guess so. You said there are things you need to tell me. Something about that Joyce fellow."

"Yes, there are some things you need to know." Michael straightened on the couch and crossed and uncrossed his legs. He clasped his hands and studied his fingers. After a long swig of his beer, he took a deep breath and looked at Kylie. "I did know Louis Joyce. He used to be my brother-in-law."

Michael let this comment register with Kylie before he continued. He watched as she sorted things through. Having a connection to a murder victim that you were arguing with only minutes before he was murdered did not exactly scream innocence. He watched as her face went from puzzlement to concentration to fear. He knew she was beginning to understand the trouble he was in. He wondered if she still believed him. He hoped so. He needed her on his side.

Her face registered shock, but only for a moment. She took a deep breath and clearly made a decision to check her feelings. Her only response was, "Go on."

"Melanie and I had only been married for a short time when I first met Louis Joyce. He was her half-brother on her mother's side. He had grown up with his father and he and Melanie were not close. But he was her brother, and she did feel a certain degree of loyalty to him. Anyway, it was the first fall after we were married when he showed up on our doorstep in Boston. Melanie was pregnant and I had only been working for four or five months. She called me and told me to come right home after work, we had company.

I knew very little of Melanie's family and I was surprised to find this scrawny kid with ripped jeans and a long blond ponytail standing in my kitchen. He must have been 18 or 19 years old at the time. He was just passing through, he said, although how one just passes through Boston when traveling from Nebraska to Georgia I'll never know. He told us that he had a chance at making some real money in Georgia. A friend of his owned a fishing boat and he needed help running his business. Louis explained that he would be working long hours, seven days a week, but it would give him enough money to make a fresh start for himself. He could go back to school for his GED, and maybe even have a business of his own someday. It sounded like a pipe dream to me, but he did tell a convincing tale and he was Melanie's brother.

We agreed to help him out a bit. I gave him some cash, not a lot—a few hundred dollars, but it was enough to get him bus fare to Georgia and allow him to eat a few decent meals along the way. I wondered if that was what he would do with the money, he looked like he might have a bad habit or two, if you know what I mean. But Melanie seemed happy for him. She said he was going to turn his life around this time. I gave him the cash and Melanie insisted we put him up for the night. By the time we woke up in the morning, he was gone.

Melanie was sad that he left without saying goodbye, but quite honestly, I was relieved. I didn't trust him. I would like to say he proved me wrong, but shortly after he left Melanie noticed her diamond and sapphire ring was missing. Other than her wedding band, it was the only piece of jewelry I ever bought her. The last time she remembered seeing it, she had left it on the counter in the bathroom. You have to understand, we didn't have much money back then. I used my family money to lease the brownstone we were living in. I wasn't using it for any of our living expenses. I had just started working and Melanie, well, she was an artist. The term 'starving artist' is quite popular for a reason."

Michael shifted his weight and settled into a different position on the couch. He looked at Kylie. "You with me so far?"

"I'm listening." Her expression gave no indication of how she was feeling.

"We didn't see Louis again for over a year. This time he showed up a few days before Christmas. Molly was almost a year old. She was a lively little girl, into everything." Michael's eyes glistened with bittersweet memories of his daughter. His voice cracked when he tried to continue, and it took him several minutes before he could start back up. "Louis had shown up with no job, no money, and no GED. The fishing job wasn't the sure thing he claimed it would be. He had big plans, though. This time he was heading to West Virginia. He heard he could make big money working on one of the crews hired to finish building the pipeline through the state. As before, he only needed a few hundred dollars to get him there. Ha, he even promised to pay us back."

Michael looked at Kylie but she remained emotionless, so he continued his story. "While he was telling us of his glorified plans, Molly was crawling around on the floor. The house was well baby-proofed, so we didn't have to worry. Plus, we never let her out of our sight. What we didn't notice was that she had crawled over to Louis' worn backpack and started pulling out the contents. The dirty socks and smelly underwear may have been funny, but when I looked over and saw my baby girl playing with a dime bag of marijuana, well, I lost it. I threw his bag and his dope and his sorry ass out on the street."

"Michael, you didn't. What did Melanie say? Was she angry?"

"Mostly she was confused. She wanted to be a good sister and help him, but he really crossed the line when he brought drugs into our home. Around our daughter. I think she was hurt more than angry. Anyway, another year went by before he showed up again. This time Melanie, Molly, and I were walking home from the corner grocery to find him sitting on the front stoop. As usual, his long, stringy hair was pulled back in a ponytail and his jeans were dirty and full of holes. His winter parka was old and worn. He wasn't wearing a hat or gloves. I figured he was here for another handout, and I wondered what it would cost me this time to get rid of him."

"Michael, that's terrible. A year had gone by. Maybe he had changed."

"Leopards don't change their spots. Melanie,

however, felt differently, and she greeted her brother with a warm hug. She invited him to come in and he only hesitated long enough to shoot me a look. He must have decided I wasn't going to kill him, so he hooked his arm through Melanie's and together they walked into the house. I brought Molly in and started getting her out of her snowsuit. Melanie and Louis were talking in hushed voices in the other room, but I could still hear them. Noise resounded well in that old brownstone. Melanie was asking exactly what he wanted, and Louis was assuring her he was off drugs for good. He was heading back to Nebraska. He had enrolled in night school and was going to get his GED. He wasn't messing around this time. I laughed when I heard him. Every time he showed up his promises got bigger."

Michael stopped talking long enough to stare off into space, clearly thinking back to that time so long ago. He swigged his beer and then returned to his story. "This time Melanie didn't sound too convinced, at least at first. But Louis told her he didn't want any money from us, and he was sorry for the way he acted before. He said he only wanted to make amends before he went home. That boy could talk a good story. He stayed with us for a few days. I watched him like a hawk, but never did I see anything that indicated he was on drugs. He seemed different. He was calmer and easier to talk to. He helped Melanie in the kitchen. He asked me about work. He was more interested in Molly than he ever was before. He actually spent some of his time playing with her. Before he left, he posed with Molly in one arm and Melanie in the other, and I took a picture with an old Polaroid we used to have. He laughed when he noticed that Molly was wearing the silver bell necklace that Melanie always wore. Melanie explained that she was already the luckiest woman around, now it was Molly's turn to claim her share of Grandma's good luck. Melanie gave him the picture to remember them by. When he left at the end of the week, I found myself insisting he take the cash I had in my hand to get home with. To this day I don't know if he was sincere, or if he played us all along."

"You did the right thing, Michael, giving him the money like that. If you were wrong, then a few dollars wouldn't destroy him. But if you were right and he had changed, well, how reassuring it must have been to know he had family that cared."

"He left on a Friday and until a few months ago, I hadn't heard from him since that night. I tried to find him when Melanie died, but the mail I sent came back as undeliverable. I searched the internet and Facebook, but nothing showed up. I didn't know how to reach him and eventually, I just quit worrying about it."

Kylie shifted in her chair, uncomfortable both physically and where this conversation was heading. She wanted him to share everything with her, but she wasn't sure she was going to like what he was about to say. For one thing, she was already upset that he had chosen to keep such a big part of his life a secret from her. She didn't understand why he would do that. Still, she stayed quiet and let him continue with his story.

"How are you holding up?"

"I can't say I'm enjoying this, but I'm fine. Just keep going."

"It gets worse, Kylie. There are things I should have told you. Things I wanted to tell you, but I didn't."

Kylie braced herself as she felt a chill crawl up her spine. "Tell me now."

"Like I said, I hadn't seen or heard from Louis since he left that night. Then, about three months ago, I got a call from him. Somehow, he knew about Melanie. At first, I figured he was going to work on my sympathy, you know, try to get money out of me. But then he congratulated me on our wedding, so that didn't really make any sense. He sounded genuinely happy for us. It wasn't long, though, before he made it clear what he was looking for. He wanted money, Kylie. A lot of money."

"What's a lot of money?"

"The figure he opened with was a cool million."

"One million dollars! Why in the world would he think you would give him that kind of money?"

"He found out something about me that next to no one knows and he threatened to go public with it. It would be hurtful if he did. Too hurtful." Michael took Kylie's hands into his own. His eyes searched hers for an indication of what she was feeling. He dreaded what he would see there because he knew whatever it was, it was about to get worse.

"Michael, you're scaring me. What could he possibly know about you that he could blackmail you for?"

"It's Molly. My daughter. She didn't die in that accident all those years ago. She's alive."

"Molly is alive? But you said, you told me, I thought she was killed with Melanie. Why would you lie about that? Why, Michael? Why?"

Michael's heart filled with pain as he watched his wife's body start to tremble. How could he ever explain why he kept his daughter a secret from her, especially since he wasn't even sure why himself? He had kept this secret for so long, from so many people, that it no longer felt natural to talk about her to anyone. But now, as he stared into his wife's green eyes, eyes that stared vacantly past him, he knew he was wrong. He should have told her.

Michael spent the better part of the next hour telling Kylie about the accident, Molly, and why Molly's being alive was kept hidden from the public. He tried to explain how he couldn't bear the thought of Molly's picture being splattered across television or the internet, or how the thought of reporters hanging around the facility where Molly lived just so they could get a picture of the 'poor little rich girl' made his skin crawl. It sickened him to think of his daughter being exploited as an object of pity and he would not subject her to that. She had already suffered so much in her life. He would not allow anyone to hurt her even more.

Kylie sat in silence as he talked. Her emotions ranged from anger to sorrow to fear. The more he explained about Molly, the more she understood his choice to whisk her away from the media in Boston and hide her in a private hospital in Maine. What she couldn't understand was why he decided to keep that secret from her. She was his wife. She was the one person to whom he could tell anything. She loved him more than anyone in the world. Why would he lie to her? But as she looked at her grief-stricken husband, she couldn't sustain her anger. Who knows how she would act in the same situation? It's not like she's never had secrets of her own. She sat there, unmoving, not sure what to do next. She wanted to hug him, but her body refused to cooperate. She couldn't quite get past the lies. Yet.

What she did grasp was the peril that Michael was now in. Once the police uncovered this connection, it would provide them with a motive for Michael wanting Louis dead. This information would make it difficult for Phil to prove Michael's innocence, yet she believed him wholeheartedly. She didn't doubt for a moment that Michael was innocent. He simply was not the kind of man to resort to murder.

She looked at her husband, but he didn't speak. Her mind worked frantically to try to sort through the information he had just provided to her. Try as she might she simply did not know what to say.

Michael also sat in silence, looking younger than his 38 years. His vulnerability touched her and she reached her hand to his. Finally, Kylie broke the silence. "Where is Molly now?"

"Ah, yes, my beautiful little Molly. She is still alive, thank God. She lives in the same facility she was brought to ten years ago. It is her home now. Most of the staff are the same as they were at the beginning. See, Father pays them very well for their excellent care and, of course, their discretion."

"Is she okay?"

A bitter laugh came from Michael's parted lips. "Okay? Define okay. Does she run and play and laugh like other little girls her age? Hardly. Will she grow up and go on dates and get married and have a family of her own? No. So, if you mean okay like you would mean normal, then no, she's not okay. She'll never be okay. But if you mean okay in that she can breathe and eat and walk on her own, then she's more than okay. She can live in a hospital her entire life and be okay."

Michael jumped up from the couch and paced the room with fists clenched and a dark, worn scowl on his face. Kylie remained curled up on the couch, her eyes never leaving him as he walked. "I'm sorry." Kylie's voice was soft, barely audible. "I just wanted to know how she was. I didn't mean anything by it. I just wanted to know."

Michael stopped pacing and approached Kylie. He knelt on the floor next to her and laid his head in her lap. Almost at once her hands found their way to his hair. "Molly has the mind of a four-year-old, but she will never improve. She will never live the life of a normal child. She can walk and get around, but her fine motor skills are severely limited. She will never hold an adult conversation. She won't go to regular school or learn to read or write. She will enjoy a picture book, but she will never understand a great work of literature. She can listen to music, but she can't remember the words enough to sing along. Sometimes when I visit her, I take her outside and she throws a ball to me. I can throw it back, but she can't catch it. I will hold her hand and take her for a walk, but she isn't allowed to ever go alone.

She has extremely limited speech capabilities. Her vocabulary is limited, as is her memory. I visit her every week and she knows who I am. When I walk in she smiles and calls me dada, but that's all. She seldom says more than that. That's what's left of my little girl, Kylie. The little girl that used to run into my arms and hug me when I came home after work now sits in a special chair and says dada like I'm nothing more to her than the staff member who brings her lunch. But she's still my girl. And that bastard was going to take that away from me."

Kylie remained silent, her hands busy smoothing Michael's hair as he remained on his knees by her side. Tears rolled down his cheeks and soaked Kylie's black skirt. Her heart ached as she listened to the sobs pour forth from him, each one touching her deeper than the last. Finally, he lifted his tear-streaked face and looked at his wife. "I'm sorry for not telling you about Molly. I've kept her a secret for so long that it felt like a betrayal to tell someone about her. I'm sorry, Kylie. I should have told you."

"It's okay, Michael. Really. But just promise me that you won't keep any other secrets from me. I love you and I'm here for you. I'll do whatever I can to make your life complete, but no more secrets. Please."

"No more, I promise."

Michael pulled himself up from the floor and rejoined Kylie on the couch. He leaned against the pillows that were piled high against the couch's wide arm and pulled Kylie with him so her back was resting on his chest. He wrapped his arms around her waist and she crossed her hands over his. After a moment she said, "You still haven't told me about how Louis was going to blackmail you. How did he find out about Molly?"

"Louis called me a while ago. He said he had been traveling around the country trying to find work. As always, he was scraping by, working one odd job after another. He had made his way up the coast working on lobster boats. Remember, he did have a little fishing experience. He heard the big money for lobstering was in Maine. He was having lunch in a little restaurant in Latchy Harbor when a couple came in with a little blond girl. He figured she was ten or eleven. Tiny, blue eyes, exceptionally pretty. He said she looked familiar, but he couldn't quite place her. He took pleasure in telling me he watched her for a while, something about her intrigued him, but it wasn't until he heard the couple say something that made him realize they weren't her parents that he started to figure it out. They said they were her caretakers, and that she required long-term medical care due to an accident that happened a long time ago. Then it came to him. She looked like Melanie. He wasn't sure at first, so he kept talking to them. He kept the conversation light so they wouldn't suspect he was trying to get information out of them. He was slimy, but he sure knew how to play people. While they chatted, he noticed the necklace Molly was wearing. It was a silver bell. The bell was long and shiny and flared out at the bottom. It was the same necklace that Melanie used to wear. At that moment, he knew that the little girl sitting before him was his niece. He told me when he got up to leave, he leaned over and whispered 'Goodbye Molly' to her, and she smiled. That confirmed what he already knew."

Michael shifted his position on the couch and stared straight ahead, his expression blank. It took a minute but then he continued. "He didn't tell me what happened next, but I assume he followed Stacy and Francesco, they are Molly's caretakers, when they left the restaurant and took Molly home. I don't know if he befriended them or worked for them or stole from them, but the next thing I knew, he was calling me for a million dollars. He told me he had Molly's necklace, a little silver bell that she always wore. It used to belong to Melanie. I believed him. The staff had reported to me that it was missing. He told me that if I didn't give him the money, he was going to take the necklace and the picture of Melanie, himself, and Molly wearing that necklace to the press. While it may not have been enough to prove that Molly was my daughter, or more importantly, C. C. Bell's granddaughter, it was enough for the press to start snooping. It's a precarious lie, Kylie. It wouldn't take long for them to put it all together and expose the truth. Everything I tried to hide, everything I tried to protect her from, would be out in the open. Molly's life would never be the same. She would never be able to go outside and play ball or go to a restaurant. There would always be reporters. I couldn't risk it. So, I paid him. It was a lot of money, but at the time, it seemed worth it. I thought he would go away."

"But that wasn't the end of it, was it?"

"No. That wasn't the end of it. I didn't hear from him for a couple of weeks. Then he called again. He wanted another million. I couldn't believe it. That punk never had a dime to his name and now he wasn't satisfied with a million friggin dollars? I didn't know what to do. At first, I told him no. He wasn't getting another dime. I called his bluff and life went on as always. I continued to visit Molly and no one had seen him hanging around." Michael paused and shifted his position. He finished his beer and faced Kylie. Holding her hands, he said, "Again, I am so sorry I never told you this. I can see now what a mistake that was."

Kylie shook her head no, but her down-turned mouth and furrowed brow gave away her anguish. This deception had deeply hurt her. "Let's not talk about that now. Let's talk about Louis Joyce. I can only take so much at a time, and right now, this is what we need to focus on. So, you refused to give him more money. Then what happened."

"He left a message on my cellphone. He told me my time was up. Either I give him the million or he goes to the press. I finally agreed to one more million, but this was the end of it. I told him I wanted the necklace and the picture. I knew he could make copies, but they would never be as believable as an original. I also started making arrangements to move Molly. The staff at Latchy Harbor could hide her for a short time if the press showed up, but they wouldn't be able to keep up that charade for any length of time. If I had other arrangements made, as soon as the first reporter arrived, I would sneak her out, and hopefully, they would think they were following a false lead."

Kylie could sense how hard it was for Michael to talk about this, but she remained seated on the couch and quietly waited for him to begin again. He got up and walked around the room for a minute, like a caged animal looking to escape, but with nowhere to go. He returned to her side and ran his hand through his hair. He turned to her and put his hand over hers. Then he resumed his story.

"I put the money together and agreed to meet him one last time. I would give him the money, he would give me the necklace and the picture. I made it very clear this would be the last time I would ever talk to him. I had already decided to move Molly. If he tried to blackmail me again, he wouldn't find her. She would be gone. I talked to her caretakers, Stacy and Francesco. They agreed to move. I had my people looking for another location. Once they found something, the property at Latchy Harbor would revert to my father. It is in his name. He can sell it or convert it to a resort, whatever he chooses. Either way, Molly won't be there. I've even toyed with changing Molly's name. It could be the safest thing for her, but it could also be confusing. She knows her name. She might not do well with change. Anyway, the only thing left to do was to meet with Louis. I was just waiting for his call."

"That was him that called you in the car on our anniversary, wasn't it? That was why you didn't want me to answer the phone."

"Yes, when you read the number off, I knew that was him. But I didn't want to meet with him. Not that night. Not on our night. I didn't want to deal with him. I didn't even want to think about him. I swear, Kylie, I didn't know he was going to be at the restaurant. I don't know how he knew where we were going to be."

"Oh, God, Michael. You saw him when you left to get the vehicle. You saw him when I went to the bathroom." Kylie started to shake. "I should have been with you."

"No, Kylie, no. I didn't know he was going to be there. I promise you. I went outside to go to the garage and there he was. It was almost like he was waiting for me. I saw him and we had words. I told him to leave me alone. This wasn't the time. I didn't even have the money with me. We argued. It got loud. People stared at us. He dangled Molly's necklace in front of my face. I wanted to grab it. I wanted to take it away from him, but there were people all around. They were stopping to watch. I just told him later. Then I turned my back on him and walked away. That was all, Kylie. I walked away and he was alive. I don't know what happened to him. I never looked back. I was angry. Hell, I was mad enough to kill him, but I didn't. I swear. I never touched him. I went to the garage, got in the Lexus, and came back to get you."

Michael stopped talking and stared at Kylie as if trying to read her mind. What was she thinking? Did she believe him? He had to know.

"You must have been going out of your mind all this time. Why didn't you tell me? I'm your wife. Maybe I could have helped."

"How, Kylie? What could you have done? Realized what a fool I had been to get messed up with the likes of him? He took me for a million dollars and here I was, ready to give him more. It's just that I was so afraid Molly would be hurt. I didn't want her to suffer because I screwed up. She's gone through so much already."

"I know, babe. I just feel sad that you had to go through this alone. I married you for better or for worse. I will stand by you no matter what, Michael. I love you."

"You're right, I should have told you. I thought I could take care of this alone, but I messed everything up. But Kylie, do you believe me?"

"I do, Michael. Of course, I believe you."

"Oh, thank God. It was all so strange. I didn't plan to see him that night. Like I said, it was our anniversary. I wouldn't spoil it with the likes of him. But he was acting like I had been expecting him. He demanded his money and said he would give me the picture right then and there. I told him I didn't carry that kind of money on me, and he would have to wait. He was upset and started to yell some nasty things at me. Like I said, we had words, but that was the end of it. After all, I had a beautiful woman waiting inside the restaurant for me."

Michael took a deep breath and sank further into the couch, relieved that Kylie finally knew the entire truth. It would be easier to face what was ahead knowing that

Kylie would be standing by his side. He put his arm around his wife and pulled her close to him. He closed his eyes and nuzzled her head. He almost cried when he heard her whisper, "I do believe you, Michael. I do."

"Well, you may be the only one."

At that moment, a soft chime interrupted their conversation. Kylie rose and stretched before going to the front door to see who rang the bell. They weren't expecting any visitors and she didn't think a reporter would be so brazen as to come right to their door. Anyway, she thought, she could use a break from their conversation. Her head was spinning.

She pulled open the solid oak door and peeked out to see Phil standing there in the bright sun. The look on his face, however, was anything but bright. It was dark and ominous. "May I come in?"

"Phil, please." Kylie stepped back and motioned him in. Michael joined them in the front foyer.

"Phil, I thought we weren't going to see you until later in the week."

"You weren't, but this is important. I have to ask you a question."

"Okay, what is it? Michael tapped his foot nervously against the hardwood floor. Phil didn't look like he was here to share good news.

"Michael, are you the registered owner of a .38 Special?"

7

"My gun? You came all the way over here to ask me about my gun?" Michael stared at Phil with a look of astonishment on his face. He walked to Kylie and stood behind her, gently grasping her upper arms with his hands.

Kylie didn't move when Michael touched her. Even when he pulled her up against him, she didn't react. The shock of what Phil was saying surrounded her, suffocating her with fear. Why was Phil asking about Michael's gun?

"A gun was turned into the police. A .38 Special. It washed ashore on the beach. The same beach you and Kylie went to on your anniversary. It's your gun, Michael. The police traced it. It's registered to you."

"I don't know what to say. I never even fired the damn thing. I haven't seen that gun for months; not since we moved here. Before that, it just sat in a box in my closet. When we bought this house last spring, I figured it was lost in the move. It might have been in one of the boxes that went to my parents' house. Or maybe one that was donated to Goodwill. I guess it's even possible that one of the movers took it. I just know when we unpacked, it didn't show up. Kylie doesn't like guns, so I didn't worry about it."

"That's the best you can do? It was lost in the move? A mover took it? Why didn't you report it missing? Most people advise the police when something as valuable as a gun is missing."

"I didn't really think about it. I never thought of it as stolen, I just figured it was lost. And like I said, Kylie doesn't like guns. She said it's against her profession. She was an emergency department nurse when I met her. Said she's seen too many gunshot wounds to be comfortable with a gun in the house. So, when it was lost, I didn't really care about finding it. It didn't seem that important."

"Well, it sure seems important now. That piece of evidence ties you directly to the crime scene. I have to tell you, Michael, this doesn't look good. If your fingerprints are on that gun, you're done."

"They're not on the gun. I haven't touched it in years."

"That's not your only concern. If ballistics determine that gun is the murder weapon, it's going to hurt your case. They didn't find any shell casings at the scene. Do you know why they didn't find any? Because the gun used was a .38 Special. Do you know what that means? It means the shell casings are still inside the gun. Now that they have the gun, they may be able to match the casing with the bullet in the body. If they do, there will be no doubt that the gun they found on the beach, your gun, is the weapon that killed Joyce. That's not good for you."

"I don't know how many times I have to tell you this. You're my friggin lawyer. You should listen. I didn't kill Joyce. I didn't fire that gun. Ever. I don't know who did, but instead of accusing me, maybe you should figure out who the hell is trying to set me up. Did you ever think of that? That someone is working very hard to make me look like the killer?"

"Settle down, Michael. Of course I thought of that. I've got an entire team of lawyers working on it. But until they find something, our immediate problem is the gun. Right now, they can place you at the scene, with a motive, and with the gun. Your gun. It's not going to be easy going against that much evidence. I'm not sure even the Bell money can get you out of this one."

"I'm not looking for the Bell money to get me out of this. I'm looking for you to do your job and prove my innocence." Michael let go of Kylie and started to wring his hands together. Anxiety shadowed his face and beads of sweat appeared on his forehead. He turned to Phil. "I know it looks bad and I can't explain the gun, but I didn't kill Joyce. Can't I take a lie detector test to prove it?"

"Not admissible in court, and if you take it just for my benefit, it will look like I don't believe you. If I can't trust my own client, why should anyone else?"

"Do you believe me, Phil? Do you believe that I didn't kill Joyce?"

"What I believe really doesn't matter. It's what I can make the jury believe that counts. And quite honestly, Michael, you aren't giving me much to go on."

Throughout this conversation, Kylie remained quiet. She was starting to think that Michael wasn't going to get off. She was terrified. What would she do if he went to prison? Would they lock him up for the rest of his life? He wouldn't be able to stand that. It would kill him to be locked away. Then another thought crossed her mind, more horrible than the one before. Did Maine allow for the death penalty? Could Michael be put to death if he was found guilty? Oh, God, what was she going to do? How could she live without Michael? He was her reason for being.

She shook her head and tried to clear these thoughts from her mind. She was jumping to conclusions. Michael swore he was innocent, and she believed him. Somehow the jury would see that. She turned her attention back to the conversation that was at hand. Phil really didn't have any other news for them and after promising to call as soon as he heard the ballistics result, he left.

Kylie and Michael spent the next few hours reviewing the case, but eventually, they got tired of repeating the same information and they moved on to other topics. "Michael, when do you usually go to visit Molly?"

"I go once a week. Why?"

"I was thinking, you said that you wouldn't be able to go now that you are out on bail. What if I went instead?"

"You would be willing to drive all the way to Latchy Harbor to see Molly? After I kept her from you all this time? Why?"

"Don't misunderstand. I am furious that you kept your daughter a secret from me. That you didn't trust me enough to tell me about her. I'm your wife. She's a part of you. I know it was your secret and you didn't want to betray Molly, but you should have told me."

"I know, Kylie. I know, and I am so sorry. Honestly. You are right. I should have told you."

"Damn straight I'm right. What did you think I was going to do? Call the press? Sell her picture to the highest bidder? And let me ask you something. Were you ever going to tell me? How long were you going to keep this little charade up? What were you thinking, Michael?"

Kylie's voice got louder as she jerked away from Michael and paced across the floor. Her green eyes burned with a fire Michael had not seen before. She was angry, no, she was beyond angry. She was enraged.

"You're right. I should have told you. I don't know how to tell you how sorry I am."

Michael's voice was not enough to appease Kylie as she circled the room. She ran her hand through her hair and turned to face her husband. "I have been faithful to you since the day I met you. I was a good girlfriend, a good fiancé, and now I'm a good wife. I deserve your trust. Haven't I proven that there isn't anything I wouldn't do for you? God, Michael, I love you. I wouldn't hurt you. And I certainly wouldn't hurt an innocent little girl. Surely you must know that."

"I do, Kylie. I do. And I'm sorry. I don't know what made me act like this. I should have told you. I wish I had told you. You had a right to know. But I promise you, there will be no more secrets. None. Ever. I promise."

She turned to face him, consciously trying to keep her breathing slow and steady. She didn't want her anger to overtake a logical thought process. After all, he made a mistake, he was sorry, and he promised he wouldn't do it again. What else could he do? And under the circumstances, with the court case that would decide his entire future looming over him, she didn't want to waste any time on anger. Seeing him looking so forlorn, so remorseful, she chose what she considered to be the high road. She forgave him.

"Let's move on. I can't deal with this conversation right now, so please, let's just move on. Tell me about Molly. Tell me where she is, what she's like, anything you can think of that I should know. She won't understand why you stopped going to see her, but maybe it will help if I fill in until you can resume your visits. Plus, I would like to get to know her. I would like to be a part of her life, too. If it's alright with you, I will go see her tomorrow."

Michael's face brightened as he thought about his daughter. He turned toward Kylie, but his eyes seemed to be looking at something only he could see. "Molly is the world to me. She is an absolute beauty. Wavy blond hair, big blue eyes, trusting smile. She's small for her age, very delicate looking. Like you. When she's sad, you just want to take her in your arms and make all her troubles go away. But when she's happy, her entire face lights up. She has a smile that can light up your world. She's amazing, Kylie. She really is."

Michael went on to tell Kylie all about his daughter. Her home is a small, private facility with round-the-clock staff to ensure she is receiving the best of care. Her caretakers are as much like family to her as they are like medical staff. Each employee was carefully screened and selected. Before being hired, they had to sign a contract agreeing to keep everything about Molly strictly confidential. Additionally, they were paid generously enough to ensure they wanted to continue their employment. Over the past ten years, very few staff members chose to leave. If they did leave, they would continue to receive an annual stipend to keep Molly's secret. So far no one has ever talked to the media about Molly.

Molly requires a great deal of assistance. She needs help to feed and dress. She can speak, but due to her finite ability to learn and understand, her speech is limited. She mostly makes sounds instead of words to express her feelings; laughter when she is happy, babbling when she plays, crying when she is unhappy. Sometimes, when something truly delights her, she will clap her hands together and giggle. Those are the best times.

She likes some people better than others. She loves chocolate but hates lima beans. She has a stubborn streak. When she is served something to eat that she doesn't like, she will not open her mouth. She prefers pink teddy bears over brown ones and she enjoys her bath but is terrified of the pool. Her life today is the same as it was five years ago, as it will be five years from now. She will never recover but instead will remain a vulnerable, trusting child for the rest of her life.

Medically she is prone to seizures, but otherwise stable. Michael expressed to Kylie that he worries about when she is older. It's one thing to take care of a beautiful little girl, but would these people be willing to take her to the bathroom and give her a bath and feed her when she's 40 years old?

Kylie tried to reassure Michael, to explain that people don't stop loving those they care for simply because they grow old. After all, she would love him when he was old and gray. Didn't he feel the same about her?

Before they ended their conversation about Molly, Michael gave Kylie directions on how to get to Caroler's Square in Latchy Harbor. Molly's home. He also called the staff at Caroler's Square and advised them that his wife, Molly's stepmother, would be arriving there late tomorrow morning and to please make her feel welcome.

Kylie fixed a quick dinner and shortly after she and Michael went to bed. They made love that night as much out of a need to be close to each other as out of passion. Although neither of them wanted to say the words, they both knew that their time together could be cut short, and they wanted to make the most out of every minute they had. When they finished, Kylie clung to Michael, her arm on his chest, her head on his shoulder. Eventually, they both fell into a troubled sleep.

The sun was shining brightly when Kylie opened her eyes. It felt so right to have Michael lying by her side. She thought about lounging next to him, relishing the touch of his body against hers, the scent of his skin, but she couldn't. She had something important to attend to. She climbed out of bed and dressed quickly in rust-colored pants and a creamy white sweater. Michael joined her in the kitchen and together they ate breakfast. Then, after a hug and a kiss, Kylie left. She was off to meet Molly, her stepdaughter.

The drive to Latchy Harbor was a little under two hours. It was uneventful and Kylie enjoyed the winding roads that led her through the woods and fields of Maine. She was surrounded by trees in the bright yellows, oranges, and reds of fall. While this was the season for leaf peepers, most vacationers stayed on Route One, so the narrow roads Michael had recommended to her were relatively traffic-free.

Eventually, she found herself clearing the deep forests and traveling on flatter ground. Soon the salty smell of the ocean was in the air. The day was warm and the ocean provided a cool breeze, making the temperature comfortable.

She found Caroler's Square without difficulty and parked her Jeep next to the quaint, three-story building. The building was an old mariner's house with severe lines and angles, softened only by the gingerbread trim that was common along the coast of Maine. A round turret replaced the harsh right front corner of the house and provided a side wall for the large front porch. The clapboard gleamed with a fresh coat of clean, white paint, in stark contrast to the dark green of the porches and shutters. Green and white striped canopies covered the front and side windows.

The red brick walkway was lined with azalea bushes, no longer blooming due to the lateness of the season, and the lawns were expertly manicured all the way to the thick evergreens that surrounded the large, rectangular lot. A rose-covered trellis in the shape of an arch marked the front entrance to the estate. It provided the only break in the solid green hedge that separated the front yard from the sidewalk. Clay pots filled with wilted geraniums were placed along the wide front stairs leading up to the porch. It looked more like a well-kept bed and breakfast than a state-of-the-art medical facility created for one young girl.

Kylie walked up to the entry and crossed the front porch. As she approached the door, a young girl in jeans and a bright red sweatshirt opened it for her. "Mrs. Bell? Hi. I'm Halie. We've been expecting you."

"Hello, Halie. Please, call me Kylie."

"If you would like to follow me, I will take you out to the backyard. We're having lunch set up for you and Molly. I believe Molly is already there. I think Stacy brought her out."

Kylie followed Halie across the foyer and down a short hall into a bright, cheerful kitchen with shiny silver appliances and red and white flowered curtains. They turned right into the dining room, which was also done in red, but this time with much deeper, richer shades than the kitchen. The back of the dining room had French doors leading onto a large, multi-tiered deck. The top tier was enclosed by screens that allowed the breeze in but kept the insects out. It held three white wicker tables, each surrounded by four cushioned chairs and covered with green and purple flowered tablecloths.

At one of these tables sat an exquisite little girl. She was slender and impish, almost frail in her appearance. Her long blond hair was pulled into a ponytail that hung all the way to her waist. Her small, heart-shaped face was smooth and clear, and her eyes were as blue as the ocean. Although she bore no physical resemblance to Michael, she was exactly as he had described her. Kylie put on her kindest smile and slowly approached the table.

"Hello, Molly. My name is Kylie." Molly smiled. Encouraged, Kylie sat down and leaned forward, arms and elbows resting on the table. "I know you don't know me, Molly. I'm married to your daddy. I am his wife. Do you know what that makes me to you? I am your stepmother. Do you understand, Molly?"

Molly's smile broadened and she reached out a delicate hand in the direction of Kylie. She made soft noises with her mouth that could have been 'Hello, Kylie, how are you?' or they could have been 'Purple donkeys can fly.' The sounds, per se, made no sense at all, but the tone with which they were spoken sounded calm and happy.

Kylie raised her hand slowly in Molly's direction, hesitating in midair, until Molly pointed to Kylie's large diamond ring and laughed.

"She likes sparkly things," said a voice behind Kylie.

Kylie turned and a thin, middle-aged woman stood there. She had short, dark hair and hazel eyes. She was small but with a solid, athletic build. "Hello, Mrs. Bell. I'm Stacy. I'm Molly's caretaker."

"Hello, and please, it's Kylie. Michael told me all about you. You've been here with Molly since the beginning."

"Yes, since she blessed us ten years ago. I've been here along with my husband, Francesco, as well as several other staff members."

"It is nice to finally meet you, Stacy. Molly's quite beautiful, isn't she?"

The two women turned appreciatively toward Molly. Molly was jabbing Kylie's ring with her fingers, babbling happily at the sparkling jewel. Stacy smiled at the girl and asked, "Molly, are you hungry? Would you like to eat?" Molly continued playing with the ring, completely oblivious to Stacy's question.

Stacy turned to Molly and tried again. "Molly, are you hungry? Would you like to eat? Eat? As Stacy said this, she acted out raising a fork to her mouth, pretending to take a bite.

Molly clapped her hands and said "Eat. Eat."

Halie came over with a large tray filled with sandwiches and fresh fruits and vegetables. Following her was a ruggedly built man carrying a smaller tray with a pitcher of lemonade and three glasses, two crystal and one plastic with a special, non-spilling lid placed loosely over it. He carefully set the tray on the table and held his hand out to Kylie. "Hi, I'm Francesco. I'm Stacy's husband and Molly's physical therapist."

"Hello, Francesco. It's nice to meet you. Will you be joining us for lunch?"

"No, ma'am. I'm afraid I can't today. In addition to providing Molly with her therapy five times a week, I also tend to things around the estate, like the plumbing and the electrical problems and other maintenance. If I don't get the overhead lights in the laundry room functioning soon, Halie tells me she'll be stuffing the dirty laundry in the back of my truck for me to take home and clean. Somehow, I don't think that would go over well with my lovely wife, so I'd best get it fixed today."

Stacy rolled her eyes and Kylie said, "Perhaps some other time."

"That would be nice, ma'am. I look forward to it. Ladies." Francesco reached over and gently patted Molly on the head before he went back inside. Molly smiled at him and yelled something that sounded an awful lot like 'see ya' to Francesco.

After the three finished their lunch, Kylie and Stacy each took one of Molly's hands and went onto the sweeping lawns that constituted the backyard. Stacy explained that the estate's land went all the way to the sea; however, there was no longer direct access to the water from the old homestead. Michael had ordered the construction of a high privacy fence all around the house on the slight chance Molly wandered off unnoticed. It would also serve to keep intruders from entering. The fence was built on the other side of the numerous evergreens that lined the property's perimeter. That way it wouldn't seem quite so prison-like.

After their walk around the backyard and a leisurely stroll through the west gardens, the trio made their way back to the house. Halie came for Molly, explaining that she would clean her up and take her to the sun porch for some quiet playtime. After this Francesco would go through his physical therapy routine with her which would conclude with him taking her back outside to run and play ball.

Following outside activity time, there would be a rest period and then more schoolwork. This mostly consisted of reading stories, drawing and painting, and other work designed specifically for Molly. Later a family-style dinner would be served in the dining room. After dinner, Molly would be bathed and readied for bed. One of the staff members would read her a story and then she would be allowed to watch an hour or two of television. Stacy laughed as she explained that Molly seemed to have a special fondness for reality shows. Another story would follow and she would be given her evening medications, brush her teeth, and go to bed. Every weekday was the same. The weekends had a little variance. Sometimes Stacy and Francesco would take Molly into town for lunch or walks on the beach. Other times they would go for drives, especially now that the fall leaves were so vibrant. But mostly Molly's life consisted of minimal exposure to different people. Especially since last May when they were so easily tricked by Louis Joyce.

Kylie avoided talking about Joyce and instead tried to make suggestions about different things they could do with Kylie. While Stacy listened politely to her comments, everything she came up with had already been tried or was already being done. Kylie could suggest nothing new to add to Molly's quality of life. Fortunately, the child was the focus of the entire staff and they all seemed genuinely concerned with doing what was best for her. Kylie went back to see Molly one more time before she left and was pleased that Molly so readily agreed to accept a hug. Then Kylie thanked the staff and said goodbye, relieved to know that she could honestly report back to Michael that the trip was a success. She felt good about her first visit with her stepdaughter.

She started up her Jeep and made the long drive back home. She parked in the garage and went through the side door into the mudroom that led to the kitchen. Michael was waiting for her at the table, anxious to hear about Molly.

"What did you think? Did you see Molly? Did you like her? How is she?"

"Michael, please, let me get through the door before you barrage me with questions."

"Oh, I'm sorry, honey. I guess I'm not being very considerate. How was your trip? Did you have a nice drive?"

"Michael!"

Kylie tossed her purse on the table and poured herself a glass of juice. Only after a couple of big gulps did she sit down and invite Michael to join her. "First, let me start by telling you that you are right. Molly is wonderful. She is gentle and sweet and we had a lovely afternoon."

Kylie told Michael every detail of her time with Molly, watching him beam with pride as she spoke. She talked about her first impression of Molly and how beautiful she is. She provided him with every detail of their lunch, their walk around the yard, and the quick tour she made of the estate. She made sure she spoke highly of the staff that put so much effort into making Molly's life as happy as possible. After she finished telling her story, she excused herself and went upstairs to take a shower. She told Michael it had been a long drive and she felt hot and grimy. In actuality, she was far more moved by her meeting with Molly than she had expected. The sweet, gentle little girl tugged at her heartstrings, and after telling Michael about her visit, she needed a few minutes to regroup. She was sure about one thing, it wouldn't take long before she could love that beautiful child like she was her own.

She climbed up the stairs and went into the bathroom. She immediately stripped and climbed into the big tile shower. The warm water felt good against her tired body. She let the water run over her thick, red hair, matting it in heavy wet strands over her face. She fumbled with the shampoo bottle and poured a puddle of it into her hand, then massaged it into her hair, careful to keep it away from her eyes. She just stood there and let the warm water rinse her hair and pour over her tired limbs. She finished up her shower, dried off, and slipped into a short, flannel nightgown.

By the time she left the bathroom, Michael was already lying in bed. He held his arms open and she lay down next to him, her body curled into his. She felt happy and her dreams would be peaceful. There would be plenty of time tomorrow to worry about how their wonderful life together could all come tumbling down. She didn't know how to prevent that from happening, but tonight she wasn't going to try to figure it out. Tonight, she was going to take a lesson from Molly and simply live for the moment.

****

Every year for the past twenty years, George and Penny Appleton left their home in the small town of Salem, Virginia, and traveled 800 miles to visit their son in Kabascet, Maine. They were immensely proud of their son, Evan Riley Appleton, because he currently held the esteemed distinction of being the youngest judge to ever serve on the Maine Superior Court. This year had been no exception, George and Penny had both enjoyed their time with Evan and his wife, Kay. They especially enjoyed their time with their granddaughter, Katy Rae. They played miniature golf, walked along the beach, dined in fine restaurants and seaside lobster shacks, went whale watching, and shopped in the many stores that lined the downtown streets. They took lots of pictures and this year, George had purchased a brand-new GoPro HERO12 so he could take videos. They couldn't wait to show their daughter, Celeste, and her husband, Mark, all the fun things they did while on vacation in Maine.

George pulled their Subaru into the garage and opened the door for Penny. It was after midnight and they were both tired from the long drive. They brought the luggage and the bags into the house and piled them in the middle of the living room floor. They decided to wait until morning to put everything away.

Penny went to take a quick shower and George said he would lie down on the couch while he waited for his turn. He said he wasn't feeling well and he probably shouldn't have eaten so much pizza when they stopped a few hours ago. It was really giving him a burning in his chest that was quite uncomfortable.

Penny finished her shower in record time. She was tired and wanted to get to sleep. Celeste would be over with her family early and she had to sort out the packages for the kids before she arrived. She yelled downstairs to George that it was his turn to get in the shower. Then she went into her room and crawled into bed. There was nothing like sleeping in one's own bed to get a good night's sleep.

When Penny woke up again it was 3:00 in the morning. George still hadn't come upstairs. Oh, that man, she thought to herself. He must have fallen asleep on the couch. It seems like he could sleep anywhere. She thought about leaving him there, but it would be easier in the morning if he had already taken a shower. Plus, she couldn't have him sleeping in the middle of the living room when Celeste arrived. Tired and not very happy with the idea of leaving her cozy bed, Penny pulled herself up and went down the stairs to the living room. She called George's name several times, but he didn't stir.

She went into the living room and clicked the light on along the way. George was lying very still on the couch. She smiled as she thought he had been lying there so long that he actually started to look like the couch, his color was also a pale shade of heritage blue. She reached down to shake him awake, gently so as not to startle him. All of a sudden, she was hit with a thought so strong, so frightening, that it caused her eyes to fly wide open and her heart to race. She shook George again, although this time not quite so gently. She practically shook him off the couch. She called his name, loudly, but he did not respond. She yelled and pulled him hard by the shoulders, but he remained oblivious to her actions. Then she called 9-1-1. She called because she knew she was supposed to, but she also knew it was too late. She knew that her husband of 53 years was gone. Her life would never be the same. What she didn't know was that the death of her beloved husband would also affect the lives of a wealthy young couple who were destined to cross paths with her son, 800 miles north in Kabascet, Maine.

8

The rest of Kylie and Michael's vacation week remained uneventful and they agreed to take the stance that no news was good news. On Phil's advice to maintain as normal a lifestyle as possible, Kylie returned to work on Monday morning. The first few days were difficult as she could sense her co-workers whispering and talking about her. On more than one occasion she would walk unexpectedly into the break room and everyone would suddenly stop their conversations. She just smiled and chose to ignore them. Eventually, things returned to normal. The one change she made right away, though, was her schedule. She could no longer work her five 8-hour shifts. She changed to three 12-hour shifts instead. This would give her Mondays off to visit Molly.

Michael, forced to remain within a 50-mile radius of the courthouse, had more time to concentrate on his work contracts to provide biostatistical expertise to various organizations. His turnaround time was better than ever, but his business did not exactly flourish. Most of his associates continued using his services, but he did notice a few stopped all contact with him. This upset him. Not because he needed the money, he could live a life of luxury if he never worked again. He knew the only reason he was losing business was because of the murder charges. So much for being innocent until proven guilty, he thought.

With so much time on his hands, he toyed with the idea of going back to school. He liked the sound of Dr. Bell, and it would only take him three or four years to make that distinguished title a reality. There's something his father could be proud of. He looked into a few programs, but then he put his computer away. He realized that was not a good plan for this time in his life. There was a very real possibility that he would be found guilty of a crime he did not commit. He wondered if he could get his PhD while serving time in prison.

With minimal work and Kylie being gone all day, plus not being allowed to visit Molly, Michael walked around the big house in a zombie-like fashion. He couldn't wait for Kylie to get home from work. He wished she would quit her job and stay home with him, but he would never ask her to do that. Especially since their future looked so uncertain. Her work provided her with self-fulfillment and socialization that he may not be able to offer once his case went to court. As much as it scared him, he knew she may need that if he was sentenced to life in prison.

Early Saturday morning Kylie and Michael were having coffee in the family room, enjoying their time together. Kylie had a magazine sprawled across her lap; she was quizzing Michael on what household chores men found most sensual when their solitude was interrupted by the beep of his cellphone.

"Hello."

"Michael, it's Phil. I've got news for you."

"Hello, Phil. What news?"

"I'm not sure how they got this so fast, but the ballistic results are back. It was definitely your gun, the gun they found on the beach, that killed Louis Joyce. But we already knew that from the serial number."

Michael fell to the couch, stunned. It was one thing assuming it was his gun, but knowing for sure, that was another thing. It didn't make sense. "I don't know what to say. How can that be? I didn't kill him, Phil. I'm telling you; I can't even remember the last time I saw that gun."

"Hang on, it's not all bad news. They also ran it for fingerprints. The gun was clean. Not a print on it. The prosecutor will say that you cleaned it before tossing it in the ocean, but she can't prove that. She can also suggest that being in the ocean could have removed the prints. Again, no proof. Just speculation. It would have been better if someone else's prints showed up, but at least your prints weren't there. That helps."

"I guess that's good. I was a little worried that my prints from when I bought it might show up. I guess the real killer's prints would have covered mine. I don't really know how this works. I don't know if they could have lasted that long."

"Well, we're clear there. The rest of the news isn't so good. When you fire a .38 Special, the casing stays in the gun. That's why these guns are so popular. We don't find shell casings at the scene. Now that they have the gun, they also have the shell casing. There's a good chance they will be able to match it up with the bullet that killed Joyce. Once they do that, there will be no doubt that it was your gun that killed him."

Michael nodded his head, understanding, not thinking that Phil couldn't see this gesture over the telephone.

"I have to be honest with you, Michael. It looks bad. We've got the entire team working on it, but the only way I can see out of this one is if we can figure out who did kill him. If you didn't do it, someone has gone to great lengths to make it look like you did."

"But who would do this to me? Who would be able to do this?"

"I don't know, but we had better figure it out. We're running out of options."

Kylie watched as the color drained out of Michael's face. He hung up the phone, his hand trembling so much that it took him several tries to hit the off button. He looked at his wife and for the first time since she met him, she saw the look of raw fear on his face. "Michael."

She walked over to him and pulled him toward the couch. Once he was seated, she sat next to him and put both arms around his shoulders. With her face close to his she said, "We'll figure this out. Somehow, we'll make them understand. They'll see that you couldn't have killed him." She held him and they both remained silent, each lost in their own thoughts.

Weeks passed and there were no new developments in the case. For the prosecutor this wasn't a problem. There was already enough evidence to convict Michael. For the defense, time was running out. Kylie and Michael spent hour upon hour trying to figure out who could have killed Louis Joyce, but no matter how many ways they pieced the puzzle together, the answer always came back to Michael. He maintained his innocence, but he was sure that no one else would believe him. After all, he said there were some days he didn't believe himself.

Their focus was that someone was trying to frame him, but who disliked him enough to want him in prison for the rest of his life? He didn't have any enemies. He ran his own company, so there weren't any work colleagues that he didn't have a good relationship with. There were no cast-aside girlfriends from his past. No jealous boyfriends of Kylie's. He was an only child, so no siblings were plotting to keep the family fortune for their own. No matter how many times they went over who would want him out of the picture, they came up empty. Who despised Michael enough to do this to him was the question, and they were running out of time to find the answer.

While Michael delved into every relationship he ever had, Kylie continued working. Some days she felt this was the only way she could keep some semblance of reality to offset the horror that she and Michael were facing at home. On one cold Monday in December,

Kylie arrived for work at her usual time and got report from the outgoing nurse. She was assigned two patients. Don Vanderbilt was a 77-year-old gentleman who would be spending the next week or two in the unit due to a gaping hole in his abdomen that refused to heal following his intestinal surgery. He was stable, and other than a rather large dressing change, wouldn't be any trouble.

Her second patient, Shawn Winslow, was another story. Shawn had recently been released from prison where he had served three years of a six-year sentence for selling drugs. The parole board thought that three years had been long enough for him to break the habit, so they released him from prison and ordered weekly meetings with his parole officer, as well as mandatory drug testing. Unfortunately, three years wasn't long enough for Shawn, and within days of hitting the streets he was back with his old gang, and his old habits.

At first, Shawn found it relatively easy to pass his drug screens. He knew what drugs would be out of his system in time for the Friday drug test and he planned his drug use accordingly. Before long, however, that didn't allow him enough 'high' time, so he had to find other methods. This, too, was not a problem. He simply wore a special belt designed with a slit along the inside that had a thick rubber container. He filled the container with warm urine provided by a 'clean' friend, and when he was asked to void, he simply filled the test bottle with the clean urine.

Shawn's parole officer was fooled for several months, but he noticed that Shawn displayed many indications of drug use, so he changed the testing plan. From now on, he would accompany Shawn into the men's room and watch while Shawn provided a sample. The first time this happened Shawn was unprepared, so he stood over the urinal for almost twenty minutes and claimed he was unable to void. His parole officer provided him with six glasses of water to drink and turned every faucet in the bathroom on to let the water run freely from them, but still, Shawn insisted he could not void. He even tried to stick Shawn's hand in warm water, but still, no results. Frustrated, he let Shawn go but told him next week to be prepared to stay until the sample cup was full.

Shawn thought long and hard about his predicament and the following week he was prepared when he met with his parole officer. As he did the week before, Shawn's parole officer accompanied Shawn into the bathroom and watched while Shawn voided into the sample jar. Several days later the test results came back and Shawn was clean. His parole officer knew he was missing something, but he didn't find out what until a few days later.

Shawn had been brought to the emergency department with chills and an extremely high fever. He was disoriented and having difficulty breathing. His throat was swelling closed, his eyes were protruding from their sockets, he was dying. Shawn's girlfriend realized this and told the triage nurse everything Shawn had been doing.

In addition to his continued drug use, Shawn had been purchasing clean urine from an acquaintance of his.

First, he would void in the usual fashion. Then he would insert a catheter and inject the clean urine into his bladder. When he went to his drug screen, his parole officer would watch him void, not realizing that the urine coming out of his bladder was not actually his urine. As disgusting as this was, it worked for a while. But then Shawn's acquaintance got less picky about who he obtained the urine from, and the last batch came from a very sick ex-drug user. Not only was the urine laden with bacteria, but it also contained a trace of iodine. Apparently, the supplier didn't think the urine was yellow enough on its own. Shawn knew he was highly allergic to iodine, he just didn't know there was any in the urine, so he filled his bladder like always.

Lucky for Shawn, his girlfriend was with him, and when he collapsed. She called 9-1-1. Shawn suffered an anaphylactic reaction. Additionally, the bacteria in his bladder made its way into his bloodstream and now he was septic. Drugs may not kill Shawn Winslow, but because of them, he was closer to death's door than he had ever been before.

Kylie scribbled a few notes on a pad and went off to see her patients. She tried to act casually about receiving Shawn as her patient, but she wondered if Shawn's prison history played a role in her assignment. If so, it was a cruel prank. If not, it was an unfortunate coincidence. Either way, she held her head high as she entered Shawn's room.

Next, she went to Carl Vanderbilt's room. Carl was a pleasant man and took his medication without difficulty.

Kylie said she would gather the supplies to change his dressing and be back in about half an hour. She hadn't been feeling very well all morning, again, and wanted to complete as much of her work as she could as early as possible.

She returned to Carl's room and stripped off the old dressing. Dried blood mixed with gelatinous green drainage clung to the bandages and oozed out of the orange-size hole in Carl's abdomen. Kylie began placing a fistful of wet dressings into the hole but the odor from the drainage seeped around her face mask and she felt the nausea that had been lying low in her stomach start to make its way to the top. Unable to finish his dressing change, Kylie ran into his bathroom and vomited. Carl rang the call bell for the nurse and almost immediately Morgan appeared at his door. She sent Kylie to the charge nurse and donned gloves so she could finish Mr. Vanderbilt's dressing change.

"I don't know what came over me. Really. I've changed a lot of dressings and they've never had that effect on me."

"I understand, Kylie, but we can't have you vomiting into patients' wounds. JCAHO would frown on that."

"Don't worry, it won't happen again."

"I do worry. I have to. It's my job. Why don't you go home today and rest? Maybe you'll feel better tomorrow."

"I'm fine, really. I've just been a little nauseated the last few mornings. It will clear up in no time. Really."

Understanding crossed into the charge nurse's eyes

and she smiled at Kylie. "Listen to yourself, Kylie. Listen to what you are saying. Now go home and get some rest."

Kylie went to the nurses' lounge and hung her stethoscope in her locker. What had Carina figured out that still eluded her? All she told her was that she had been nauseated in the mornings, but it always cleared up after a few hours. Nauseated in the mornings. Sick in the mornings. Morning sickness. Oh, God, Carina thought she was pregnant! No, that can't be. We're careful. Well, we're usually careful. She left the hospital and swung by the drugstore to pick up a pregnancy test kit. She hid it deep in her purse and went home.

The next morning Kylie rose early, much earlier than was necessary to get ready for work on time. She grabbed her purse and went into the bathroom, trying to be quiet so she wouldn't wake Michael. After carefully following the instructions, she sat at her vanity and timed out three minutes. It was the longest three minutes of her life.

With two minutes down and one to go, Kylie heard a tapping on the bathroom door. "Kylie, honey, are you alright?"

"I'm fine. Go back to bed."

"Can't sleep. What are you doing in there?"

"Geesh, Michael. What do people usually do in a bathroom?"

"Can I come in?"

Kylie hesitated a bit too long and Michael pushed the door open. "What are you doing?"

"Nothing. Just sitting here."

But it was too late. Michael's eyes were immediately drawn to the pregnancy test kit sitting in the middle of the bathroom counter. "Are you pregnant?"

"Well, if you wouldn't have come in, I would know by now."

Realizing that Michael wasn't leaving until he knew, Kylie reached over and slid the box closer to her. She pulled the stick out of the container and glanced at the bottom. There, in the center of the stick, was a little pink plus sign. She looked up at Michael as he was trying to see the stick from over her shoulder. "Well, my dear, looks like you're on the hook for a Mother's Day gift next year."

"You're pregnant? Oh, Kylie, that's wonderful news. I can't believe it. We're going to have a baby. Kylie, isn't that wonderful?"

Kylie didn't think it was possible, but there in front of her, her 6'2" husband who weighed in at a good 195 pounds, who was usually reserved and distinguished, was now frolicking around the bathroom. Not pacing, not walking, but frolicking. She put her hand over her mouth to cover her laughter. It was nice to see him happy. It felt like they had been living a nightmare for so long now, this was a welcome reprieve.

Kylie called out from work and she and Michael spent most of the morning lounging in their bed. It seemed like as long as they stayed in their room they could revel in the joy of her pregnancy. Once they opened the door and stepped out, however, the whole court case would be staring them in the face, robbing them of their happiness.

Kylie made a quick trip to the kitchen and returned with a tray of cheese and tomato sandwiches. As they sat in bed eating, Michael's cellphone rang. Neither of them wanted to answer it, but finally, Michael reached over and snapped it open. "Hello."

"Michael, it's Phil. I've got news for you, and this time, it may not be all bad."

"What is it? Did they figure out who did it?"

"Calm down, Michael. I said not bad news. I didn't say a miracle."

Michael tightened his grip on the phone while Kylie sat unmoving on the bed next to him. "Go on."

"It's about Molly. They don't know about her. The prosecutor doesn't know she's alive. With all the investigating they've done, they haven't figured out your secret. She is still safe."

"How can that be? They know that Joyce was Melanie's half-brother. They seemed to have it all figured out."

"They know that, and they figured it was some type of extortion. Of course, they have looked at your telephone records and bank statements and matched up the money being withdrawn after several of his calls, but they don't know why. Your calls to Latchy Harbor have been very limited, and for all they know, you are calling to order lobster."

"That's incredible, Phil. They are going to lock me up for a murder I didn't commit, yet they can't find a person who isn't hidden all that well. And I'm supposed to trust my life to these people?"

"No, you're supposed to trust your life to me. And right now, well, let's just say I'm glad that Maine doesn't have the death penalty."

"So much for your happy news."

"I'm sorry, Michael. But the more time that slips by, the less likely we are to uncover anything new. I have private investigators working round the clock on this, but they keep coming up empty-handed. If you didn't do it, then someone sure wants it to look like you did."

"If, Phil? Thanks for your vote of confidence."

"I'm an attorney, Michael. In all the years I've been practicing, I've never yet had a client tell me they were guilty. It's my job to represent them, not to believe them."

Michael hung up the phone and filled Kylie in on everything Phil had said. Even though the news was good, the mood changed, and together they finished their lunch in silence.

Time went by, and winter turned Maine cold and gray. Still, the anticipation of a baby brought joy to Michael and Kylie. They endeavored to make their lives feel as normal as possible. Kylie continued working at the hospital, and by Christmas, her baby bump was starting to show. Although it wasn't necessary, she was excited to start wearing her maternity clothes. She found them both stylish and comfortable. News of her pregnancy reached Michael's parents. It was quite a surprise when C. C. and Cynthia Bell invited both Michael and Kylie to Christmas dinner. While it wasn't a warm, family-type meal, it was enjoyable, and they lavished Kylie with expensive maternity ensembles.

Kylie had made several trips to visit Molly and their relationship continued to grow, but once the winter snow settled in, she explained to Michael that she was no longer comfortable driving the winding roads that led to Latchy Harbor. It was one thing to wade through lobster-eating tourists, but even with four-wheel drive, driving through snow and ice in the middle of a Maine winter was foolhardy at best. Michael, given his past history with severe weather driving, agreed.

The spring melt finally made its appearance in April. The weather warmed and Kylie resumed her weekly visits to Latchy Harbor. She had managed to visit Molly three or four times over the winter, but now that spring was here, her visits would be more routine. Phil had become a permanent fixture at the Bell house, but surprisingly very little progress was made on Michael's case. The private detectives that were hired did checks on everyone from family members to friends to employees, and still, they found no connection to Louis Joyce other than Michael. Kylie and Michael tried to find happiness in their everyday life, but none as much as an early morning at the end of June when Kylie woke Michael up in the wee hours of the morning. "Michael, wake up. My water broke. I think it's time. Michael."

"No thank you, honey. I don't want any water."

"What? Michael, wake up! I'm not talking about a glass of water. I'm talking about Niagara Falls. My water broke."

"Why are you talking about Niagara Falls? We can't

go there."

"Michael. Wake up. It's time for the baby!"

"Oh, the baby. The baby! Are you okay? Is it time? Are you having contractions?"

"Yes, but they're not bad. They are only coming every ten minutes or so."

"Kylie, we need to go to the hospital." Michael jumped out of bed and ran to his closet. He quickly appeared wearing jeans and his favorite L. L. Bean sweatshirt. This would have been perfectly natural if the sweatshirt hadn't been on inside-out.

"Michael, calm down. I've already called Dr. Saylor. She said that I'm fine. Once my contractions are every five minutes apart, we should head to the hospital. Otherwise, we should stay here, and you should try to relax."

"Okay, if that's what she said. How are you feeling?"

"I'm okay. Excited. A bit scared. But okay. How about you?"

"I can't wait. I love you so much, Kylie. Can I get you anything?"

"No, Dr. Saylor told me nothing but a few ice chips, and I don't really want that. Just come and sit here with me. But first, fix your sweatshirt."

They sat together for another hour or two and dozed, but then Kylie felt an increase in the intensity of her contractions. She could tell from Michael's slow, steady breathing that he had fallen back asleep. She wriggled out of his arms and went into the bathroom to freshen up. Then she put the last few items in her overnight bag and woke Michael. "C'mon, honey. Let's go meet our son."

Michael helped Kylie to the vehicle and together they rode the short distance to the hospital, as excited as teenagers out on their first date. Michael drove carefully, but kept one hand clasped tightly around Kylie's smaller hand. When they arrived at the hospital, a nursing assistant helped Kylie into a wheelchair and brought her to the maternity floor. Michael tagged along behind with her overnight bag. Kylie was brought to a private room and provided with the standard-issue blue hospital gown. Then she spent the next fourteen hours walking in the hall, lying in the bed, and even letting out an occasional yell or two. When it was all done, Kylie and Michael were the proud parents of a seven-pound, ten-ounce son. Benjamin Clifford Bell.

"He's gorgeous," Kylie gasped as they gently placed her newborn son in her arms. She touched his soft cheek with her finger and ran her hand over his fuzzy little head. She laughed when Michael tucked his big index finger into the baby's tiny fist. Her two favorite men in the world. When she looked into Michael's face and saw his eyes glistening with tears, she started to cry. Never had her life seemed so perfect. If only it could last.

They had only been home from the hospital a week when Kylie found herself dressing Benjamin, or Benji as he was now called, in a blue terrycloth romper and matching cap. She and Michael were going to visit Michael's parents. C. C. and Cynthia had called just days after Benji was born and requested that the three of them come to the Bell Mansion for a family dinner. It almost

174

sounded like a sincere invitation, but experience made them both a bit leery.

Kylie was finishing up dressing Benji when Michael came into the room to check on them. As she wrapped the baby in a soft blanket, she took a minute to admire her handsome husband. Tall and lean with dark hair and eyes, he always brought to her mind a Roman god. He had high cheekbones and a square jaw which emasculated his chiseled face and slightly aquiline nose. He smiled broadly at her, and his full lips took on that lopsided grin that warmed her inside and out. She loved him so much.

Then she looked back at Benji, and her heart ached with the pride and joy she felt. He had his father's dark hair and eyes, but her fair skin coloring. With her husband standing close behind her and her son lying quietly on the bed, Kylie could not have been happier. As long as she didn't think about the charges that were filed against Michael, her life was like a fairytale. She wished it could go on just like this forever, but she wasn't naïve enough to believe in fairytales.

"Are you two ready to go?"

"We are."

Michael grabbed the overstuffed diaper bag and they went to the vehicle. In no time at all they were pulling through the iron gates at the home of Michael's parents.

"Mother, Father, you remember my wife, Kylie." Michael's voice took on a steel tone that occurred only when he spoke to his parents.

"Of course we do, Michael, don't be silly. You've

been married for well over a year now to this lovely woman. Kylie, how are you?"

"I'm fine, Mr. Bell. How are you?"

"Oh, couldn't be better. The stock market took a little turn in our favor today. Now, let's see what you've got in that carrier."

Kylie placed the baby carrier on the table in the entryway and gently lifted Benji out, loosening the blanket that was around him. Both C. C. and Cynthia Bell walked over to look at their grandson. C. C. pulled the blanket away from the baby's face and smiled. "He is very sweet. He looks quite a bit like you did at that age, Michael. What, exactly, did you name him?"

"Benjamin Clifford Bell."

"Clifford, hmm. I didn't expect you to include the namesake. I'm rather honored."

"Don't be honored, Father. It was Kylie's doing. I refused to include Michael in his name, and she wanted to name him after me. I only agreed because of Grandfather."

"Either way. I'm glad to see the tradition is continuing. He's a fine-looking young fellow. Congratulations to you both."

The tension in the room thickened as Michael and his father stood next to each other looking at Benji, without uttering another word. Cynthia, who had only given the baby a passing glance, now looked out the window. Finally, Kylie could stand it no more. "Well, at least we didn't name him Jingle."

"Or Hells," added Cynthia from across the room,

who surprised everyone by acknowledging that she had been listening to the conversation that was taking place.

"Jingle Bell. Hells Bell. I don't know if I should laugh or toss my cookies." Michael responded with a groan, but he also laughed, and this was enough to break the tension. C. C. joined in the laughter and then suggested they all go into the living room to sit down. There were drinks and hors d'oeuvres waiting to hold them until dinner.

Soon they were called to the dining room and Kylie was pleased to see that a special stand to accommodate Benji's baby carrier had been placed next to the table. At least they knew her well enough to know that she would not allow the staff to take the baby away while they ate like he wasn't even part of the family.

The roast duck was excellent and Kylie ate every bit of food that she was served, in spite of the looks of disdain she received from Cynthia. After all, a lady didn't finish everything that was on her plate. After dinner was finished and they were sipping coffee, C. C. said he had an announcement to make.

"Michael, Kylie, I want you to know that both Cynthia and I welcome Baby Benjamin Clifford into the family. He is the next generation Bell heir."

"Bell heir, like the Fresh Prince of Belair?" Kylie laughed, despite the cold looks she received from C. C. and Cynthia. Michael couldn't help but roll his eyes.

"I'm sorry," Cynthia chirped. "What, exactly, is the Fresh Prince of Belair?"

"You know, the television show. With Wil Smith. The

Fresh Prince…" Kylie stopped. There was no point in trying to explain. If they didn't understand it, she wouldn't be able to explain it to them. If they did get it, they would never acknowledge it. Instead, she mumbled an apology and sat back quietly in her chair. Michael smirked.

"Anyway, as I was saying. Your mother and I welcome Benjamin into our family, and like so many before us, we would like to establish a trust in his name to ensure he will always be provided for. We assume that neither of you have any objections to us performing this Bell family tradition?"

Michael shook his head to indicate that he had no objections. Kylie did, too, although it was a wasted effort as the question was obviously directed only toward Michael.

"Additionally, in light of your current, eh, situation, we would like to establish a second trust fund. One that will assure both Kylie and the baby will have ample funds to be raised in an appropriate lifestyle in case you are, well, there's no delicate way to put this. In case you are incarcerated."

Michael seemed to take no notice of his father's choice of words to discuss his impending trial. "No need to be delicate, Father. What are you trying to say?"

"As long as Kylie remains your dedicated wife and lives in your current home, the trust will provide for all the same living expenses you currently have. It will also provide for Benjamin's education at the finest schools, from kindergarten through graduate school."

"I see. And if Kylie chooses not to remain my wife? After all, I could be, as you so graciously put it, incarcerated for a very long time. What if she decides not to remain faithful to me?"

"The trust would cease, of course."

"So, correct me if I'm wrong. Benji deserves the best of everything only if Kylie does exactly as you see fit, but if she doesn't, if she chooses to go on and have a life of her own, then he no longer deserves everything the Bell name can bestow upon him. Am I understanding that correctly, Father?"

To everyone's surprise, it was Cynthia who spoke next. "Why must you make everything so difficult, Michael? This isn't brain surgery. It is simple. It is damaging enough to have a Bell sent to prison for a crime as heinous as murder. If your wife chooses to stand behind you 100%, then at least it will appear that she believes in your innocence. There will be doubt in the public eye that you actually killed that man. However, if she chooses to leave you, then your guilt will be all but guaranteed. How would that look to our friends? Our acquaintances? We would be ostracized by our entire circle."

"Ah, now it is starting to make sense. This has nothing to do with your feeling love for your grandson. I guess I shouldn't be surprised since you never felt any love for your son. This has to do with protecting the family image. I guess you two will never change." Michael rose sharply out of his chair, almost tipping it over in the process. "Kylie, are you ready to leave? I think we've had enough family togetherness for one evening."

"Michael, why must you act this way? We were trying to do a good thing, not only to protect us but also your son."

"You want to protect Benji? Good. I will happily accept the initial trust. After all, that's been done for every child born into this family. As a Bell, he is entitled to certain provisions. A good home. A steady income. The best schools. As far as the second offer is concerned, forget it. If Kylie chooses to stay with me, it will be because she loves me. And because she believes in me. Not because she wants to secure a future for herself, or our son."

"Don't be foolish. Love is only so important, Michael."

"You know, Father, I'm sorry you feel that way. Maybe if you felt the way I do, that love is most important, you wouldn't be quite the cold-hearted bastard you are today."

With that, Michael grabbed the baby carrier in one hand and put his other hand on the small of Kylie's back and the three of them left the dining room. Neither C. C. nor Cynthia tried to stop them as they made their way to their vehicle and drove off the estate without another word to Michael's parents.

Kylie was glad to stand by her husband. After all, he had his pride. His parting remarks to his father were a fine example of it. Deep inside, however, she felt quite differently. She feared that Michael was not going to beat the charges that were filed against him. She would much rather have C. C. Bell on their side, fighting for them, instead of against them. She didn't care about the money for herself. She already had more than she ever dreamed of. But she didn't want Benji to grow up with less than he was entitled to. She worried that his life would change drastically if it turned out she was supporting him on her income alone. Then she got angry at herself for even thinking that way. This was never about money. She didn't care about it when she married Michael and she wouldn't care about it now. If Michael lost his trust, whether by his father or by lawyer fees or by any other means, then so be it. She would raise Benji on her nurse's salary. They would be fine. Benji would still have a mother and father who loved him, and that would be more than enough. She was going to stay with Michael forever. Not for money, but because she loved him. She loved him and she believed in him, and nothing would ever change that.

After they got home, Kylie fed and rocked Benji for two hours before he settled down to sleep. She gently laid him in his crib and crawled into her own bed. Michael pulled her close to him, but the best she could do was snuggle against him before she fell asleep.

The night passed quickly, especially since Kylie only slept a few hours before Benji decided it was time for her to get up again. Michael had tried to hire a private nurse to help Kylie with the baby at night, but she would have none of it. Benji was her son and she wasn't going to have him raised by a nanny. Eventually, they would have to hire someone to help watch him while she attended court and work, but for today, Benji was all theirs. These were the thoughts that played on Kylie's mind in the wee hours as she sat feeding her son, but when she looked at his big eyes staring at her in the predawn light, she couldn't help but smile. She fed him and rocked him and soon he was back in his crib.

Finally, it was morning and Benji was still asleep. Kylie sat across from Michael at the kitchen table. Her eyes were red with fatigue, and she yawned frequently as she clung to her mug filled with hot coffee. "So, how much were you up last night?" Michael asked her.

"The better question would be, how much wasn't I up."

"You should let me hire a nurse, Kylie. You're going to overtax yourself."

"Don't be silly. Lots of women take care of babies without any help at all. And they certainly don't hire nannies."

"Well, I don't care about lots of women. I care about you. I hate seeing you look so tired."

"There is a solution to that, my dear. You could take a turn getting up with Benji, too."

"I know, and I'm more than willing. But you'll either have to wake me or let him cry for a second so I can hear him."

"Let him cry? I don't think so."

They continued their casual banter while having their morning coffee, but finally, Kylie could stand it no more. She was tired, but not so tired that she couldn't recognize the grim look on Michael's face. "What's wrong?"

"I hate to tell you this, but I talked to Phil. My trial has been placed on the docket. It begins in two weeks. Kylie, I could be going away for a very long time. I don't want to leave you. Or Benji. Or Molly. They're going to find me guilty and I'm going to lose my family and I didn't do it. I swear, I didn't kill him."

Kylie watched in horror as Michael, her pillar of strength, broke down and cried. She felt helpless as she sat there watching him, her heart being wrenched right out of her chest. She loved him and she believed him. She just didn't know how to save him.

9

It was another two hours until the case began but already the courtroom was overflowing. Townspeople, interested attorneys, reporters, and even a few people from the tabloids were there to watch the opening statements of Michael's trial. And of course, Kylie. Phil had warned her it would be a circus, but she hadn't anticipated this kind of turnout. She felt small and vulnerable as she sat alone on the first wooden bench behind the defendant's table. She wished she had someone to hold onto and help her get through this, but the only person she had ever counted on would be six feet in front of her. And while it was only six feet, it may as well have been the other side of the world.

Kylie fidgeted with the hem of her linen skirt. She wished they would start, although she had hoped for so long that this day would never come. She was acutely aware that so many eyes were on her. She would have preferred that C. C. would be present for his son's trial. Not only would the support have shed a positive light on Michael, but it would also have taken some of the focus away from her. Unfortunately, he was nowhere to be seen.

Suddenly, the doors opened, and a flurry of activity occurred in front of her. The players entered the courtroom. Kylie wrung her hands together but a quick warning look from Tim Stone immediately halted her action. She was supposed to appear confident. She had to show that her faith in her husband was unquestionable.

When Michael entered, he looked at Kylie and let out the smallest of smiles. That was just like him, he was trying to reassure her so she wouldn't be anxious. Her return smile wasn't staged, it was genuine. Kylie thought he also looked around the busy courtroom for his parents, or at the very least for his father. She wasn't sure if the look of disappointment that registered on his face was real or if it was just her imagination.

The proceedings began and Kylie spent the entire day, except for a one-hour lunch break, listening to the prosecutor, Meredith Tyson, ramble on about why Michael was guilty. She already hated that woman. She hated her black suit and her gray silk blouse and most of all, her heels that clicked every time she walked across the floor. Did every pair of shoes that woman owned have to click that way? But the worst thing of all about Meredith Tyson was her eyes, her piercing blue eyes. She didn't just look at a person, she looked through them. Just the thought of her made Kylie shiver. Kylie spent much of the morning wishing Meridith would trip and break her leg. She was sure the assistant prosecutor could not be as terrifying, or as efficient, as Meredith Tyson.

It took all of Kylie's willpower to sit still and listen to Meredith go on about the evidence she was going to present to prove Michael's guilt. She was going to tell the jury how Michael had such an easy life and was used to getting his own way. She would embellish how he hated his brother-in-law and didn't want to part with even a meager amount of money to help the poor man when he was down. She would explain how Michael lured Louis to the restaurant that September night, laughing to himself that he was doing this on his anniversary, and then how he killed him in cold blood. How he casually disposed of the gun while walking with his wife on the beach, and then returning to his high-end hotel room without the slightest bit of remorse about what he just did. Kylie couldn't listen to another word after that. She couldn't understand how this woman could talk about Michael this way. She didn't know him. She didn't understand that he could never do the things she was accusing him of doing.

As Meredith rambled on with her ridiculous speculations, Kylie's mind drifted. First, she stared at Michael. She was so proud at how tall he sat in his chair, how stoic he remained as he listened to these lies. He looked sad, but he held his emotions in check. Phil had trained him well. Then she looked at Phil. He was supposed to be the best defense lawyer in New England, yet she thought he was failing. Why was he just sitting there letting Meredith go on and on about how Michael deviously and cold-heartedly killed Louis Joyce? Couldn't he object? Kylie wished she had paid more attention when Phil had explained about opening statements and what to expect this week at court.

Somehow Kylie managed to sit on the hard, wooden bench and appear supportive throughout the day. She kept all emotion inside as instructed, both anger and sorrow. By 4:00 PM she was tired, sore, and anxious to go home. While the defense team was staying in a hotel near the courthouse, Kylie and Michael opted to make the drive back home each day. They wanted, no, they needed to be home with Benji.

Kylie sat in the car and watched Michael as he expertly guided it around the hordes of press that had been waiting outside the courthouse. Sneaking out the back door was no longer a choice now that court was fully in session.

"How do you think it went today? Are you still sure of my innocence?"

"Of course I am. You know I believe in you, 100%."

"I love you, Kylie. I am so sorry that you have to be dragged through this. I don't understand why this is happening to me. To us."

"It's not your fault, Michael. I know that. And we'll get through this. You'll see. We'll not only get through it, but we'll end up stronger than ever."

Michael reached over and squeezed her hand. He was so lucky to have her by his side. They drove in silence the rest of the way home and just over an hour later Michael pulled into their driveway. As soon as they went inside, Kylie went to get Benji and Michael checked on the supper Cassie had prepared. Then the household staff was dismissed for the evening and Kylie, Michael, and Benji tried to make the most of their time together.

Cassie had left a fresh garden salad in the refrigerator and a casserole warming in the oven. The table was set and the wine glasses were filled by the time Kylie came downstairs with Benji. She put him in the swing close to the dining room table and sat down with Michael for dinner. Although the food was delicious, neither one of them had much of an appetite.

They spoke little about the case. They were both present for the day's proceedings and knew how grim the outlook was. The prosecutor was very convincing. They would be glad when she was done and it was Phil's turn to speak.

Neither of them wanted the evening to end so they played with Benji and took turns holding him until he was exhausted. Eventually, the baby couldn't keep his eyes open. After putting him in his crib, there was really no choice but to go to bed and let the new day come forward.

After a full week of hearing Meredith Tyson explain why Michael must have murdered Louis Joyce, the prosecutor finished her opening statement and Phil had a chance to present the statement he had prepared. His depiction of Michael was much different from Meredith's. He showed Michael as a well-behaved child who was quiet and respectful. A child who was educated in boarding schools and always received excellent grades, who never had any behavior problems. Michael was a man who loved and cared for his first wife and child and grieved their loss for years. He was a man who tried, on several occasions, to help his brother-in-law, and even now, when Louis resorted to blackmail, Michael simply paid him instead of arguing. The money didn't matter.

Phil explained to the jury how Michael lived a normal life. He worked, he raised a family, he did his part to make the world a better place. He explained that Michael and Kylie got up and went to their jobs every day, just like the jury members did. He managed to bring up Benji, playing on the jury's sympathy. His hope was that they wouldn't want to take a new father away from his infant son, especially a father who lost his other child in such a horrible accident. Some of the time Phil was talking, he paced back and forth in front of the jury box. Other times he stood with his hands resting on the brass bar in front of them where he took the time to look into the eyes of each juror. Like Meredith, Phil spent several days on his opening statement, and while Meredith made Michael seem evil, Phil made him out to be a saint. For Kylie, the days that Phil spoke were much easier to sit through than the others.

After opening statements, the actual trial started. Phil had prepared both Michael and Kylie for this and they knew what to expect. Still, knowing didn't make it easy. They sat there day after day, week after week, sitting quietly and calmly, leaving all expression at home. Every day Meredith Tyson found new ways to paint a dark picture of Michael, from the time he was a child until now. She showed him as nothing more than a spoiled, shallow, self-centered man who cared about nothing but his own pleasure. Anyone who knew him understood this wasn't even close to the real Michael, but sadly, very few people truly knew Michael. He distanced himself from most people. Meredith then went on to paint a picture of Michael, angered by an ex-brother-in-law blackmailing him for money. The prosecution hedged on exactly what the blackmail was about, but they did have a witness from many years ago who recalled Michael complaining about his wife's brother showing up at their house and demanding money. They brought in telephone records and bank statements for scrutiny by the jury. They spent a great deal of time confirming that it was Michael's gun that killed Louis Joyce. They questioned a middle-aged woman who claims she saw Michael and Kylie on the beach the night of the murder and they appeared to be in a celebratory mood. Of course, Meredith never mentioned that Michael and Kylie were celebrating their anniversary.

A parking lot attendant said Michael seemed upset that night when he picked up his car. The police detective who arrested Michael testified that proper police procedure was followed and that Michael was properly mirandized. The transcripts of Michael's conversation with the police before Phil arrived were introduced into evidence.

Kylie squirmed when they covered Michael's previous marriage and more so when they discussed the deaths of

Melanie and Molly. She now knew everything there was to know about that marriage, but she didn't like it being discussed so openly. By the time the prosecution was done, Michael appeared to be a self-absorbed, spoiled man who would let nothing stand between him and his money. A man who had no conscious about taking the life of a young, hard-working relative, his only tie to the woman who had once been the joy of his life. Michael merely wanted to avoid giving his brother-in-law a few measly dollars.

These were the longest, most difficult weeks of Kylie's life and when she and Michael left the courtroom on one particular Friday, they both felt defeated. Kylie believed that Michael did not kill Louis Joyce but at this point, she knew she was the only one who felt that way. "Michael, let's go out tonight. Let's do something fun and take a break from this. We can get all dressed up and go dancing, or to a movie. Anything."

"Please, sweetheart, don't ask me to do that. I don't want to share the time I have left with anyone other than you and Benji. If the Pope showed up right now on our doorstep, I would turn him away because I want to spend my time with just the two of you."

"If the Pope shows up here, honey, then I would suggest you invite him in. He's not exactly on the side you want to tee off right now."

"I'll tell you what. You go get Benji dressed, and I'll take the three of us out for a casual dinner. Some kind of a family restaurant. Then we'll come back here and spend a nice, relaxing weekend at home. Just the three of us, okay?"

"That sounds wonderful. Just give us two minutes."

Kylie ran upstairs and dressed Benji in a pair of red plaid coveralls with a matching cap and sneakers. Then she stripped out of the print dress she had worn to the court and threw on a tee shirt and an old pair of jeans. It felt so good to be out of heels. She quickly packed the diaper bag and joined Michael downstairs. He, too, had changed into more casual clothing. Together the three of them headed out for dinner on the town, just like any other normal family.

In the past, their usual restaurants included places like Chez Honore or The Steakhouse, restaurants that were considered to be fine dining for the financially secure. Tonight, however, they opted for Texas Roadhouse. No time like the present to start getting used to places Benji would prefer as he got older.

Once they were away from the dismal atmosphere of the courthouse and surrounded by the noise and bright lights of a cheerful family restaurant, Kylie and Michael relaxed. Kylie ordered potato skins and barbequed chicken. Michael laughed when she not only ate everything on her plate but went ahead and ordered dessert, too. It was a fun evening and for a brief time they were able to forget their troubles.

Just as they were getting ready to pay the check, a little girl of about seven came up to their table. "Cute baby," she said.

"Why, thank you. His name is Benji."

"Benji, like the puppy dog?"

Kylie smiled. "Well, his real name is Benjamin. We just call him Benji."

"Like me. My real name is Rebecca, but everybody calls me Becky."

Suddenly a woman appeared out of nowhere and grabbed the girl by the arm. "Honey, haven't I told you not to talk to strangers?" She snatched Becky away, but before they were out of earshot Kylie heard the mother add, "That man murdered his brother. He's dangerous. Now maybe you'll listen to me."

Kylie's stomach twisted in knots as she heard those words. What kind of mother would point to a man in a restaurant and tell her little girl that he was a murderer? Apparently, the same kind of mother who could believe that a man like Michael could kill someone.

Kylie glanced at Michael and realized he must have heard the mother's comments, too. Although he didn't say anything, his head seemed to hang a little lower as they paid the check and left the restaurant.

The rest of the weekend was quiet and they cherished every minute they were together. Monday came all too soon. It was time to leave Benji with the nanny and make their daily appearance in court. This week it would be the defense's turn to negate every point the prosecution had made.

Michael stood in front of the mirror perfecting the knot in his conservative merlot-colored tie. Kylie watched him from her side of the bathroom wondering how many more chances she would have to share getting dressed in the morning with him. It wasn't right, what was happening. She knew he didn't kill Louis Joyce. He was far too good and honest to complete such a horrendous act. Especially over what he would consider to be an insignificant sum of money. But as she watched him flick his tie around his collar and fashion it into a small, neat knot, the sick feeling in her stomach grew. Whether it was fair or not, she suspected the jury had already convicted him.

Their arrival at the courthouse brought the usual flock of reporters hovering around their car. They made their way into the courthouse with their only comment to the press being 'no comment.' Phil met them inside and took them to a small room with nothing but a table and chairs. He looked at Kylie. "Do you remember everything we've gone over?"

Kylie nervously tugged at the pale-yellow jacket she wore. "Yes, I remember everything." Her hands moved from her jacket to smoothing her skirt.

"Good, now stop fidgeting with your clothing. Remember, confident and trustworthy, kind and down to earth. You need to relate to the jurors. You don't want them to think you believe you are better than they are because of the Bell name."

"Phil, you know me better than that. I don't think I'm better."

"That's good, Kylie. Just maintain that persona in front of the jury. Also, try to make eye contact with the jury. It shows you are trustworthy. Especially Juror Number Five. I think he finds you attractive and he seems the type who might appreciate a little acknowledgment."

"Phil, that doesn't exactly sound appropriate. Shouldn't the jury be focusing on the facts, not on my wife?"

"The way this is going, Michael, we better use any trick we can. The prosecutor is so confident, she won't even entertain a plea bargain."

"A plea bargain! I'm glad she won't entertain it. Neither will I. I didn't kill him."

"That's good, Michael. Maintain that attitude in front of the jury, too."

They entered the courtroom and took their respective seats. Kylie looked at the jury, at the seven women and five men who held the fate of her husband in their hands. She looked at their faces and watched their responses to the questions Phil was asking the server who had taken care of them at the restaurant the night of the murder. Most of them appeared to be concentrating on the case, although Juror Number Two looked like he was going to doze off at any minute.

She folded her hands on her lap to keep from twisting the white pearl buttons on her jacket. She hated sitting here, watching these people, these strangers, judge her husband. Listening to details about Louis Joyce's murder could never reveal to them the kind of man Michael was. Is. If they knew him, they would find him innocent without a moment's hesitation. She wished this day, this whole trial, would end. But as soon as she wished it, she took it back. She had a sick feeling that what she was dealing with now would be nothing compared to what she would be facing when the jury read their verdict. She again glanced over at the jury and smiled at Juror Number Five.

When the noon recess arrived, Michael was shuttled into one of the private meeting rooms off the back hall of the courthouse. Kylie joined them and they ate turkey subs while discussing the case. Phil, along with an entire team of attorneys, was trying to find any additional tidbit of information that could swing the trial in their favor. He was presenting the evidence in the best possible light, but he explained that he didn't feel it was enough. He needed something more to go on.

Tim, the second chair, spoke up. "What if we told them about Molly? I know it's a gamble, but I feel like we have nothing to lose. They could see the dedicated, compassionate kind of man Michael is."

Michael stood up from his chair, fists clenched at his sides. "Absolutely not. I will not have her involved in this."

"But we have to try something. We're losing in there."

"I don't care." Michael's brown eyes took on an intense, piercing look as he stared at the attorney. "I will go to jail for the rest of my life before I let you involve my daughter in this. She has suffered enough in her life, so keep her out of it. Is that clear?"

Kylie stared in horror as she listened to Michael's words. No one had said 'go to jail for the rest of my life' aloud before. It was Phil, however, who responded. "Sit down, Michael. We are not going to talk about Molly. It is too much of a gamble. While the jury could see you as a loving father who only wants to protect his daughter, they could also see you as a cold-hearted aristocrat, so embarrassed of his injured daughter that he pays to keep her hidden and then easily lies about it. That's not exactly the image we want to portray, is it?"

"Then it's settled. Now go in there and find another way to win this for me."

Court was back in session and went on until well after 5:00 PM. The judge, a rather young man, seemed hesitant to end the proceedings. It was as if he wanted to give the defense every opportunity to provide all of the evidence they had to defend Michael.

Kylie liked the judge. He seemed focused and fair. Throughout the entire trial, he took notes, asked questions, and made fair rulings. Kylie wondered if she should smile at him, too.

As the week went on, Kylie grew more hopeful. Phil was making one good argument after another about why Michael could not be the murderer. He discussed such points as there was not enough time for Michael to murder Joyce, retrieve the car from the parking garage, and get back to the restaurant in the timeframe allotted. No fingerprints or footprints that matched Michael's were found in the alley where the murder occurred. No gun residue was found on Michael's hands the night they arrested him. There was no real motive other than an alleged blackmailing, but what was Joyce blackmailing Michael about? Perhaps the previous sum of money paid to Joyce was merely a gift to the only remaining family member of a deceased wife.

Finally, Friday arrived. It had been a grueling week and both Kylie and Michael were exhausted. They were anxious to go home and spend a quiet weekend with Benji. No lawyers. No nannies. Just the three of them.

They didn't want to go out in public because of the press. It was easy to see who recognized them because of the hushed whispers that occurred as they walked by. Instead, they lounged in the yard and played in the family room. Michael cooked a couple of meals on the grill and on Sunday morning Kylie served him breakfast in bed. Granted it was only cold cereal with a sliced banana and coffee, but it was fun, and they both enjoyed it.

Shortly after Michael finished breakfast and Kylie was clearing the dishes, Michael sat in bed thinking about who could be setting him up for murder. He kept running the facts through his mind. It had to be someone who knew him, and knew him well. Someone who knew his connection to Joyce and knew that he was being blackmailed. No matter how many times he went over it, he could only come up with one name. C. C. Bell. But would his own father let him go to prison, quite possibly for the rest of his life, for a murder he didn't commit? Sadly, Michael knew the answer to that was yes. Father would do anything to protect the precious Bell name, even if it meant sacrificing his only son. After all, he felt no guilt about controlling his wife for the last 40 years. Cynthia never had the nerve to stand up to C. C., but Michael did, and C. C. didn't deal well with people who did not bend to his will. Also, C. C. knew about his connection to Joyce. He could have easily known about the money. For all Michael knew, C. C. may have access to all of Michael's financial records. And while Michael didn't share his anniversary plans with his father, it wouldn't surprise him if C. C. was aware of them. His father had all kinds of information about people that they didn't know he had. Yes, C. C. was the most likely person who would have had Joyce killed, but why would he have set Michael up? That was the one piece of the puzzle that Michael couldn't understand. Why didn't he just have him killed and keep Michael out of it? Was it a safety net in case he got caught? Was he that upset with Michael that he would have him thrown in prison for the rest of his life? For the millionth time since this mess began, Michael tried to figure this out, but as always, the answer eluded him.

Monday morning came all too soon. Kylie hated handing Benji over to the nanny as she and Michael headed off for court. Kylie was wearing the same forest green pants suit she had worn twice before. Phil thought it would look better if she didn't show up in a new outfit every single day of the trial. The defense would rest soon and then closing arguments would begin. After that, Michael's fate would be in the hands of the twelve people who made up the jury.

When they arrived at the courthouse Monday, Phil called them aside to give them what he referred to as 'unpleasant' news. He had tried to arrange a deal with the prosecutor's office, but the prosecutor wanted no part of it. She felt her case was strong and she was counting on a guilty verdict. Phil explained this was a bad sign. He also said that while the actions of a jury could never be known for sure until they occurred, the outcome looked bleak. Then he laughed and said that if Michael was ever going to skip town, now would be the time. He laughed, but at the same time, he stared intently into Michael's brown eyes.

Kylie felt a chill as cold as ice travel down her spine. Phil may have said the words in jest, but his eyes were dead serious. She had a strong suspicion he was trying to tell them to run, now, before it was too late. She almost wished Michael would consider doing just that, but even now he was already shaking his head from side to side saying he was innocent and he was going to see this through to the end.

Court on Monday continued in much the same fashion as it had every other day. Tuesday was more of the same and finally, on Wednesday, the defense rested. All that remained were closing arguments and the verdict that could change Kylie and Michael's lives forever.

The night before the jury was expected to reach a verdict, Michael dismissed the household staff early. He wanted to be alone with Kylie and Benji, two of the most important people in his life. He would have loved to have Molly join them, but he refused to give the press any trace of her existence, so he kept his distance. After a quiet supper and several hours spent holding Benji, Michael tucked the baby into his crib and turned to Kylie. "Come with me. I need to talk to you."

Kylie followed him into their bedroom, pulling her robe tightly around her. She glanced around the room where they shared so much love. The king-size bed with the big, padded headboard. The mossy green comforter and the ubiquitous pillows of greens, mauves, and creams. The windows that flooded the room with light during the day and the fireplace that warmed the room at night. The whimsical landscape pictures, their wedding photos done in black and white. The room was comfortable, almost enchanting. She always felt at peace here. Until now. Now she looked at Michael and she knew he was scared about the verdict tomorrow and that terrified her. What was she going to do if he was found guilty? She couldn't just stand by while the absolute love of her life was locked behind bars, possibly forever, for a crime she was sure he didn't commit. She loved him and the thought of living without him made her sick to her stomach. How could something as right as celebrating their wedding anniversary turn into something so wrong?

"Kylie, I've been thinking about this for a long time, and I want you to listen carefully to what I have to say. I don't want you to answer. Just listen."

Kylie didn't like the feeling that was starting to swell inside of her stomach. She was sure she didn't want to hear what Michael was going to say but she was also aware that he had to say it, so she forced herself to sit quietly. She wrapped her arms around herself trying to find comfort in the warmth of her chenille robe, and focused on her husband.

"I have reviewed the trial over and over in my mind and no matter how I look at it, I don't think it looks good. I think they are going to find me guilty tomorrow."

"Michael, don't say that."

"Let's be realistic, Kylie. The evidence all points to my guilt, not my innocence. I'm not trying to say I'm giving up. Believe me, I don't want to spend the rest of my life in prison. I will have Phil start working on any appeal he can come up with the second they turn the key in the lock. But for right now, I can't see it turning out any other way. But there are things I need to say to you."

Kylie didn't answer but shook her head in the affirmative.

"First of all, and most importantly, I love you. You have been the greatest joy of my life and I love you more than anyone has ever dreamed possible. You have brought me more happiness in the few short years we have been together than most men have in a lifetime. You have been my reason for wanting to face each day and the biggest part of my prayers every night. Regardless of what happens tomorrow, I will love you forever. Nothing can change that."

Kylie nodded as tears started to glisten in her eyes. Still, she remained silent, sensing that Michael wanted, no, needed to continue.

"Second, I want to thank you for Benji. There's not a man on earth who could be prouder of his son than I am of mine. I wish for him only the best things in life, and with you as his mother, I know he is off to a great start. He is beautiful and I love him. Please promise me, Kylie, that he will always know that. I need for him to know how much I love him."

With tears spilling onto her cheeks, Kylie shook her

head affirmatively. "I promise."

"Next, I know we have already reviewed finances, but I want to make sure you understand that even if they sentence me to life, you, Benji, and Molly will always be provided for. You can live here, in our home, for as long as you want. Your expenses will be covered. You'll never have to worry. You and Benji will always be comfortable. Benji can attend the finest college. His future is well protected. Molly's, too. Her lifestyle can continue throughout her entire life. My father will see to that. You don't have to worry about money."

"Michael, I don't want to talk about this. I know we are all set financially. But I don't care about that. I care about you. About us. I want you to be here with me. Without you, none of this matters."

"It does matter. We have to be realistic. Please, Kylie, this is difficult enough as it is. You need to understand how the finances are set up. Also, you know that Phil can help you. He has a full understanding of my share of the income and trusts of the Bell family. He works closely with our accountants and financial planners. He'll look out for you. And Benji."

"I understand, Michael."

"Lastly, and this may be the most difficult one of all, for you and for me. I need you to promise me something."

Kylie stared into his brown eyes, so full of emotion. Whatever he wanted her to promise, she would. If he told her she must love him forever, she could easily say yes. If he wanted her to fight for him, or just wait for him, she would. She loved him that much. She would do anything for him. Surely, he must know that by now.

Michael scooted closer to her and took her hands in his. He stared into her eyes, leaving her no room to look away. "I need you to promise me that no matter what happens tomorrow, you will go on. If we are destined not to live our lives together, then you must live yours without me. And if that means divorcing me, so be it. I love you too much to force you to stay in a hopeless situation. It would be better if you didn't waste your life, or Benji's, by clinging to a man you can no longer have. If I must spend the rest of my life in prison, then I need you to promise that you will divorce me and move on. Find happiness for yourself and Benji. Find someone who can give you everything I won't be able to. You need a best friend, a lover, a confidante, and if I can no longer be that for you, find someone who can." Michael's voice started to fade, but a stubborn look appeared on his face, and he cleared his throat. He found the strength to continue and said, "Benji needs a father. More than anything I want to be that man, but if I need to sacrifice that role for his happiness, I am willing to do that. Do you understand, Kylie? Do you understand what you must promise? What you must do?"

Tears flowed freely from Kylie's eyes. She could no longer hold back the raw emotion she was feeling. "Michael, I can't. I don't want anyone else but you. I love you. Don't ask me to promise that, Michael. I can't. I won't."

Michael took Kylie in his arms and pulled her close to

him. He rubbed his hands over her back while he buried his face in her thick hair. He wanted to savor the way she felt under his fingertips, the scent of her freshly washed hair, the sound of her voice, the taste of her skin. He clung to her in a desperate attempt to ingrain all these images in his mind so deeply that he could never forget any of them. Despite the confident appearance he had been trying to portray these last few weeks, deep within his soul, the cold, harsh truth tore at his every movement. He would be found guilty tomorrow and he was going to be taken away from his family for a very long time. Possibly forever.

"You must, Kylie. I need you to promise this to me. I won't be able to survive if I know that I have ruined your life, too. Please, babe, please promise me. Please."

Kylie nodded her head, but she couldn't bring herself to say the words. She knew she could never commit to a promise that she would never keep. She leaned into him and put both hands on his face, tracing the corners of his mouth with her thumbs. She brought her lips to his and kissed him. It was a deep, soulful kiss, full of passion. She moved her hands to his hair, entwining her fingers in his dark curls.

He held her tightly in return, his arms encircled around her. His return kiss was hot and passionate. It was the kiss of desperation. The kiss of a man who knew it may have to sustain him for a lifetime. Kylie returned this kiss, matching his passion, but with tears streaming down her face.

Afterward, they lay on the couch together,

comfortable with their bodies entwined. They each drifted into their own version of a dark, troubled sleep. Tomorrow morning would come all too soon, and with it, the verdict that could change their lives forever.

10

"All rise." The words Kylie dreaded but had to hear were spoken loudly by the bailiff. Court was in session. The jury had reached a verdict. She focused on each of the twelve jury members as they entered the courtroom in a single file and took their seats in the jury box. These twelve people held not only the fate of Michael in their hands, but her own as well.

Kylie stared at the faces of the seven women and five men who made up the jury, trying to read what secrets were locked in their minds. She saw nothing but blank expressions. They all stared at the judge, their eyes never wavering. Kylie didn't take that as a good sign.

The time had come and the jury foreman passed a folded white paper to the bailiff to pass to the judge. The judge opened the paper, read its contents, and refolded it. Then he looked to the jury foreman and said, "In the case of the State of Maine vs. Michael Clifford Bell, to the charge of murder in the second degree, what say you?"

Michael turned back to look at Kylie. How could he stand there looking so calm? So proud? He winked at her and mouthed the words, 'I love you.' She managed a half smile as she said them back, but inside she was falling apart. She watched as he turned back to face the judge. She could do nothing but stare at the back of Michael's head. Her hands were clenched by her sides. She was no longer worried about how she would look to the jury. It didn't matter. She was a mess. Standing there without toppling over was a challenge. She had to rest her hand on the wooden rail in front of her to keep her balance. Every muscle in her body was taut. She bit her lip hard enough to draw blood, but she didn't feel the pain. She was holding her breath.

The courtroom took on a surreal tone and everything around her played in slow motion. There were no longer background noises. No shuffling of papers, no coughing or clearing of throats, no murmuring or shifting of positions. There was only silence. Kylie couldn't even hear the sound of her own breathing. The only thing that mattered was the next words that came out of the jury foreman's mouth. Everything else had been blocked from her mind. Her attention was completely focused on the balding little man with the thick black glasses and the charcoal gray suit coat, otherwise known as the jury foreman. He was preparing to read the verdict that could lock her husband up for the rest of his natural life or put this yearlong nightmare to rest once and for all.

Kylie shifted her attention from the jury foreman back to Michael. He stood straight with his shoulders back and his head held high, looking handsome in his navy suit with the crisp, white shirt and dark red tie. He had taken Phil's advice for weeks on what to wear to the trial, but today, when it really didn't matter anymore, he arrived wearing his favorite tailor fit, Ralph Loren suit. Kylie was sure he had taken the breath away from more than one female attending the proceeding. The only indication of what Michael was really feeling inside was the constant movement of his fingers on either hand.

The foreman cleared his throat and adjusted the glasses that sat atop his large, bulbous nose. He mumbled an entire sentence in response to the judge, but Kylie didn't hear any of it except the last word. She only heard when he said, "Guilty."

****

Penny Appleton was having great difficulty deciding what to do. She wanted to go to Maine like she always did but this year, her first since George died, her daughter's family was going on a cruise to the Caribbean, and she insisted that Penny go with them. Penny wasn't sure the idea of a cruise appealed to her, especially since she was still grieving over losing her husband almost a year ago. But Celeste could be very strong-willed when she wanted to be.

What Penny really wanted was to make the journey to Maine this summer just like she did every summer before

George died. She always enjoyed visiting with her son and his family and she didn't imagine this year would be any different. Of course, she didn't want to drive alone. Being on the road for twelve hours didn't appeal to her. But a flight from Roanoke to Portland would get her there in about four hours. That she could manage.

She and Celeste had been arguing about this trip for months now and the time had come to decide. Maine or the Caribbean. What should she do?

Finally, unable to decide on her own, she called her son, Evan, to see what he thought. Evan was smarter than she was, smarter than anyone in the family, and she would trust his opinion.

She called Evan late on Friday night and asked what she should do. She listened carefully as he told her to take the trip. After all, how many chances did she have to go on an all-inclusive, week-long cruise to the Caribbean? She was sure to enjoy it, as were Celeste and her family. It was time she did something different, something fun. Maine will always be there next year. Plus, Evan explained that he was in the middle of a very important trial right now and would probably be tied up for weeks. He wouldn't have time to visit with her. Instead, he would plan to spend sometime in Virginia later this year and they could all get together then.

Penny hung up the telephone and smiled. It was such a relief to have the decision made for her. And it really was the right decision with Evan being busy in court and all. She called up Celeste and told her she would be happy to go on the cruise with them. Then she went to the closet in the spare bedroom and pulled out two black suitcases, one large one and one overnight bag. She had less than a month until they left so she had better start packing.

She pulled out a few articles of clothing and placed them in the suitcase. Then she took the new book out of her drawer that she hadn't started to read yet and put it in the overnight bag. She tucked the camera into the bag. She started to reach for the GoPro that George had bought just before he died. The only time it had ever been used was on their last visit to Maine. She finally decided against bringing it. She hadn't even been able to figure out how to watch the movies he already made, so there was really no point in taking more. Celeste would have her hands full with the children and she didn't want to bother her by asking for help with it. She placed the bag back in the closet and instead went in search of her favorite beach blanket.

She was excited about going on this vacation. She had never been on a cruise before. She had never been to the Caribbean. She would miss Evan and his family, but she would see them soon. They would come to Virginia and she would spend plenty of time with them then. What difference did it make if she missed one trip to Maine? It's not like she couldn't go next year.

11

Hours had passed since Kylie drove home, alone, and still the tears poured freely down her cheeks. For the first time since she was a child, she felt totally lost. She didn't know what to do or to whom to turn. There seemed to be no options in front of her. No path to choose. No choice seemed acceptable. Michael was going to prison, possibly for the rest of his life. And there was nothing she could do about it. How was she supposed to go on when the only man she had ever loved was gone? In the blink of an eye, her entire life was destroyed. Everything she had ever wanted, ever dreamed of, was gone. Her perfect life was over.

She walked around the big, empty house, clothing disheveled, hair a mess, mascara streaking down her cheeks. She had sent the staff home and tended to Benji by herself, but now he was tucked safely into his crib for the night. There was nothing to distract her from the pain that seared through her heart.

Someone rang the bell at the front door but she didn't answer it. There was no one she wanted to see. The ringing cellphone also went unanswered. If she couldn't talk to Michael, she wouldn't talk to anyone.

Using the app on her phone, she locked the doors. Then she went from room to room and closed the blinds. Loneliness surrounded her but it was better than seeing anyone. Her life was essentially over. She understood that and the sooner other people did, the better off she would be. All she had left in this world was Benji and other than him, she had nothing. Isn't that what she expected out of life? Nothing? Isn't that what her parents taught her she deserved all those years ago? She wondered now why she ever thought she could do better than what she had been destined for.

Darkness fell upon the house and still she paced. Weariness attacked her body and her pacing became muddled. She staggered, but she continued. The clock ticked past bedtime and moved into the early hours of the morning. Exhausted from crying and walking, Kylie finally gave into her fatigue and fell across her bed. She was sure there was not another teardrop left inside of her, but as she succumbed to sleep, tears continued to roll down her face.

Benji must have sensed the turmoil inside of his mother, for he slept later into the morning than ever before. When he awoke, his tiny whimpering turned into full-scale cries. Kylie was pulled from her dreamless sleep and hurried into his room. Her son, Michael's son, deserved nothing less than her full attention.

She picked the crying baby up from his crib and brought him close to her chest, cuddling and soothing him with her words. He calmed under her gentle touch. She changed his diaper and brought him into the kitchen. It was after 8:00 AM and Cassie was hard at work. Cassie had heard the baby's cries, so she warmed his bottle. Kylie merely had to retrieve it from the counter, settle into the big recliner in the family room, and feed her son. As watched him greedily suck on the nipple of his little blue bottle she smiled, and for a brief moment, the blackness in her heart paled to gray.

After his breakfast was complete, Kylie bathed him and carried him into the backyard so he could enjoy the beautiful weather. When he fell asleep, she laid him in his stroller and sat next to him, staring at his perfect little head, his tiny hands and feet, his diaper-clad rump propped up in the air. He was her only purpose in life and she was going to do right by him. She would be the best mother possible.

Kylie spent the rest of the day with Benji, holding him, feeding him, changing him, and at times, just staring at him. Day turned into night and Kylie tucked Benji into his crib, relieved that the darkness cloaking their outside world now matched the darkness she felt inside. She gently kissed her tiny son and lay down on the bed next to his crib, glad she had the foresight to include a twin-size bed in the nursery. She was sure sleep wouldn't come to her, wouldn't let her escape the pain she was feeling that easily, but in the end, her body proved wearier than her mind and she succumbed to its beckoning tranquility.

The next day passed in much the same fashion, with Kylie tending to Benji and refusing to accept company with anyone else, whether it be by cellphone or letter or even in person. She hoped her leave of absence from work was continuing but if it wasn't, she didn't care. There wasn't much she cared about.

Days turned into weeks, although Kylie still had no conscious knowledge of the passing of time. She was living moment to moment; every step was centered around Benji. He was the one constant in her chaotic life. The one thread that kept her woven into the perfect life she and Michael had shared.

On one particularly sunny day, Kylie sat on a wicker chair on the rear deck, Benji sleeping contentedly in his stroller by her side. Suddenly Cassie burst through the back door wringing her hands as she hurried to Kylie's chair. "I'm sorry, ma'am. I told him you still weren't up to receiving visitors, but he insisted."

"Who insisted? What are you talking about?"

"I did. You need to see me, whether you are up to it or not."

Kylie looked through her darkened sunglasses, surprised to see Phil standing there, fully clad in a three-piece gray suit, the always present briefcase clutched tightly in his hand.

"It's alright, Cassie. I know how persuasive Mr. Ackervale can be."

"Thank you, ma'am." Cassie turned and practically fled to the safety of the house.

Kylie turned her attention from the fleeing girl to the confident, demanding attorney who had seated himself without being invited. "Have you come to tell me you know a way to free Michael?"

"I wish I did but so far we haven't found enough to even bring an appeal."

"Then I don't understand why you're here. We really have nothing to say to each other."

"I know you're angry, Kylie. I understand. But you knew it was a long shot going in. There was just so much evidence against him."

"You understand? You understand? Who the hell do you think you are coming here and telling me you understand? Did you ever watch your spouse be ripped away from you, from your infant son, on the whim of twelve people who know nothing about how kind, how decent, how innocent…"

"I'm sorry, Kylie. You're right. Saying I understand was not appropriate. I can't even pretend to understand what you are going through. But please don't attack me. I'm on your side."

Kylie relaxed, slightly, and leaned back into her chair. She glanced at Benji who was still sleeping in his stroller. She knew that none of this was Phil's fault. Phil and his team had done a remarkable job, considering the evidence that was stacked against Michael. It just wasn't enough and she was tired of holding in so much anger.

"What did you come over for? Do you have news about Michael?"

"He was wondering if you were going to be visiting

him soon. He would like to see you and the baby."

"I can see him? I can visit with him? With Benji?"

"Yes, Kylie. That's why I needed to see you. We applied for visitation weeks ago and it has been approved. I've been trying to reach you. Your scheduled visitation day is Saturday. We can go tomorrow. I thought I could pick you and Benji up around 9:00 AM and you can see Michael around 11:00 AM.

"I can see him? It's been so long."

Phil fished a two-page typed document out of his briefcase and put it on the glass-topped wicker table in front of Kylie. "Read these rules carefully because any exception to any of the rules could prevent them from letting you in tomorrow. Make sure you dress appropriately, no camouflage, no hoods, no zippers, nothing too revealing. Nothing too tight or too short. No scarves, no bandanas, well, it's all there. You can bring a bottle, a diaper, and a few wipes for Benji, but nothing else. Extra clothing, toys, more diapers--that will all have to stay in the car. You can talk to Michael, but no other prisoner. You can give Michael a quick hug and kiss, but not much more than that. Trust me, the guards won't be shy about breaking you up. Let's not get on their bad side on your first visit. Michael will be allowed to hold Benji. Take comfort in that. I won't be joining you during your visit. It's for family only. This is your time with him. Make the most of it. Oh, and one more thing. Don't be surprised when you get to the second page. Some of the, uh, procedures, you may have to endure as a visitor may not be very pleasant, but from the prison's point of view, they are necessary."

Kylie picked up the document and immediately turned to the second page. Her face remained calm as she read where Phil had indicated. She folded the paper in half and placed it back on the table. "Phil, I've been a nurse for a long time. Trust me, I've done worse things to patients that I actually cared about than these guards will ever do to me."

"That's the spirit, Kylie. Stay strong. For Benji, for Michael, but most of all, for yourself. I'll be by at 9:00 AM sharp."

"Goodbye, Phil. We'll be ready. And thank you. Thank you for taking me to Michael."

"Of course, Kylie. Anything I can do to help you." Phil stared at her, perhaps a bit too long, before he crossed the deck and went back inside the house. Without even glancing his way, Kylie picked up the rule sheet and began reading every word. She wanted to understand everything that was going to happen tomorrow. She didn't want to make a mistake that might prevent her from seeing Michael.

That night Kylie tucked Benji into bed with a different attitude than she had in the previous weeks. For the first time since Michael was taken away, she felt like her life had a purpose. At least a purpose other than taking care of Benji. She crawled under the sheets of the twin bed and instantly fell into a sound sleep. Tears didn't follow into her dreams.

Kylie was up and dressed in khaki pants and a simple lilac top with no ties, no scarf, and no belt. She skipped any type of stocking and slipped into closed-toe, flat shoes. When Benji made his first whimpering sounds of the morning she responded quickly. She fed and bathed him and dressed him in a one-piece terrycloth sleeper. She stuck a bottle and diaper in her purse and packed a diaper bag to leave in Phil's car. Then she sat and rocked him for the next hour while waiting for Phil to arrive.

When Kylie was sure 9:00 AM would never get here, Phil's black BMW pulled into her driveway. Benji's car seat and diaper bag were already on the front porch so all she had to do was throw a blanket around Benji and head outside. Phil never even made it to the front door.

"He's all buckled in. Let's go."

Phil started the vehicle and waited until Kylie fastened her seatbelt. "Are you prepared?"

"I can recite every rule forward and backward if that's what you're asking."

"Partly. But are you prepared for everything? You look like hell and this hasn't been easy for Michael, either."

"What do you mean, I look like hell?"

"Oh, c'mon, Kylie. How much weight have you lost? Ten, fifteen pounds?"

"So, I've lost a few pounds. What woman doesn't want to hear that?"

"You're skin and bones. You need to pull yourself together."

Not wishing to pursue this conversation further, Kylie chose not to address Phil's last statement. Instead, she asked, "What about Michael? Is something wrong?"

"He's lost weight. Most people do when they first go to prison. They adjust. He will, too."

They remained silent for the rest of the trip and soon the prison loomed before them. It sat far from the road on a knoll surrounded by green fields. From a distance, with blue skies, flowering meadows, and finally a deep forest in the background, the landscape looked more like it should be housing a five-star resort than a state penitentiary. Once they drove closer to the gray stone building, however, that impression changed. The building looked cold and foreboding. It was built of thick, gray stone, patched with worn cement. There were iron bars and reinforced glass with chicken wire over every window. Kylie could see cameras over every door. There was a dual, high-energy fence around the perimeter of the building, only interrupted with heavily guarded gates. Guard towers were scattered across the property. Everything inside the fence was gray. The building was gray, the asphalt was gray, even the uniforms of the guards were gray. A cold chill ran down Kylie's spine.

It took just over an hour to get through the fences on the outside and the numerous security checks on the inside, even with Phil by their side. Kylie didn't flinch when she was wanded and patted down. Then she was subjected to having a large dog sniff her to ensure she wasn't smuggling drugs into the building. She had to force herself to remain still when a guard removed Benji's diaper to check for contraband before Benji was allowed to enter with her. Finally, Kylie sat with Benji on her lap in a square, gray room surrounded by other families. There were a few guards scattered around the room. She tried to stay calm as she waited for Michael, but inside she was a big bundle of nerves. Would he look the same? Would he act the same? Would he love her the same? She was feeling both excitement and fear escalate inside of her but she didn't show any of it, she remained seated at the table she was assigned to. Just like the rules had instructed.

She heard a loud click and just like other family members, she jerked her head up and looked toward the door at the far end of the room. It opened and a line of prisoners started to file through. They kept their heads down and walked to the table where their families were seated. Then she saw him. Michael. Her Michael. He looked thin and tired, dark circles had formed under his eyes and his cheeks had sunken in. His complexion was pale, almost gray. He had aged ten years. His thick, dark hair sat flat and greasy on his head. He needed a shave. When he saw Kylie, he started to hurry toward her, but the guard that had escorted him into the room redirected him to the opposite side of the table. Michael immediately lowered his eyes and acquiesced to the guard's unspoken demand.

Michael took his seat and quickly put his hands on the table. Kylie forgot this was one of the rules. She smiled and she reached one of her hands out toward him. The other she kept firmly clutched around Benji. "Kylie, God, Kylie." Michael looked like a man who finally found water after crossing the desert. He could barely speak. He could only stare at his wife while clutching her hand. He was desperate for her touch.

"Michael. I can't believe you're sitting here in front of me. I've missed you so much." Kylie leaned over and kissed Michael. She kept it brief, afraid to break any rule, but she managed to convey both tenderness and passion just the same. It was enough to bring a smile to Michael's face.

Suddenly it felt like it always had. It was just Kylie and Michael. The same Kylie and Michael it had always been. They tried to squeeze as much love into a short visit as they could. Michael held Benji, amazed at how much he had grown in such a short time. He also kept one hand covering Kylie's. For this brief visit, he managed to forget where he was. Maybe next time they would talk about the case and what she should be doing to help Phil and how they could bring an appeal, but for today, it was just about Kylie and Michael. And Benji and Molly.

"So how are you doing in here, really?"

"I'm adjusting. Can't say I like it much, but I'm alright."

"I didn't come all this way for you to lie to me, Michael Bell. Now, how are you really?"

"I'm okay. Trust me. It isn't easy but I'm getting the hang of it. I'm more concerned about you, my love. How are you holding up?"

"I'm lonely. I miss you. You're all I think about. But other than that, I'm doing okay. I'm not sure it has all set in yet. It still doesn't feel real."

"I'm sorry, Kylie. Truly sorry."

"I know, but this isn't your fault. You didn't do

anything. I believe that."

Just then Benji woke up in Michael's arms and made his presence known. Kylie quickly handed Michael his bottle so he could feed his son. Her heart simultaneously filled with joy and sorrow when she noticed the tears glistening in Michael's eyes.

Far too soon, before Kylie could find the words to convey to Michael how much she loved him, how much she missed him and wanted him home, and possibly most importantly, how much she believed in him, the guard standing closest to the door announced it was time for all prisoners to return to their cells. Visitation was over. Michael immediately stood and passed Benji back to Kylie. Then he turned and fell into line with the other prisoners. They were led back through the same door where they had entered just a short time ago. While Michael was returning to his cell, Kylie and Benji were escorted out of the visitation room and reunited with Phil in the main lobby. The three of them made their way to Phil's BMW in silence.

The ride home was quiet. Benji slept and Kylie stared out her window. Even Phil stayed quiet, easily able to feel Kylie's pain from his side of the vehicle. When they arrived back at her house, Phil carried Benji, still tucked in his car seat, into the house, but he didn't linger. He sensed that Kylie wanted to be alone. She thanked him and he left, but only after he made her promise to call him if she needed anything. Anything at all.

Kylie spent the remainder of the night wondering if it was harder to see Michael and have to leave him than it was not seeing him at all. Watching the way her strong, confident, independent husband fell into that line without the slightest hesitation made her cringe. It was unbearable, seeing what prison had already done to him. What would he be like after a year? Ten years? A lifetime? The finality of their situation was suddenly undeniable, and it was sucking her into a deep, dark abyss that she didn't think she could ever crawl out of. Her only hope was Benji. He was her salvation.

Soon Kylie realized she would not be able to be a good mother if she did not find a way to pull herself out of the dark hole she had fallen into. It wasn't doing her or her son any good to have her sitting around the house moping. First, she focused on nothing except Benji and working on her new life plan. Weeks passed. It was time to make some major decisions. The first thing she knew was that she would never leave Michael. That was for sure. She owed him that much. It wasn't his fault he was in this situation. She believed in his innocence and of course, she still loved him. She married him for better or for worse and she would live up to those vows.

Her next decision was to return to work. She still had more time on her leave of absence and money wasn't a problem, but she needed to feel the sense of accomplishment that only her work as a nurse seemed able to provide. She also decided that she would rather see Michael across a cold, metal table once a week than not see him at all, so every Saturday she would dress Benji up, and together they would go and visit Michael. She made a silent vow that she would go to that visitation come hell or high water.

When she called Carina to make arrangements to go back to work, she advised her that she needed a firm commitment that she could keep her previous hours. She had to keep Mondays off to visit Molly and Saturdays to see Michael. That was not negotiable. Carina was understanding of Kylie's special situation, plus Kylie was an excellent nurse and the ICU was short-staffed, so she agreed.

Since Michael had been taken away to prison, Kylie's life had been filled with turmoil and emotional highs and lows, but now that she started to make some decisions about her future, she found she could sleep when her head hit her pillow at night. Her choices were now the routines in her life. She worked her usual three days a week at the hospital and hurried home after her shift to take care of Benji. The nanny was very capable, but Kylie wanted to spend as much time as possible with her baby. He was already growing and changing so quickly. On Mondays she would visit Molly, and on Saturdays, she went to see Michael. It wasn't the life she dreamed of, but she could make it work.

Every Saturday, she took great care in dressing both herself and Benji in their best outfits to visit Michael. Michael wouldn't care what they wore, but somehow it made her feel like their time together was more special if she treated it like a date instead of a routine Saturday morning. Once they were seated at the table in the visitation room of the prison, Kylie and Michael would spend most of their time expressing their love for each other and for Benji. They held hands and took advantage of the initial hug and kiss they were allowed. Michael would hold and feed Benji, and then cuddle him as much as possible. Kylie would give him an update on Molly and tell him how close she was getting to his daughter. During the last few visits, though, Kylie noticed a change in Michael and it concerned her. He started commenting that perhaps she should consider moving on with her life and that if she wanted to be free of him, he would understand. She would shake her head no immediately; she would never leave him. She would never even consider it. But it concerned her that he even brought it up. How could he be giving up so quickly? He needed to fight. There had to be a way to get him out of prison. It was after these visits that she vowed to call Phil and push him even harder.

Christmas came and went and barely made a dent in her life. There was the usual Secret Santa game at work and she bought rather lavish gifts for her household staff, but she and Benji spent the actual holiday alone. He was too young to care and she was content to spend Christmas Eve doing nothing but rock Benji and sing him Christmas carols. A couple of the girls from work invited her for Christmas dinner but watching them with their happy, intact families didn't appeal to her, so she lied and said she had plans. It wasn't all that bad and she did have an extra visitation with Michael on Christmas. She was working hard to adjust to this lifestyle.

She never missed her weekly visits with Michael. She didn't like being searched, and she despised it when they searched Benji, but it was a small price to pay to see Michael, so she simply accepted it as part of the process. Mostly the guards did it as quickly and respectfully as possible. She wondered how this process would be for Benji when he was older. Would the kids at school make fun of him for having an incarcerated father? Would they tease him? It wouldn't matter. She would teach him what a wonderful man his father truly was, and he would love him no matter what the kids at school said. Plus, Michael always seemed so happy to see them. She would never take that joy away from her husband.

Work remained as busy as ever and Kylie devoted herself to her patients. When Mr. Hendrix needed a chest tube, she was right there to assist. When Mrs. Elwood came in for her cardioversion, Kylie was the one setting the joules for Dr. Wise. When Jane Doe coded from a drug overdose, Kylie did CPR tirelessly until she was revived. This was not the life she wanted, but she was learning to make it work.

Kylie's dedication and long, solid work history did not go unrewarded. She was promoted to assistant manager of the intensive care unit. This happened at the same time her husband was getting library privileges in prison and her son was celebrating his first birthday. She baked a cake and brought lots of presents for Benji but her accomplishments, as well as Michael's, went unnoticed by everyone but each other. It was a solitary life for all of them, but to be fair, it always had been.

When Michael first went to prison, Phil would drop by frequently to discuss Michael's case with Kylie. They would review the court transcripts to try and find a way to file an appeal. Often, he would bring dinner. At times he would try to convince her to grab Benji and go out for dinner with him, but she always said no. His overly warm handshakes and extended hugs and goodbyes made her uncomfortable. Eventually, his visits became more infrequent. He still had his attorneys working on Michael's case, but they kept hitting dead ends.

Summer turned into fall and on a beautiful, bright sunny day, with blue skies and puffy white clouds, Kylie reported to work to find her supervisor, Carina Evans, waiting for her.

"Kylie, come into my office. We have to talk."

Kylie walked into the small room that was barely large enough to hold the desk, filing cabinet, and two chairs that it contained. Papers were scattered across the desk, some being held by framed photographs of Carina, her husband, and their two daughters. Every nursing administrator was overworked, Kylie thought to herself.

Carina signaled to Kylie to take a seat. Kylie pulled her mint green scrub jacket closer around her as she sat, wondering what was wrong.

"Thanks, Carina. What is it? Is there a problem?"

"Oh, no, nothing like that. You are doing an excellent job with the ICU. Both your patients and your staff think so."

"Well, that's good to hear."

"It's just that, I wasn't sure if you knew or not. I thought I should tell you before you got to the floor."

"What is it, Carina?" Kylie started to feel a wave of

panic form in the pit of her stomach. She twirled her wedding band around and around while trying to maintain her composure.

"We had an admission early this morning. Seventy-six-year-old male brought in with a severe case of pneumonia."

"So? That's not unusual. What's special about this case?"

"It's not because it's a pneumonia case that makes it unusual. It's the patient. It's Clifford Bell. Your father-in-law."

If Carina had bopped her on the head with a mallet, Kylie would not have been more surprised. Michael's father was here, a patient on her floor. Her head was spinning. How serious was his condition? Was he going to live? Was she supposed to see him or pretend she didn't know him? Was Cynthia here? Did she care? Would Michael? More questions than answers sprang into her mind.

Since before the trial neither she nor Michael had any contact with him. Granted, he didn't try to do anything to disturb her financial security since Michael was incarcerated, but he also made no effort to contact either of them. He hadn't even bothered to try and see Benji.

She took a deep breath and tried to collect her thoughts. She was acutely aware of Carina staring at her, waiting for her to say something. She finally managed to ask, "How bad is he?"

"He's stable. He's on the usual drugs. They are keeping his vitals within normal limits. He's only been here for an hour or two so it's too early to predict how he'll make out."

"Okay. I think I'll assign Morgan as his nurse with Diego as backup. I'll stay in the background on this one."

"That sounds like a good plan. Kylie, I know you and your father-in-law aren't close, but are you okay? Can you handle this or would you like some time off?"

"Thanks, Carina, but I'm fine. Really. Like you said, we aren't close."

Kylie headed down the hall toward the ICU. This wasn't going to be a problem for her. She was going to treat him just like every other patient. No more. No less. She went to the nurses' station and quickly got report from the night supervisor. Then she took her usual seat near the patient charts and began reviewing each one of them, jotting notes on a small pad of paper that she carried in her pocket. She prided herself in having more than a casual knowledge of every patient on the floor. She hesitated when she got to C. C.'s chart, but she was a professional. The fact that she knew him was not going to prevent her from doing her job.

The day wore on and Kylie busied herself by completing the ubiquitous paperwork and assisting her nursing staff wherever she was needed. Things were running smoothly until shortly before it was time to go home. That was when she was struck with a situation that was a terrible error, that could have been a life-threatening error.

It started in the medication room. Morgan was preparing an infusion of Vancomycin for one of her patients. This was such a familiar sight that Kylie thought nothing of it. A few minutes later, Kylie was walking by C. C.'s room and she saw Morgan through the glass with the Vancomycin in her hand. Again, this was a common sight in the ICU, so she continued to walk by. Suddenly the seriousness of what was about to happen stopped her in her tracks. A cold chill ran down her spine all the way to the tips of her toes. Morgan was about to hang the Vancomycin and Kylie read in C. C.'s chart this morning that he had a severe allergy to it. Kylie ran into the room, yelling at Morgan to stop. Morgan was so startled by Kylie's abrupt entrance that she immediately stopped what she was doing."

"What is it, Kylie? What's wrong?"

"Morgan, don't you realize what you're doing? C. C. is allergic to Vanco."

Morgan pulled the paper with the information on her two patients from her pocket. "No, Bell's not allergic to Vanco. Simpson is. She pointed to the words that fell on the crease of the paper, but even as she denied the error, she realized her mistake. She had written that C. C. had an allergy to this common antibiotic, but she had written it in the wrong space. In her haste, she hadn't noticed the arrow she drew earlier that morning, indicating that the allergy belonged to Bell, not Simpson.

"Oh, God, Kylie, I could have killed him." Morgan started to shake as she realized the seriousness of her mistake. C. C.'s breathing was already seriously compromised. No telling what an anaphylactic reaction would have done.

"Morgan, come here." Kylie pulled Morgan by the arm to the foot of the bed. She turned toward Morgan so they were standing face to face. "Settle down. Take a deep breath. We'll go over this together, later. But first, calm down, and let's look at your patient's chart and review the order sheet."

Morgan took a couple of deep breaths and slowly her breathing returned to normal. "Oh, God, Kylie, I've never done anything like that before. Honest."

"I know. You're a good nurse. You made a mistake, well, you almost made a mistake. No one got hurt. Now, let's go pull C. C.'s chart and see what medication he needs. Okay? Then we'll get it together."

"Thank you, Kylie. You're a lifesaver. Literally. He should be grateful to have a daughter-in-law like you."

"Well, right now I'm not acting like his daughter-in-law, I'm acting like your manager. Let's go take care of the patient first, then we'll get this documented."

Together they walked out of the room, neither of them looking back to see C. C. Bell open his eyes. 'Kylie saved my life', he thought to himself.

Kylie's day finished with no further incidents and no further interaction with her father-in-law. She went home with plans to do nothing more than play with Benji. She pulled her Jeep into the garage, glancing at Michael's unused Lexus, as she did every time she drove in. Then she entered the house through the back kitchen door and noticed two things that immediately lifted her heart. The first was Benji, toddling toward her saying Mama. The second was the amazingly large bouquet of flowers, deep red roses and purple orchids, sitting on the kitchen table. Michael, she thought. She scooped up Benji and rushed to the table. She laughed as Benji scrunched up his nose in an attempt to smell the flowers. A small white card was inside the sealed envelope addressed to Kylie. With nervous fingers she pulled the card out, expecting to find words of love from Michael. She didn't. Instead, what she found in small, disjointed handwriting was just two words. Thank you. Thank you for what, she wondered. Who sent these? There was no return address on the envelope, not even the florist's address who delivered them.

"Cassie, did you happen to notice the van that delivered the flowers? Which florist?"

"I'm sorry, I didn't notice. Actually, I don't think it was a van that delivered them. I think it was just a black car. And I'm pretty sure the man who brought them to the door was just wearing regular street clothing. Wasn't there a card?"

"There was, but it didn't really say who they were from."

"Not Mr. Bell?"

"They may be. I mean, who else would they be from? I just wonder how he managed to send flowers."

"Oh, a man in love can transcend all kinds of opposing forces."

"I guess." Kylie glanced again at the beautiful flowers. "But the card didn't say anything about love."

Soon Kylie's mind was distracted from the flowers. Benji, who had now mastered the art of walking, was trying to wriggle free of Kylie. She put him down and he immediately headed for the family room. He was old enough to know where the bulk of his toys were kept. Kylie followed him, but only after asking Cassie to put the flowers in the formal dining room. The flowers didn't exactly upset her, but they didn't make her feel good, either. If Michael had found a way to send her flowers, she was sure he would have found a way to have them signed with the word love.

12

It was pure and simple, Penny Appleton missed her son. She missed her granddaughter. She even missed Kay, her daughter-in-law. Oh, sure, they all flew down last Christmas and spent a few days with her, but it wasn't the same. She missed going to their house for a few weeks like she did when George was alive. Their long weekend in Virginia just didn't give her enough time with them. Katy Rae was growing so fast. She wanted to spend time with her while she was still little.

It was her visits to Maine that gave her time to bond with Kay. They would go shopping and have long talks. In the summer they would take Katy Rae to play on the beach, but that wouldn't be a good idea for this trip. It would be too cold. They could find other things to do. They could shop, watch movies, bundle up and go for walks, or just make cookies and sit by the fire with hot chocolate. It would be wonderful.

She would also try to spend a day or two at the courthouse. She loved watching Evan as he passed judgment on people. He looked so handsome wearing that long black robe and rapping his gavel on that little block of wood. He had always been a smart boy and she knew he would go far in life. As a superior court judge, he had proven her right.

She hesitated for only a minute before calling the airline to book her flight. She would have preferred to have her car there, but it had been many years since she had driven in a Maine winter and she wasn't sure if she could still handle the snow and ice. Better to fly and let Evan and Kay chauffeur her around.

She finally got through to an actual person and reserved her flight. She would arrive at the Portland Jetport one week before Christmas and stay until the middle of January. The flight was ridiculously expensive, that's what happens when the day of departure is only a week away from the date of booking. She didn't care. George left her a tidy sum in the form of a life insurance policy. Next, she made a quick call to Evan and Kay and gave them the date and flight number of her arrival. Then she pulled out her worn black suitcases and laid them on the bed. It was never too soon to start packing, she thought.

Before pulling out any clothes to take on her trip, Penny went to the big closet off the front living room and started pulling out the gifts she had bought for Katy Rae. If she didn't have enough warm clothes while she was in Maine she would buy more, but every gift in this closet was going to fit into her suitcases. Once she cleared out everything, which more than halfway filled the large suitcase, she glanced up at the top shelf. Sitting there, having not moved for over a year, was the GoPro that George had bought. Well, this would be an excellent opportunity to look at that video George had filmed the last time they were in Maine. She pulled the GoPro out of the closet and added it to her suitcase. She was sure Evan would have no difficulty working the machine and together they could all watch what turned out to be George's last days on earth.

****

The snow had been falling since mid-afternoon and showed no sign of letting up. Kylie wasn't worried. There was plenty of food in the pantry and there were fireplaces if the heat went out. Not that fireplaces would be necessary, there was a generator that could be turned on with the flick of a switch. Plus, this was Maine, and no matter how many feet of snow fell today, by tomorrow the main roads would be clear. Even if they were still piled high with snow, it wouldn't matter to Kylie. Tomorrow was Christmas and she and Benji had no plans to leave their comfortable home. They were both content to celebrate with only each other.

Kylie smiled as she watched Benji running around the family room in his fuzzy, footed pajamas. He was currently kicking a stuffed teddy bear up and down the strip of hardwood flooring between the carpet and the couch. This must have been far more amusing to perform than to watch because each time he kicked he let out a burst of loud, wet giggles. It was still a little early to put Benji to bed, even though he was tired. They had spent the morning with Michael and the afternoon running errands. When they got home, they played outside for a bit in the freshly-fallen snow. Benji was worn out. His increasingly loud giggles were evidence of that. He became quite silly when he was tired. Kylie knew from experience, however, that before long that lovable silliness would turn into extreme grouchiness, and it would be best if she tucked him into his bed before that happened.

Kylie sipped the deep, red merlot she had poured earlier from one of her best lead crystal wine glasses and thought back over their day with Michael. Prisoners with records of good behavior were allowed to have their immediate family members join them for a Christmas party on their regular visiting day. Michael had been a model prisoner so Kylie and Benji were at the top of the guest list.

They had arrived at their usual time at the prison, but this time they wouldn't have to leave after only an hour. The search was as thorough as always, although it was a bit more difficult to search an active 18-month-old than it had been when Benji was a tiny baby. Luckily, Maddie, the guard responsible for the search, was quite familiar with both Kylie and Benji. Intimately familiar, Kylie sighed to herself. Next, they were escorted into another visitation room, only this one was much larger than the usual one they went to. There were a few paper Christmas decorations hanging from the gray walls and bright Santa Claus paper cloths had been spread over the metal tables. Place settings of red and green plates lined every table along with paper cups and plastic spoons.

The guests were quickly seated as they were all well accustomed to prison protocol and soon the prisoners were escorted in. This time, however, Michael didn't immediately walk to the seat across from Kylie and put his hands on the table. This time he walked right up to her and hugged her, holding her tightly and refusing to let her go. After what Kylie felt seemed like a cross between an eternity and not nearly enough time, Michael released her and bent over to scoop Benji into his arms. Benji rewarded his dad by running his chubby little hands across Michael's cheeks and through his hair. Kylie hadn't seen Michael look this happy since he was locked in this hell hole over a year ago.

Next, the families were served meals of sliced turkey, mashed potatoes, corn, bread, and fruit punch. The prisoners ate the food wholeheartedly, commenting that it was exquisite, especially when compared to their usual dinner selections. Kylie, however, only picked at hers, thinking the pressed turkey and instant potatoes slathered with congealed gravy left a lot to be desired. It didn't matter, though. Any time she spent with Michael where she could reach across the table and touch him was more life-sustaining than any food could ever be.

After dinner, the families congregated in their own private areas, ignoring everyone else in the room to focus on their loved ones. Michael presented Kylie with a purple and green beaded bracelet that he had made during one of the prison's activity sessions. He seemed rather embarrassed by his inexpensive, handcrafted gift, but Kylie assured him it meant more to her than all the diamonds in the world. He gave her a second bracelet for Molly, and he gave Benji a small wooden train set painted in bright primary colors that he had made. Benji seemed to favor the red caboose saying 'fast' as he rolled it around the floor.

All too soon the party ended and Michael clung to Kylie and Benji in a desperate attempt to make what he was feeling now last forever. His love for her, and of course for his son, hadn't wavered one iota since his confinement. He missed them terribly. He often thought they should break away from him, they should move on to their own lives, but every day he was thankful that they chose not to. He knew it was selfish of him to want them to stay by his side. He wanted them to have more out of life than he could provide, but he just couldn't let them go. Not yet. Maybe in the future he would refuse their visits, or serve Kylie with divorce papers, but right now he chose to remain selfish, and he clung to them as if his life depended on it.

Forcing the thoughts of her visit with Michael out of her head, Kylie set the wine glass on the table and wiped a tear from her eye. Benji's silliness was starting to mingle with a bit of crabbiness, so she picked him up and headed for his bedroom. Even before she laid him down, his eyelids started to close over his brown eyes. The stuffed giraffe he had been clinging tightly to had slipped from his hands. She gently pulled the quilt over him and brushed a brown curl away from his forehead. She kissed her finger, then transferred the kiss to her son's rosy cheek. She loved this beautiful little boy so much. She had always hoped there would be more babies to join him, but for right now, she would be content with just the one.

She left his room and quietly pulled the door shut. As she walked toward her own room the telephone started ringing. Who would be calling her on Christmas Eve, she wondered.

"Hello."

"Kylie, it's me, Phil. I was calling to see how you are doing. I know you saw Michael today but I figured you would be sad tonight so I thought I would call."

"Phil, I'm fine. Really. I just put Benji to bed and now I'm going to arrange gifts under the tree."

"Santa's work is never done, right?"

Kylie laughed. "Right. But it's truly a labor of love."

"I was thinking if you're too sad, or too lonely, I could swing by. Maybe have a drink. Or I could even bring dinner if you'd like."

"No, I'm fine. I already had dinner. And a drink. Now I'm going to finish with my Christmas Eve chores and then pamper myself a bit and think about Michael."

"I know you love him, Kylie. And I know how dedicated you are to him. But do you really think that's in your best interest? And Benji's? I mean, he was sentenced to 25 years to life and that's a very long time.

Even if he gets out early on good behavior, we're still looking at close to twenty years."

"Phil, how can you talk that way? I love him and nothing will change that. Nothing. If I have to wait twenty years for him, so be it. I'll wait."

"I'm sorry, Kylie. I shouldn't have said that. I just worry about you."

"Well, there's no need. Trust me. I am doing quite well. And so is Benji. And if we have to wait until the end of time for Michael to come home, then that's what we'll do. Now please, I have things to do. Good night."

"Good night, Kylie. And don't be too upset with me. I'm looking out for Michael's best interest as well as yours. Merry Christmas."

With a beep, the line went dead. Kylie stared at the cellphone still clutched in her hand with hatred. How could Phil even suggest such a thing? Was he out of his mind? What kind of lawyer would suggest that his client's wife give up on his client? Phil was supposed to have private detectives looking for evidence for an appeal. Had he given up on Michael? The nerve. And to invite himself over for a drink? She was furious. She couldn't imagine what Michael would think. She pushed the off button and put her cellphone on the table. Then she went to the closet and pulled out two large bags full of gifts for Benji. This was supposed to be a fun process, but Phil had ruined it for her with his phone call. She just didn't understand what made him call and say those things to her.

Still, it was Christmas Eve, and she had a

responsibility to Benji. She returned to the bags of presents. Half of the gifts were labeled from Santa Claus; the other half were from Mom and Dad. She put everything under the massive Douglas fir that stood majestically next to the oak stairwell on the main level. Then she went back upstairs for a long, hot bath. When everything was done she went to bed, alone again, on Christmas Eve.

Benji's cries yanked Kylie out of a sound sleep and she was surprised to see light streaming through the skylight in her room. Seldom did she sleep an entire night without waking several times. She pulled her robe on and hurried down the hallway to Benji's room. It was Christmas morning and there was a large array of gifts waiting for him.

Excited, she gathered Benji into her arms, cleaned him up, and fed him a quick breakfast. He may not understand what all those presents under the tree were, but she did. She brought him to the beautifully lit Christmas tree and smiled as his little face stared at the sparkling lights in awe. She picked up a brightly wrapped box and sat on the floor next to Benji. She pulled the ribbon and ripped off the paper. Then she pulled out a bright yellow school bus with little 'students' that could be moved from one seat to another. When she put the bus on the floor and pushed it, the Happy Face Bus started singing. Benji, delighted with the toy, clapped his hands together and did his own special version of a dance. Kylie laughed and took lots of pictures to share with Michael.

Next, she unwrapped a stuffed superhero followed by a plush, blue car that sang a variety of traveling songs. Benji was catching onto the fun of unwrapping presents. He started picking up packages and piling them on Kylie's lap for her to open. It took several hours to get through the gifts, mainly because each time one was opened there was a bit of play time before proceeding to the next gift. By the time the gifts were opened, the stockings had been taken down from the fireplace and emptied, and the torn wrapping paper stuffed into a large, plastic bag, it was time for Benji's nap. There was no lunch to be had today because they had been snacking the entire morning on bananas, Cheerios, and special Christmas cookies. Kylie tucked him into his bed and then went to her room to get dressed. Just because they were alone didn't mean they couldn't dress up to celebrate this special day.

She pulled on deep burgundy pants and a rich golden blouse made of the smoothest satin. Then she accented her outfit with a sparkling necklace made with both diamonds and rubies. She added the beaded bracelet Michael had made and looked in the mirror. She felt quite festive. Once Benji was up she would dress him in his red velour Christmas outfit and together they would have dinner in the formal dining room where Cassie had already set the table in Christmas reds and silvers.

Kylie started down the stairs to check on the meal that was all prepared, just waiting for her to heat it up and serve it on a silver Christmas platter. Just as she reached the landing, the front doorbell rang. Odd, she thought. She wasn't expecting visitors. Her mind quickly flashed back to the telephone conversation she had had the previous night with Phil and she hoped he hadn't come to check on her. For the first time since she had known him, she was feeling a bit nervous in his company. Why couldn't he understand that she was content to spend Christmas with just Benji?

She walked to the front door and peeked through the side glass. Her mouth dropped in amazement. There, standing only a few feet away from her on the other side of the door, was C. C. Bell. In all the years she had known Michael, C. C. had never ventured to their home. She wondered what brought him here today.

She hesitated for a moment before pulling the door open to greet Michael's father. C. C. stood there, shopping bags in both arms, waiting to be invited in.

"Mr. Bell, what a surprise. Please, come in."

"Hello, Kylie. Merry Christmas."

"Merry Christmas to you, too. May I take your coat?"

C. C. shrugged out of his wool coat and put it in Kylie's outstretched hand. "I hope I'm not intruding. Are you going out? Do you have plans?"

"No, Benji and I are having a quiet day celebrating together."

"Benji. My grandson. Where is he? May I see him? I brought a few things for him. And you, Kylie.

"He's napping, but come in. "I'll get you a drink. He'll be up soon. He loves unwrapping gifts."

Kylie quickly set up a small tray of refreshments while C. C. took several packages from the shopping bags he had placed on the floor and began arranging them under the tree. Then they went into the sitting room to wait for Benji. At first, there was an awkward silence and the two mostly stared at each other. Then the conversation drifted to the weather. A good Maine storm was always a topic of conversation. The small talk progressed from the weather to Kylie's work to Benji and finally, C. C. got to the reason for his visit. "Kylie, I've made many mistakes over the years and I've never stopped to look back and see what they were. But today I'm here to correct at least a few of them. Because of you. You have made me want to make some changes."

"Me?" The look of surprise on Kylie's face was genuine. She couldn't imagine what she had done to make C. C. want to change anything about himself. After all, this was a man who didn't even want to change enough to see his own son, his own innocent son, who was sitting in prison. She crossed her arms and leaned forward, listening intently to what he was going to say.

"When I was in the hospital, I heard the nurse say that you saved my life. My life. I've never done a thing for you. I've never been kind or accepting. I've never given you a reason to care about me at all. But when given the chance, you saved my life. You made me start looking at things in a different light."

"That's my job, Mr. Bell. I'm a nurse. Saving lives is what I do."

"But you saved mine. I want to thank you for that. I knew flowers weren't enough. Especially since I've been so awful to you. Like I said, I never gave you a reason to care whether I lived or died, but you did. Thank you."

"Of course you gave me a reason. You gave me Michael. So, I guess I should be the one thanking you."

Then, in true Christmas fashion, a very unusual moment occurred. C. C. rose from his chair, crossed the room, leaned over, and hugged his daughter-in-law. The man who had never even hugged his own son, found enough love, enough caring in his heart, to find love for the wife his son had chosen. Kylie, letting down her guard to enjoy having an extended family moment, freely hugged him back.

They were spared the awkwardness of the time immediately following this show of emotion by Benji, who had woken up and was now demanding to be released from his room. "May I?" C. C. asked Kylie while indicating his desire to go up and get Benji.

"Sure. He is always so happy to be let out of his room that he'll go to pretty much anybody." Kylie realized the harshness that statement implied and quickly tried to soften it. "I'm sure he'll be delighted to have you get him. He's upstairs. Second door on the left."

A few minutes later, C. C. emerged from the stairway carrying a brown-haired, brown-eyed little boy. Benji was pointing at every picture along the way saying, "Wassat?" C. C. was happily explaining each detail of every picture to him. Kylie smiled and wished that Michael was here to see this incredible site.

Whether it was because of the extreme kindness that C. C. was showing or the stacks of fun gifts he brought, or maybe just because it was Christmas, for some reason

Benji took to C. C. like he had never taken to a complete stranger before. Kylie enjoyed watching the two of them together, grandson and grandfather. They both seemed so happy to be with each other. She considered asking C. C. where Cynthia was, but she decided that the day was not worth spoiling, so she let Benji's grandmother slip from her mind and focused instead on the wonderful scene playing out before her.

Benji enjoyed opening another round of gifts and Kylie was truly impressed with the royal blue dress and sapphire necklace and earrings that he had brought for her. She wondered if he picked it out himself, or if Cynthia did. Then it dawned on her that they had people for that, but she didn't care. It was an amazing gesture, and it made her happy.

As grandfather and grandson played, Kylie slipped out of the room to add another place setting to the dining table. Soon the three of them were enjoying a scrumptious dinner, thanks to Cassie's careful planning. The day passed quickly and all too soon it was time for C. C. to leave. He stood at the door, still holding Benji, while Kylie was retrieving his coat. "So, you'll bring that other bag of presents to Molly the next time you visit?"

"Of course, I'll be happy to."

"And you'll explain to Michael that I didn't bring gifts for him because I didn't know what would be allowed?"

"I'll explain to Michael, although you could always visit him yourself and tell him."

"I know. And I will. Soon."

C. C. gave a squirming Benji yet another kiss and then

exchanged him for his coat. His reluctance to let the boy go was obvious.

"I enjoyed having you here today, Mr. Bell, and I hope we can do it again soon. You don't have to wait for a major holiday to visit your grandson. And of course, you can always bring your wife if she would like to come."

"I can assure you, it will never be that long again. I missed out on watching Michael grow up. I don't plan on missing any more of watching Benji grow up, too. As for Cynthia, well, for a woman who's never had an original thought in her life, she's been quite content to stay at home lately. But maybe we'll take this one step at a time. Oh, and Kylie, please, can we think of something other than Mr. Bell for you to call me?"

"Okay, sure. What did you have in mind?"

"Well, dad would be my first choice. Or pop, papa, or at the very least, C. C."

Kylie hesitated. What did she want to call him? Dad seemed a little too personal, although she wasn't sure why. It's not like she held any respect for her own father. C. C. was too impersonal. Then she finally decided.

C. C. pulled on his heavy wool coat and leather gloves. Then he turned back to Kylie. She leaned forward and kissed him on the cheek. "You come back and visit us again real soon. Okay, Pop?" The smile that was on the face of C. C. stayed there as he drove back home.

****

Michael leaned his head against the flat, rectangular object that sat at the head of his bed. The guards referred to it as a pillow, but he refused to even put it in the same category as the soft, puffy, satin-covered pillow he enjoyed at his home with Kylie. He closed his eyes and thought about yesterday's Christmas party. It was incredible, spending that time with Kylie and Benji. If he could have seen Molly, his day would have been complete. Funny, what made his day complete now. Just a few years ago he would have described a good Christmas as one filled with friends and fine dining, expensive alcohol, and extravagant gifts. Now all he needed were his wife and children.

He opened his eyes and looked around the small cell that he now called home. He couldn't say he had adjusted to prison life, but he was trying to make the most of it. He spent as much time as he could in the prison library. Thanks to Phil, he was able to take advanced graduate courses online. At the rate he was going, in another few years he would have his PhD. For all the good it would do him.

His first few months in prison were difficult. He was a big guy and as muscular as anyone else in lockup, but it was obvious that he wasn't the 'hard time' type. A few of the other prisoners tried to intimidate him, but soon he found his niche. Since then, they left him alone. First, he quickly learned that if he stood up to these guys, most of them backed down. They tended to prey on the weak and surprisingly enough, there were plenty of those to go around. Also, it didn't take long for his sad story to spread around the cell and for some reason having a beautiful wife and a new baby growing up without a dad seemed to play on the other inmates' sympathies. When all else failed, Michael did have that never-ending bankroll and on occasion, he would instruct Phil to do something nice for one of the other inmate's family members. No inmate wanted to risk losing the chance for Michael to do something for his family, so instead of going after him, they looked out for him. Overall, it was a system that worked.

Today was Christmas, his second away from his family. He spent the majority of the day thinking about Kylie. He tried to imagine her opening presents with their son. Would Benji like the new toys he received, or would he prefer to play with the wrapping paper? He tried to picture Kylie walking down the hall to get Benji, hair tousled, and big, fuzzy slippers. He could almost see her playing with him, her eyes alight with joy. He wondered if she would put on the white frilly apron she liked to wear when she served dinner, even though they both knew full well that she didn't do any of the cooking. He started thinking about her lying in their big bed. Maybe she would be wearing the red silk nightgown with the plunging neckline and the Santa hat. He quickly pushed that image from his mind. Prison was no place for those kinds of thoughts.

He was so in love with her and even these past 18 months that they were apart didn't change that. He thought she felt the same way, too. It was amazing, her faith in him. She never doubted him, she was sure he didn't kill Louis Joyce. When no one else believed him, she did. Faith like that was hard to come by.

Then his mind switched gears and he thought about the same thing he had thought about every night since he was incarcerated. Who did kill Joyce? He had gone over it a million times and still, he didn't know the answer. He was almost convinced that Joyce's killing was not the tedious planning of someone with a grudge against him but a freak coincidence that happened simply because Joyce was in the wrong place at the wrong time. That didn't explain how it was that his gun was the murder weapon.

He had talked to Phil about it on several occasions, but Phil could not offer any answers. All he said was that he had the feeling they were missing something obvious. Their conversations usually circled back to C. C. He had motive, to protect Molly, and he certainly had the means. The only part that didn't fit was letting Michael take the fall. That may have protected Molly, but would C. C. really do something that was so detrimental to the family name? He said he still had detectives looking for clues, but so far, they had found nothing new. He had a team of attorneys trying to find cause to file an appeal. They would continue, but it didn't look promising. After that conversation, Phil didn't talk about the case quite as often as he had previously. Michael figured that Phil didn't like to linger on the biggest case he had ever had, or more likely, the biggest case he ever lost.

Eventually, sleep overtook Michael, which was a good thing. The cell lights went on at 5:00 AM and Michael was not given the option of lying in bed trying to make up for lost sleep. The last thought on Michael's mind as he drifted off to sleep was of his wife. Merry Christmas, Kylie. I love you.

****

C. C. Bell buttoned the last of the buttons on his pajamas and slipped in between the 1,000 thread count percale sheets of the large, king-size bed. He pulled the heavy brocade spread to chest level and leaned over and picked up his cellphone. He quickly opened the gallery and clicked on to the three newest pictures he had from earlier that day.

The first was of Michael, Kylie and Benji when Benji was born. The picture had been taken only minutes after the birth, and the joy on Kylie's and Michael's faces was contagious as they held their son. C. C. smiled just looking at the photo. The next picture was one of Benji. He was sitting in the living room by the fireplace playing with a wooden train set. Kylie said she had taken the picture on Christmas Eve. The last picture, quite possibly his favorite, was of him holding Benji. Benji's chubby little finger was pointing to a shimmering silver vase in a curio cabinet in the front hall and he was explaining the difference between gold and silver to his grandson. Benji seemed to be clinging to his every word. C. C. studied the picture to see if the camera picked up the tear that was in his eye. This beautiful little boy had charmed him so completely that it turned him from a cold-hearted businessman to a proud, blithering grandpa. Boy, the Grinch has nothing on me, he laughed to himself.

He glanced over his reading glasses at his wife. Cynthia was sitting far across the massive bed, paging through a gossip magazine. There had been nothing between them for so long, he wondered why he felt the need to try to change that. But it was Christmas and even she deserved a chance to understand the joy of having a grandson.

"I have pictures. Would you like to look?"

"Pictures. Of what?"

"From today, Cynthia. I told you I was going to visit Kylie and Benji. Our family."

Cynthia stretched out her slender arm and took the cellphone from C. C., barely taking her eyes away from the magazine. C. C. watched her as she looked at the three photos. She only briefly glanced at the first photo, the one that had Michael, Kylie and Benji in it. She also breezed by the one with just Benji. So much for trying to reach out to her, C. C. thought. Then she looked at the third picture and this one held her attention. Her forehead creased as she brought the photo closer to her face. She seemed genuinely interested in it. After several minutes she finally removed her glasses and handed the pictures back to C. C. "You look happy," she commented.

"He's an incredible baby, Cynthia. Our grandchild is truly a joy."

Cynthia didn't respond but the slightest trace of a smile did fall upon her lips. Nothing else was said and C.

C. turned off his light. He resumed his usual sleeping position, arms and legs drawn close to his body, back toward Cynthia. Her reaction wasn't much but it was more than he expected. Maybe he would be able to get through to her after all. Wouldn't it be nice if just once she could step out of her role of perfect wife and actually be one?

C. C. closed his eyes. His last thoughts before drifting off to sleep were first of Kylie, then of Benji, then of Michael. Good night, children, and Merry Christmas.

****

It had been an amazing day, just about the best Christmas that was possible without Michael. Benji was an absolute joy and she couldn't have been any prouder of her son. He loved all the glitter and glitz of Christmas and that was fun. What was even better was the way he took to C. C. Pop. No, C. C. It would take a while before Pop rolled off her tongue smoothly.

She had been so surprised when C. C. had shown up on her front porch. She had considered not opening the door, afraid his cold, selfish demeanor would ruin their Christmas. Instead, she was thankful she did. He turned out to be delightful. He arrived with perfect Christmas presents, and while she doubted he had much to do with picking them out, she was still appreciative that he had brought such lovely gifts for both her and Benji. He was witty and fun throughout dinner, and both Kylie and C. C. had to laugh when he offered to assist her with the dishes. As if he had ever done dishes in his entire life.

The best part of entertaining C. C. was, without a doubt, watching him with Benji. He was a natural and Benji took to him like he had known him all his life. They seemed to have connected on a level that even Kylie didn't understand but knew enough to be grateful for it. Family was so important and Benji's was on shaky ground. A grandfather-grandson bond could only add to her son's life, and she was thrilled to see it develop.

Kylie pulled on a warm flannel nightgown and climbed into bed. The only thing that could make her life perfect was if Michael was home. She didn't see that happening, at least not for another twenty years. She turned off her light and sank into the soft, comfortable mattress. She closed her eyes with only one last thought on her mind. Merry Christmas, Michael. I love you.

13

Evan Appleton was a good son. His parents had always provided well for him and his life turned out better than he could have imagined. He graduated from high school and college with highest honors and was accepted into all three law schools he applied for. Upon graduation, he was offered a position at an esteemed law firm in Portland, Maine, which is where he had always hoped to live. He met Kay, fell head-over-heels in love with her, married, and eventually had a daughter. His daughter was already showing signs of being a talented, exceptionally bright young girl.

Most recently, he was appointed to the Maine Superior Court. This was quite an accomplishment for a man of his relatively young age. And he knew that his parents made all of this possible. They supported him, both financially and emotionally, in every way possible. He owed them a great deal and he took this debt very seriously. That is why when his mother, Penny, said she would like to visit him for three weeks over the holidays, he immediately agreed. When she asked if they could pick her up at the airport and chauffeur her around for those same three weeks, he didn't hesitate to say yes. And when she requested that he and Kay give up their weekly Saturday night date to stay home and watch home movies with her and their daughter, he jumped at the chance.

The fireplace was keeping the large living room warm and toasty as it cast dancing shadows of yellow and red across the room. Penny and Kay were curled up on the overstuffed sofa, and Katy Rae was plopped in her beanbag chair in front of the television. Evan stood at the kitchen table, occasionally muttering under his breath as he tried to turn on the GoPro. He was unable to accomplish this relatively simple task, however, because the battery was completely dead. Luckily his mother had brought all the cords that go with it. He untangled the mass of black spaghetti and plugged everything in the correct way. Then he was able to start up the GoPro.

Penny's gasp was audible to everyone in the room as George's voice came blaring over the television. He was instructing the target of his camera to smile and wave. Only Katy Rae did so without a stiff, posed look. After endless minutes of Penny, Evan, Kay and Katy Rae waving, the picture blinked, went black, and then restarted. This time the screen was filled with images of Kay helping Katy Rae ride her new, hot pink tricycle. At one point the camera wriggled and filmed the sky, the side of the house, and the ground before becoming focused again. Suddenly George appeared out of nowhere, very close to the camera. He said, "That's my granddaughter" and then he was gone from the picture. The camera zoomed in on Katy Rae riding her trike before blurring and filming the edge of the picnic table. Once again, it went black.

Soon the camera blinked back on. This time the picture focused on Penny. She was standing in front of one of the town's better restaurants, Alexander's. Penny was wearing a bright turquoise dress and white sandals. "Oh, I remember that. I wasn't sure if I should wear white sandals in September, but it was such a nice day. Ha, I look like a tourist," Penny said.

In the film, Penny and George, who remained unseen behind the lens of the camera, could be heard arguing.

"Why can't you just ask someone to hold the camera so you can be in the picture, too?" Penny was asking George.

"No, Penny. I just paid hundreds for this GoPro thing. I'm not going to put it in the hands of someone who might run off with it."

"Oh, c'mon, George. Give it to one of those ladies over there."

"Those two?" The camera bobbed slightly to the left and briefly focused on two elderly women before returning to Penny. "They must be in their nineties."

"So, at least if they run you could catch them."

George muttered something undecipherable, followed by "doesn't matter, they already went inside."

"Well, how about one of those men?"

This time George swung the camera slightly to the right. Two men could be seen talking to each other not twenty feet away. "I don't know, Penny. They look like they're angry about something."

The camera continued to shoot as one of the men, an attractive man in his late 30s wearing a navy-blue suit and white shirt yelled something at the other man, a small, thin man with long hair and ripped jeans. The attractive man then threw both of his hands up in disgust, turned, and walked away from the smaller man. The smaller man yelled something at him, but the attractive man didn't look back. He just kept walking toward the camera, head down. The smaller man suddenly turned to his right and then scurried into the alley. Just as the attractive man got very close to George's camera, a loud bang was heard. The attractive man kept walking, obviously lost in his own thoughts. George aimed the camera back at Penny.

"What was that noise?" Penny asked. "It sounded almost like a gunshot."

"Oh, Penny, don't be ridiculous. It was probably just a car backfiring."

Then the camera went black and this time nothing else appeared. George's first attempt at capturing a movie for all of posterity was very short-lived.

Kay switched the lights back on and smiled as Katy Rae was saying, "I saw me learning to ride my trike. I saw me!"

"You did, honey. And what a good job you did. And now you can ride a bike all by yourself."

Penny added, "And get a load of George. He just had to stick his head in front of the camera, but when I practically begged him to get in the picture, he had every excuse in the book."

Penny, Kay, and even Katy Rae laughed loudly, obviously enjoying the movie. It was only when they looked at Evan that their laughter stopped. Evan, still sitting in the lounger holding the remote, hadn't moved. His face was pasty white, his blue eyes bulging. He had a look of intense shock on his face.

"Evan, honey, what is it? What's wrong?"

"Oh my God. Do you know who that was?"

"Who? What are you talking about?"

Evan finally blinked and leaned forward in the lounger. "Kay, do you know who that man on the camera was? The man in the navy suit?"

"No, should I?"

"Mom, what day was this movie taken? Is the date on the screen accurate?"

"Well, yes, I'm sure it is. I can still hear George going on about how amazing it was that the date was built right into the picture. Why?"

"Evan, what's going on?"

"That movie, that man. That's Michael Bell."

"Michael Bell. Isn't that the guy who murdered some family member of his because he was being blackmailed? You were the judge, right?"

Evan jumped out of his chair and walked briskly across the room. He ran a hand through his hair causing it to stand up on end. He replayed the camera again. And again. Each time he shook his head in disbelief. "Don't you get it? Don't you see what this means? This movie was taken at the same time that Michael Bell was supposed to have murdered Louis Joyce. But in the movie, he walked away from Joyce, and Joyce was very much alive. He isn't the killer. He was clearly visible walking away when the gunshot went off. Oh, God. We locked up the wrong man. Michael Bell is innocent."

****

Michael was escorted into the library like he had been every weekday morning for the past year. He took his usual place at the second computer station on the right. Jerome, the young guard who was a cross between Herman Munster and a bull moose, took his usual spot behind the bullet-proof glass at the guard station. The prisoners who were allowed to use the library were considered non-threatening and of the best behavior, so while they remained heavily guarded, a guard was not required to remain in the room with them.

Michael switched on the computer and signed into his Biostatistical Analysis in Human Subjects Research distance class. He was hoping to finish reading the last two chapters of the assignment and then get started on his paper. It wasn't difficult work, although it did require in-depth thinking, but it certainly was tedious. Some days he felt this was such a colossal waste of time, working on his PhD. But then again, what else would he do with his days? He knew he would get through the coursework, but he did have doubts about completing the thesis.

He was so completely immersed in his reading, that at first, he didn't hear Jerome rapping loudly on the glass. Finally, Blaine, the big, blond prisoner sitting next to him reading a third-grade primer, nudged him. Anytime touching was involved, Michael's self-preservation instincts kicked into gear, and he jumped out of his chair, muscles flexed.

"I don't want nothing, man," Blaine said. "Jerome wants you. He's been banging on the glass and pointing at you."

"Oh, sorry." Michael lowered his fists and glanced over at Jerome who had left his station and was walking around toward the locked library door. Michael looked back at Blaine and felt bad for being so harsh with him. After all, Blaine was more like Bam-Bam from the Flintstones than he was a threatening inmate.

"So, Blaine, good book?"

"I like this book, Michael. It has lots of pictures of real fast cars and trucks. See? I like the red one. It's real pretty."

"That one is very nice, Blaine. I like it, too." Blaine wasn't the brightest crayon in the box. Hell, he probably wasn't even bright enough to make it into the box. Dealing with him was like dealing with a four-year-old, and even though he did kill a man because he wanted to drive the man's car and the man resisted, Michael tried to get along with him. He was harmless, at least to anyone who didn't own a bright red Mustang.

"Michael, come over here now. You're not going to

believe this." Jerome had a huge smile on his face.

"What's that, Jerome?" Michael asked as he hurried toward the guard. He got along great with Jerome, almost to the point of being friends. Still, he knew when Jerome said jump, the proper response was to jump.

"The warden wants to see you."

"Me? What did I do?"

"You didn't do anything." Jerome snickered as he realized his own pun, but so far Michael wasn't in on the joke."

"Then what does the warden want?"

"I think I had best leave that to him to tell you. Now come on, Warden Tracey doesn't like to be kept waiting."

Michael allowed Jerome to handcuff him as was policy whenever a prisoner was transferred into the administrative area. He then hung his head down appropriately, not looking at anything other than his own feet. Jerome led him down one hallway after another until they reached the office suite of Warden Miles Tracey.

"Hello, Regina. I believe the warden is expecting us."

"Hi, Jerome. Let me tell him you're here." Regina looked at Michael with a knowing smile on her face, but it was wasted on Michael who was listening intently, but staring at the toes of his orange prison shoes.

Jerome watched in silence while Warden Tracey's secretary buzzed into his office. Michael stood motionless next to Jerome, head and eyes still downcast.

"Go right in Jerome. Prisoner Bell."

Michael was shocked to hear Regina call him by his

name and he glanced up at her and smiled, but only for a second. Then he immediately looked back down at the floor. The door to Regina's right swung open and another guard emerged, signaling to Jerome to enter. Michael was led to one of the large leather chairs that flanked the warden's oversized walnut desk. Jerome took a position at the rear of the room, just opposite of Tony, the warden's private guard.

Michael finally looked up and was more than a little shocked to see Phil occupying the chair next to him. Phil had a big, goofy smile on his face, but Michael had no idea what put it there. Perhaps Phil and the warden shared a joke before he came in, Michael thought.

Warden Tracey sat larger than life behind his desk, or at least that's how it seemed to Michael. He had a big, bald head and a thick, brown mustache that hung fully over his top lip. His pudgy cheeks were red, and he was peering over them with small, nondescript eyes. The warden was wearing a dark green polo shirt with the logo of the prison embroidered over a pocket on the left side of his chest. He looked more like he might be preparing for a game of golf than running a prison. Michael only glanced at him for a second before immediately lowering his head. He didn't understand why he was brought here. What had he done that warranted this visit? And why the hell was Phil here? He didn't like that being in the mere presence of Warden Tracey made his insides churl and his knees shake. Not so many years ago Michael could have seen this man anywhere and not given him a second thought.

"For God's sake, Miles, uncuff him, will you?"

In response to Phil's statement, the warden barely waved his right hand and Jerome immediately crossed the room, handcuff key in hand. Once the cuffs were removed, Michael, gently rubbing his wrists, looked up at the warden.

"Mr. Bell, I am about to say something to you that I have never said to any prisoner. Not in all my 21 years of being the warden at this prison. You are definitely the exception to the rule and as sure as I'm sitting here, I hope I never have to say this again."

Curious, Michael asked, "What rule is that, sir?"

Phil was squirming and grinning and barely sitting on the edge of his seat. Whatever he was about to say was going to be big and Michael felt butterflies swoop into his stomach.

"Now, you must understand, Mr. Bell. Our justice system has evolved over the years to protect the rights of the innocent. We have the fairest, best-designed system in the world. It is a process that has grown and morphed from the time of our forefathers."

Michael did not yet understand what Warden Tracey was trying to say. Surely, he had not been brought in here for a lesson on the history of the justice system.

"Yet, like any procedure that is continually changing, it is not perfect. While it strives to make the best decision for those that it is sworn to protect, there are those rare instances when something can go wrong. A mistake if you will. As a nation, we try hard to prevent these flaws from occurring, but…"

"For God's sake, Miles, will you get to the point?" At this time, Phil could no longer remain seated. He stood up and leaned slightly over Miles' desk. Michael felt the butterflies expand to the size of seagulls.

"What I'm trying to say, Michael, is that a mistake of the gravest type has occurred where you are concerned. Now we plan to correct that mistake as soon as possible. We will do everything in our power to make things right, but sometimes these things happen. There was just no way of preventing it.

Michael grew excited and slightly nauseated at what the warden was saying. He was trying hard not to jump to any conclusions.

"You see, we now have absolute proof that you could not be the murderer of Louis Joyce. For the first time in my 21 years as warden, Michael, a prisoner who has professed his innocence, truly is an innocent man."

Michael rose out of his seat, completely ignoring the warning looks of both Jerome and Tony. For several seconds he was too shocked to speak. He could only stare, first at Warden Tracey, then at Phil. Finally, the true meaning of what Warden Tracey had said washed over him and the same dumb smile that was present on Phil's face was now mirrored on his own. "You know I'm innocent? You know I didn't do it? You believe me?"

Phil looked Michael straight in the eye. "Yes, Michael, they know. They believe you. And do you know what that means?"

"Kylie! I can see Kylie again. And Benji. And Molly."

"Yes, Michael. You will be a free man. You are going

home."

****

This was the first Tuesday morning in a long time that Kylie was home instead of at work. She thought that would make her sad, or at least nostalgic, but she was wrong. She was happy to be home and she knew leaving her job was the right thing to do. She had thought about it for a long time before she finally gave her notice. She had discussed it with Michael during their weekly visits and he was supportive of her choice. Actually, he was more than supportive. He was thrilled that she would be home full-time with Benji.

He had listened intently while she explained to him that she no longer got any satisfaction from her job, and she was bored with it. She thought she was resentful that her nursing position took her away from Benji. She also knew that her life would be full without working. First and foremost, was Benji. She felt that if she did nothing but successfully raise her son to be a strong, independent man, she would have succeeded in life. There was also Michael, and although she couldn't have him like she wanted, she did have every Saturday at 11:00 AM and she would never give that up. She had her weekly visits with Molly, and she was becoming very close with her. She wanted to go to Latchy Harbor more often than once a week. There was also a developing relationship with C. C. Bell. Even Cynthia seemed to be coming around, albeit slowly. Once friends and perhaps a bit of charity work were added in, her life seemed as full and rewarding as she could expect. And when Benji grew up and moved away, well, she would just have to invest in a couple of cats.

So, just over a month ago, she had given her notice. It was difficult, after all the years she had spent working there, but it felt right, and she never once doubted her decision. Carina initially tried to talk her into staying, but she understood that it was time for Kylie to move on. Instead, she gave her a glowing recommendation and baked her an incredible strawberry swirl cake for her farewell party.

Now here she was, alone with her son. Kylie had just finished dressing both Benji and herself. He was getting so big so fast, she made a mental note that she would need to go shopping for new clothes for him. It was early and they were playing in Benji's room, engulfed in a wild game of hide-and-seek. Every time Benji found her and laughed, Kylie wished that Michael could be home with them. How he would love that sweet sound of Benji's laughter playing in his ears.

Kylie was actually a little worried about Michael after their last visit. Although it didn't make any sense to her, he seemed too happy. It wasn't that she wanted him to be sad, but a man locked away in prison for a crime he didn't commit shouldn't exactly be giddy. She tried to ask him about it, but he just acted like he didn't know what she was talking about. Then he would change the subject, but soon enough, he had a big, goofy grin on his face again. While his words made sense, she had the feeling he was keeping something from her. Worse, she feared he was adjusting to prison life. She had read about prisoners who accepted their fate would be life behind bars, and that the weekly visit with their family was the only thing they had to look forward to. What if that was how Michael felt? Would he give up even trying to find a reason to appeal his guilty verdict?

As Benji and Kylie continued their game, the front doorbell rang. Cassie had left to get groceries, so Kylie took Benji by the hand and led him down the stairs. She hoped whoever was ringing would be willing to wait a minute or two. Benji was at an age where he preferred to walk down the stairs like a big boy with Kylie safeguarding his every step, but it took a very long time.

As they were about midway down the stairs the doorbell rang again. Kylie wondered who would be visiting this early in the morning. She seldom had guests; for the most part only C. C. stopped by, and he usually called first. Oh well, she thought, maybe Cassie had ordered something, and it was a delivery man.

They got to the bottom stair and Benji started to run across the hardwood floor, giggling about his sudden burst of freedom. Kylie, also laughing, ran in back of him and picked him up, swooping him high over her head. She did a twirl or two with him still high in the air and then brought him close to her as she opened the front door. The laughter that she had on her face quickly faded away as she saw Phil standing there.

She debated for a second or two about whether or not she should invite him in. The last few times he had stopped by to discuss Michael's case he made her feel uncomfortable. He was always asking her if she was sure she wanted to wait for Michael. After all, he could be locked up for a very long time. What kind of lawyer focused on that? Shouldn't he instead be focusing on getting him out of prison? And then, there was the way he looked at her. Sometimes he stared at her a bit too long and in all the wrong places. She often found herself crossing her arms or pulling her sweater around her chest when he was around. Of course, she was still angry with him for letting Michael be found guilty. She knew it wasn't fair and that it made no sense, but she blamed Phil for not getting Michael off. He was supposed to be such a great attorney, yet he let her husband go to prison. Sometimes she hated him for it.

She stepped back from the door, still debating whether or not she should open it. She wasn't up to worrying about any ulterior motives he may have, and she definitely didn't want to listen to any talk about moving on and letting Michael go. She was never going to leave Michael and he had no business telling her otherwise. She looked through the glass again and noticed Phil shudder as he stood on the front porch waiting for Kylie to invite him in. On the other hand, the only time Phil ever came to the house was when he had something relevant to tell her. It would probably be better to invite him in and listen to whatever he had to say. At least it would be better than leaving him on the front porch shivering.

Not convinced she was making the right decision, she

pulled the front door open and stepped back. Her action made it obvious that Phil was to enter. Instead of walking through the door, however, Phil stepped back and looked to his side. What was he doing, Kylie wondered. She tried to glance around the large, potted plants that were on either side of the door, but before she had a chance to see around them, another man stepped in front of her.

The man was tall and had broad shoulders. The collar of his wool coat was pulled up high, and his rather old-fashioned fedora pulled down low. A plaid scarf covered the rest of his face. He not only stepped in front of Phil, but he also walked right into the house. Panic hit Kylie. She didn't know what to do. Who was this man and why would Phil bring him to her home? Was Phil being forced into this? Did this stranger have a weapon? She wrapped her arms tightly around Benji and drew herself up to her full height. She knew she was no match for the man who stood before her, but she was going to make it clear that he would never hurt Benji. She took her most defiant stance, only vaguely aware that Phil was grinning from ear to ear.

She stared into the stranger's eyes. She started to tremble as she looked into the warm, brown eyes surrounded by the dark, thick lashes. She tightened her grip on the now squirming Benji, which was good because her grip on reality was tentative. Oh my God, she muttered to herself. She reached up and grabbed the end of the plaid scarf and started to unwrap it from the man who stood quietly before her. She could see the eyes twinkle in the same familiar gesture she had seen so many times before. Knowing what she was going to find and still not believing it, she pulled the scarf away. There, standing before her, was Michael.

"Hello, my love. I'm home."

Kylie dove into Michael's arms with such force that it actually knocked him back a step. He immediately recovered and wrapped his arms around both her and Benji, squeezing so tightly she was sure she wouldn't be able to breathe. It didn't matter. Michael was home and he was holding her. She didn't need air. She only needed him.

Initially, Benji enjoyed the hugs and let out a few 'dadas' but now he was making his desire to be set free known to all of them. He wriggled and squirmed and said "Down. Down, now." Michael laughed, gave him one more hug and kiss, and put him gently back on the floor. Then Michael turned back to Kylie, holding both of her hands in his. He couldn't stop staring at her, holding her, touching her. It didn't feel like this could be real. Luckily, Phil had entered the house and pushed the front door shut. Otherwise, they may have all simply frozen in place. Phil continued to just stand there, beaming at the other three.

"I don't understand. Are you being allowed to come home for a visit? Why did they let you come home? When do you have to go back?"

"No, Kylie. I'm not going back. Ever. I'm home for good."

All of a sudden, a dark thought flashed into Kylie's

mind. She glanced toward the front door to ensure that no one else was coming through it. "You didn't escape, did you? I mean, are they going to come after you? Should we leave right away?"

Michael laughed. "No, Kylie. I didn't escape. They let me go. They know I didn't do it. I'm free."

"Free? You mean you are home to stay?"

"If you'll still have me."

"If I'll have you? Are you kidding? This is all I ever wanted. You are all I ever wanted. Oh, Michael. I love you so much! And now you are home. Oh, God. Thank you. Thank you!"

The couple again embraced, only this time Benji was having nothing to do with it. Instead, he was entertaining himself by playing with the puddle of wet snow that had melted on the floor.

Finally, Kylie and Michael parted, slightly, and the four of them made their way into the family room. Too enthralled with what was happening to even think of refreshments, Kylie listened intently while Michael explained to her why he was home. He told her about the judge's mother finding the GoPro of her late husband and the judge recognizing who was on it and realizing that Michael could not have been the killer. He had known for several days that he was going to be released but he wanted to surprise her, so he made Phil promise not to tell. Originally, he wanted to come to the door alone, but Phil thought it might be too frightening for Kylie to have a strange man standing on her front porch, or barging into her house, so he insisted on coming.

After all, it wouldn't do much good to have Michael released from prison only to be shot by a scared female while trying to bust into his own house. Kylie rolled her eyes and started to ask Phil what kind of woman he thought she was, but then she realized that she didn't really care. Michael was home to stay. That's all she cared about.

Cassie arrived home just as Phil was preparing to leave. He had a news conference to go to, especially since Michael adamantly refused to attend. It didn't take long for the news of Michael's release to spread through the town. Already C. C. called to confirm what he heard was true, and actually sounded more than a little delighted to learn that Michael was indeed home to stay.

Even though Michael had only been home for an hour, the calls started pouring in. Cassie was assigned to telephone duty as Kylie and Michael both refused to take any calls. Before long she had a huge stack of messages. Carina called to say congratulations. News reporters from every news show and newspaper were looking for a story. There was even a call from a reporter at the National Enquirer who wanted an exclusive interview and was willing to pay a pretty penny for it. Messages showed up from attorneys who wanted to represent Michael in a lawsuit against the state for false arrest. A few other people called, people who knew neither Kylie nor Michael, to offer their condolences that Michael had spent time in prison even though he was innocent. There was also a call from a shrill-sounding female who said Michael should rot in hell for all eternity because he must have used his money to buy his way out of jail. None of the calls mattered to them. Michael was free. He was home. That's all that was important.

Soon after Phil left. Kylie, Michael, and Benji retreated to Benji's room after leaving Cassie with strict instructions not to disturb them, and by no means was she to open the front door. As they had done previously, they would include a large bonus in Cassie's next paycheck for taking on these extra responsibilities. Then the three of them sat on the floor of Benji's large bedroom and played with cars and trains and action figures until Cassie knocked on the door. It was lunchtime and she had prepared a tray full of soup and sandwiches and thick, warm slices of chocolate cake. There was a bunch of red grapes, still glistening with drops of water from where she had rinsed them off, and a pitcher of fresh lemonade. There was also a pot of hot coffee. While Kylie only picked at the food, both Michael and Benji ate heartily.

After lunch, it was time for Benji to take his nap. He was reluctant to give up Kylie and Michael's undivided attention, but he could barely keep his eyes open. Kylie pulled off his shoes and socks and together they kissed his rosy cheeks and put him in his bed. Then they tiptoed out of the room and headed down the hall toward their own bedroom.

Michael pushed the door shut and locked it. He turned to Kylie and she let out a nervous giggle. After all, it had been a long time since they were together like man and wife, and she was a little shy with him standing so close. Michael fought back the intensity of the two years of passion he felt and instead gently took his wife in his arms. He held her. He kissed her. He treated her like it was their first time.

Afterward, they lay together and he gently stroked her hair. Kylie was so happy inside; her life had finally turned into the perfect fantasy she had dreamed about. Michael was home to stay. Benji was happy and healthy. Even their relationship with Michael's parents was improving. As she lay in her husband's strong arms, she knew she could never want for more.

14

Two years passed since that frosty morning when Michael was released from prison, and as far as Kylie was concerned, life just continued to get better. She grew more in love with Michael with every touch, every look, every moment they shared. Benji would soon be celebrating his fourth birthday and he was nothing less than an absolute joy. Kylie and Michael made visits together now to visit Molly. Their relationship with Pop Bell flourished and even Cynthia finally agreed to being called Nana by Little Benji. There was something different about her now. While she still succumbed to every single demand that C. C. made of her, in her own way, she seemed to be a bit stronger, a bit more of her own person. She would select gifts for Benji and Molly without C. C.'s approval. She stopped by for lunch with Kylie and Michael one day and didn't invite C. C. She even joined a women's book club that had monthly meetings and never asked her husband if he thought it was acceptable. Perhaps Kylie's independent ways were starting to rub off on her.

Michael finished his PhD and only made Kylie refer to him as Dr. Love for a few days before he decided it was just a title and he really didn't need the glory. Then, just when Kylie couldn't believe life could get any better, she found out she was expecting. Even more impressive, she was expecting twins.

Time went by quickly and in just over two months she would give birth to Alison Hope and Alyssa Faith. Michael couldn't be any prouder. Even Benji agreed that having two little sisters would be a good thing. Maybe not as good as a puppy, he added, but good, nonetheless.

It was Saturday night and Phil was on his way over for dinner. Kylie was putting the finishing touches on the place settings in the dining room while Kendra finished cooking dinner. Kendra was replacing Cassie for the next few months while Cassie was home with her new baby, Jaxon. The Bell household was just spitting out babies left and right, Michael liked to say.

With the last of the silverware in place, Kylie joined Michael and Benji in the family room. She had barely fallen into the comfortable lounge chair and put her tired, swollen feet up on a stool when the front doorbell rang, signaling Phil's arrival.

"I'll get it, honey. You keep sitting."

Michael came back with Phil in tow. After a quick round of drinks for the men, and apple juice for Kylie and Benji, they made their way into the dining room. Kendra wasn't quite as good with the housekeeping as

Cassie had been, and she was even worse at greeting guests and answering telephones, but she was an amazing cook. For that reason alone, Michael was willing to pay whatever salary she demanded for the brief period that Cassie would be out. The veal cutlet she prepared looked divine and smelled even better. Just the aroma made his mouth water. New potatoes and bowls filled with bright, green broccoli, along with warm bread, tomato bisque, and a fresh garden salad completed the family-style meal. Once seated, everyone dug in as only those comfortable with the people around them could do. They all murmured their appreciation for Kendra's cooking talents.

Eventually, the compliments of the meal had all been said and the conversation turned to the same topic it always did when Phil and Michael got together. Phil was reluctant to continue the same discussion over and over, but Michael wouldn't let it go. Who killed Louis Joyce? Michael pondered this question day and night. He wondered if there was someone out there who had set him up, and he feared whoever it was might try again. There were times when his curiosity was turning into an obsession.

Kylie listened to the two men long enough. With a sigh, she abruptly stood up and started clearing the table, like this was a task that fell to her instead of Kendra. "Michael, could you please clean up Benji?"

Michael hesitated only a moment. Then he pulled his napkin from his lap and started to wipe the dried tomato bisque off Benji's mouth.

"Michael, take him into the kitchen and use a washcloth. Please." Kylie rolled her eyes as Michael got up from his seat and picked up Benji. As he carried him into the kitchen, Kylie said, "I love that man, but I wish he wouldn't always do things the easy way."

She laughed as Michael yelled out from the kitchen, "I heard that." Phil simply sat there with a perplexed look on his face.

Michael cleaned Benji up and dressed him in his pajamas. He turned a movie on for him to watch and then returned to the table. While Phil tried to direct the conversation to Michael's work, soon it had worked back around to the same place it always ended up. Michael was again trying to figure out who killed Joyce and why he had spent two years in prison when the murderer was still free.

Phil listened but did not respond. Then he glanced at Kylie. She, too, was listening quietly. Finally, Phil rested his fork on the edge of his plate and rubbed his forehead with his fingers. After a moment he let out a sigh and looked Michael straight in the eye. His face held no trace of laughter as it had just moments before. "Are you sure you really want to know, Michael? Like you have said so many times, the killer must be someone who knows you. Someone close to you. Are you sure you want to know who it is? And if you did know, could you deal with it?"

Michael matched Phil's stare, his brown eyes never wavering. "Do you know who did it?"

"No, Michael, I don't know. But there can only be so many choices. So be content to leave well enough alone.

Move on with the rest of your life. For God's sake, put this to rest. It will be better for everyone if you do."

"But Phil, it has to be someone who knows me. Someone who knew what restaurant I would be having dinner in that night. They used my old gun. I don't think that can be a coincidence."

"Michael, it's been over two years since you've been set free and almost five years since the murder. No one has come after you. You need to let go of this. Put it behind you. Don't let it destroy any more of your life than it already has."

"I can't, Phil. I can't. I have to know."

Phil shook his head. "Let it go, Michael. It's time." Then he glanced at Kylie and said it was time for him to leave. After all, it didn't take a brain surgeon to see that the very pregnant Kylie was tired. As soon as he left, Kylie settled Benji down for the night and then climbed into her own comfortable bed. She was lying there flipping through the channels with the remote when Michael came and joined her.

"How are you, my love? Can I get you anything?"

"I'm fine. Tired, fat and a little anxious to see my toes again, but otherwise happy. Although there is something I want to talk to you about."

"What's that?"

"Try to understand, Michael, I don't mean to downplay what has happened to you. To us. Remember, while you were locked away, I was suffering, too. I fully understand the injustice that was done, you serving time for a crime you didn't commit. But Michael, Phil's right, we have to put this behind us. I don't want to spend the rest of my life looking over my shoulder to see if someone is going to try and take away what we have. And I definitely don't want Benji or our daughters to grow up that way."

"Kylie, please, I can't help it. I feel so driven. I have to know who did it. Can't you understand that?"

"I can, Michael. I do. But don't you see what it is doing to you? It's becoming an obsession. It's all you think about. All you talk about. Haven't you noticed that Phil doesn't drop by nearly as often as he used to? I think he just doesn't want to hear about it anymore. And what about us? Hasn't it taken enough from us already?"

"Phil. Right. I think he knows something. I think he knows who is behind this and for some reason he is not telling. Why would he do that?"

"Oh, Michael. Stop. Listen to yourself. Can't you see you're doing it again? Can't you just let it go? Please? For me? For our children?"

"I don't know."

"Listen to me. Whoever did this has already taken precious years from us. Years we can't get back. Please don't let them take more."

Kylie watched Michael as the sense of what she was saying seemed to be getting through to him and she breathed a sigh of relief. She, too, suspected that Phil knew more than he was letting on, but she also knew that she had no choice but to trust Phil. In the past when she had suspected him of ulterior motives, they had been completely unfounded. She had actually thought Phil was telling her to let go of Michael because he was interested in a relationship with her for himself. In reality, Phil was only acting on Michael's orders. Michael, from his lonely prison cell, was thinking that it would be in Kylie's best interest to break free of him, and he had insisted that Phil start planting that notion in Kylie's head. She had resented Phil back then. Phil, who was only trying to appease Michael. She wouldn't make that mistake twice.

"I know you're right, and I'll try to let it go. Really. I will. I have you and the kids. I don't want to miss enjoying the life we have together. I love you."

"And I you. Now, crawl into this bed with me and let's get some sleep. In just a few short months we'll be sorry we didn't take advantage of moments like this."

Six weeks later, Michael found out exactly what Kylie had been talking about. Kylie had just spent the last nine hours in labor and now, lying in her hospital bed with curls popping out of the elastic band that was meant to hold them in place, face red with excitement, sat Kylie, with two little pink bundles lying in her arms. Her smile, albeit tired, was radiant.

Michael fluttered around the room taking picture after picture until Kylie finally had to beg him to stop. Then she suggested he hold one of the babies while she nurse the other. That settled him down like nothing previously had been able to.

A week later Kylie and Michael brought Alison and Alyssa home to join Benji. What used to be their oversized colonial home was now becoming cramped as the blue space in the house quickly gave way to pink.

Alison and Alyssa were good babies and Benji reveled in being their big brother. By the following year, however, when the twins were both walking and getting into everything, Benji was just as happy to leave them behind and attend kindergarten.

The year after that, Benji proudly started the first grade. By that time, C. C. and Cynthia Bell were becoming regular fixtures in the Michael Bell household, and this beautiful spring day was no exception. The 2-year-old twins were chasing each other across the grassy backyard and Benji was playing with the newest addition to the Bell family, Rambo, a 6-pound poodle who thought he was as St. Bernard. Michael and Kylie were involved in an animated conversation about the pros and cons of piercing the twins' ears, with Michael being dead set against it. C. C. was in the backyard in his favorite lawn chair, chewing on a piece of licorice since he was not allowed to enjoy a cigar anywhere on the property. Kylie had broken off her discussion with Michael to duck inside and refill the lemonade pitcher, but now she stood in the doorway of the screened room admiring the scene. And a beautiful scene it was, she thought to herself. She knew that if Michael would just let go of the past and move ahead with the future, they could have the perfect life she always dreamed of. And now that they had it, the rewards were amazing.

She finally stepped outside and joined the others in the bright May sunshine. After a few minutes of listening to everyone laugh and play, she finally said she had something to discuss with the family. All heads turned toward her with expectant looks on their faces. It was quite comical when Kylie realized why they did that. Those were the exact words she had used when she wanted to tell them that she was expecting twins.

"No, no, I'm not pregnant. Trust me, having two 2-year-olds has cured me of any desire to have more children. No, what I wanted to talk about is, well, I would like to put the house up for sale."

"But you said you loved this house."

"I did. I do. But, let's face it, it simply isn't big enough anymore. We have no extra bedrooms. We have to squeeze into the dining room when the whole family gets together. I have something much different in mind."

"Like what? What are you planning?"

"I was thinking. What do we have to keep us in this area? Michael, you do all of your work from a home office, and I can be a mom anyplace. We don't have any close friends here, and let's face it, we both know we still get odd looks from people in most stores and restaurants." Then she shifted her gaze from Michael to C. C. and Cynthia. "We're still a fair distance from both of you. Maybe someplace closer would be better. I think it's time for a change."

"It sounds like you've put a lot of thought into this, Kylie. What do you have in mind?"

"I was thinking. What if we moved a little closer to the people we care about the most? Perhaps somewhere along the coast? Someplace closer to you, Pop, and Cynthia. And to Molly."

"Well, you have my vote," said C. C.

Cynthia smiled and nodded her head in the affirmative.

Michael stood up and walked over to Kylie. You mean someplace like Latchy Harbor? It's a much smaller town. You wouldn't have the stores and the nightlife that you have here. Is that what you really want?"

"It is. I've been thinking about this for a long time. What do I care about the stores? Anything I want I can buy online. And the nightlife? I'm more interested in good schools than I am in fancy restaurants."

"Are you really sure you want to leave here?"

"I'm sure. Especially after this week."

"Why? What happened this week?"

"I hate to mention it, but it happened to Benji. At school. One of the kids in his class, Nathan Malone, you know the Malones that live over on Pond Road. Well, Nathan was having a birthday party and he handed out invitations to every boy in class, except Benji. He said he wanted to invite Benji, but he wasn't allowed because his parents didn't want a rich boy who had a dad who killed people to come to his party."

"That's awful. What did you say to him? Is he okay?"

"He's fine. We talked about it and he's fine. But I think as long as we stay in this town, we are going to hear this kind of crap. I don't think we'll hear so much about it in Latchy Harbor."

"I agree. I say, let's call the realtor in the morning."

"Thank you, Michael."

C. C. was deep in thought. Finally, he looked up and said, "Malone on Pond Road. Is his father's name Ned?"

"I believe so. Why?"

"Ned Malone of Malone's Construction?" I do believe he put a bid on a rather lucrative project I'm developing. A strip mall down in Lewiston. It was a good bid. He was in the running. Too bad. As of this minute, his bid just wasn't good enough."

After the in-laws left and the kids were all settled into bed for the night, Kylie and Michael spent the rest of the evening talking about selling the house. They explored different areas they would like to live in and what kind of house they hoped to find. Kylie wanted at least five or six bedrooms and Michael wanted a four-bay garage. They both agreed there should be lots of fireplaces and a big yard where the kids could run around freely. The house didn't have to be right in Latchy Harbor, but at least close. Any small town on the coast where the children could grow up away from the media and vindictive parents would be fine.

The next morning, as promised, Michael called Ella Winston, the realtor, and made an appointment for her to come over and help set a price for their current house. She also agreed to search the listings for the perfect home on the coast. It was a little out of her territory, but when searching for a house in the 8-10 million range, she was inspired to stay involved with helping them find the home of their dreams.

The next several weeks were spent with tours of exclusive houses up and down the Maine coast. They looked at old sea captains' homes and English-style Tudors. They toured colonials and farmhouses and even one that resembled a European castle. They went to homes on the ocean, near the ocean and one on a small island surrounded by the ocean. It wasn't until a brisk day in early September that they found the house they felt could be their next home.

It was late in the morning when they arrived at the 20-acre parcel surrounding an old sea-faring mansion with an attached three-car garage, and an additional three-car garage beyond the main house, not far from the guest quarters. The sun was gleaming off the many tiers of the house's roof. It was a century-old home that had been updated with every modern convenience. The house sat majestically on a small bluff overlooking the Atlantic Ocean. It was surrounded by green lawns and walls of shrubbery to the north that eventually gave way to trees almost thick enough to be called a forest. The southeast corner of the property where the house sat had a path that led to wooden stairs down to its own private beach. Both Kylie and Michael loved the outside of the house. It was quintessential New England, with a touch of class and wealth.

The inside was even more impressive. The first floor had a wide entranceway with marble flooring and a curved, sweeping staircase. To the right through a pair of original 12-foot double doors was the formal living room with a massive rock fireplace and built-in bookshelves that encompassed one entire wall. To the left was a study and library combination with oak shelving and an antique Victorian desk that was being sold with the house. There was a formal dining room that could easily seat sixteen.

The rear of the house contained a large eat-in kitchen with all modern appliances. Next to the kitchen was a comfortable family room that had a full wall of glass doors. The wall of glass offered an amazing view of the ocean. The second floor had five bedrooms and an upstairs sitting room that would be excellent for the kids as they got older. The third floor was devoted entirely to the primary bedroom suite, complete with a large bedroom, a sitting room, an office, and his and her bathrooms. There was a warm, bubbling Jacuzzi that sat under a skylight that was big enough to let the stars in on cold, winter nights. Every room on this floor had stunning ocean views.

Kylie's favorite part of the house was a small staircase that led to an octagon-shaped room at the very top of the house. The room had windows on all sides but one, with that one side being a door. The door led to a walkway with a rail, known as a widow's walk. It was here that the woman of the house would watch for her husband to return from the sea. While many of them didn't return, hence the name, Kylie felt she had done her share of waiting for her husband. Now she simply could use the room to enjoy the view.

"Oh, Michael, I love it. It's so beautiful here."

"It is that, but are you sure you want to live this far away from a larger city? I seriously doubt if we will find a mall close by."

"We already covered this. I don't need a mall. I need you. This place is perfect. I love it. And I think it will be great for the kids. They can each have their own bedroom. Plus, there are four fireplaces. There's even one in our bedroom. Now I ask you, how can you turn down a place with a fireplace in our bedroom? And don't forget the guesthouse. Just think, your parents can come and stay with us if they want. Or we could see if Cassie and Joe want to move here with Jaxon. Or if you think it's even possible, maybe Stacy and Francesco could live in the guesthouse, and Molly could have one of the bedrooms. But if not, we're only fifteen minutes from her. We can visit her all the time. She's like a daughter to me. It would be lovely having her this close. And the ocean. Oh, Michael, we can wake up every morning to the sound of the ocean."

"I'm glad you feel this way, Kylie, because I love it here. Let's do it. Let's make an offer."

****

Christmas was less than a month away and Michael was determined to have the Christmas decorations out of the attic and ready to be put up before Kylie got home from her one marathon day of Christmas shopping. Kylie told him to wait until she got home, and she would help him, but Michael wanted to surprise her. She had enough to do with Benji and the twins. It was important to her to have the house properly decorated before his parents made their first visit to their new home, the least he could do was help. Phil had been invited, too, and he asked if he could bring a friend. His friend's name was Viviana and he had been seeing her for several months.

Kylie's obsessive need to have everything in storage arranged just so didn't really apply right now since the movers had unloaded boxes and stuck them any old way into the huge attic space, so he didn't even have to worry about messing anything up. Plus, he had a special surprise for her. This was probably his only chance to take care of it since he seldom had the house to himself these days.

He worked his way further back into the attic and looked around. Boxes were haphazardly piled everywhere. It was amazing how much stuff they had accumulated over the years. He pushed his way through the maze of brown cardboard, deeper into the dark, musty attic.

Finally, he arrived at what appeared to be the first of the Christmas storage boxes. He pulled open the cardboard flap and peered inside. Silver and gold garland indicated he was on the right track. He pulled the first box out, quickly followed by two boxes of green garland and another two of ornaments. Every time he hauled one box out, he felt like he found two more waiting. Just how did Kylie manage this while he was away, he wondered.

Believing he had the majority of the Christmas boxes located, Michael started carrying them from the attic to the first floor of their new home. After the first four or five trips he decided to make a stop in the kitchen and grab a cold beer out of the refrigerator. He took a few big gulps and trudged back up the staircase and into the attic, again astounded that Kylie used to handle this by herself. That woman is full of surprises, he chuckled to himself.

He sat down and took another swig from his bottle. Too tired to move, but too antsy to relax, he looked around at the variety of boxes and clear plastic bins that surrounded him. He laughed when he noticed that a few of the boxes had been newly labeled and stood in a neat row along the back wall of the attic. Apparently, Kylie had been up here after all. How did she find the time, he wondered.

He leaned forward and pulled open the brown cardboard carton that was closest to him. It was filled with baby clothing. Mostly blue, he noticed. He pushed the box aside and peeked into the next one. Another box filled with blue baby blankets, sleepers, and other items; bittersweet reminders that the time he had with his infant son was minimal. Having missed so much time with Benji still brought him sorrow. He quickly shoved that box out of the way, too.

He could feel his mood changing, so he quickly grabbed the last of the Christmas boxes and brought them downstairs. He had too much to do to start feeling sorry for himself. Benji was at a friend's house for the evening, but he did stop and check on the twins. They were still sleeping peacefully. The new nanny was sorting their laundry, also waiting for them to awaken, but he liked to peek in on them.

He went to the garage and grabbed the packages he had picked up earlier in the week and made his way back into the house. He had to hurry. It was getting dark and Kylie would be home soon. He climbed the stairs to the glass room that sat high atop the house. Once there, he took the new, fiberoptic Christmas tree out of the box and quickly set it up. He set the display to blink so when he turned it on, it would flash with multicolor lights. He was sure Kylie would like this surprise as she came down the long driveway to the house. It would be almost like a lighthouse welcoming her home, he thought.

This was truly her room. No one else ever came up here. It was small, there wasn't enough space for any furniture other than a small chair and the built-in bookshelf that lined the walls under the windows. She liked it, though. It was her hideaway when she needed a bit of peace and quiet. He sat there now and finished his beer. Then he sat back and stretched his long arms out, resting them on the window ledge behind him. It was too cold to go outside, and getting too dark to enjoy the view, but it was peaceful. He watched for Kylie's headlights.

As he repositioned himself to get comfortable, his fingers grazed against something stuck beneath the window and the window ledge. Odd, he thought, as he wondered what it could be. He switched the tree lights to white to give him enough light to peer into the small crack between the window and the worn wood to see what was tucked inside. He was finally able to see a yellowed envelope that had been shoved down where the glass did not fit snuggly into the wooden frame.

Using a ballpoint pen that was in his back pocket, he was able to fish the envelope out of its hiding place. He was curious about what secret it contained. Perhaps a

100-year-old letter to a husband lost at sea? No, he was being silly. They didn't have modern envelopes like this 100 years ago.

The envelope wasn't sealed. He opened it and looked inside. Michael had expected to discover a treasure from someone's past. What he didn't expect to find was a picture of Louis Joyce holding Molly when she was just a baby. Next to the picture was a silver chain with a small, bell-shaped necklace attached. Molly's necklace. The necklace Louis Joyce was going to return to him the night he was murdered.

Michael sat there, frozen in time. The room was spinning around him as the significance of what he just found crashed into his brain. This picture belonged to Joyce. This was Molly's necklace. She wore it all the time. Every day since she was a toddler. Every day, that is, until Joyce took it. He was going to give it to Michael in exchange for the second million dollars. He had it in his hand the night he was murdered. Joyce was dangling it in front of him for Michael to see. But Michael didn't take it. He turned and walked away. Yet here it was. In his house. His new house. The house he shared with Kylie.

He tried to deny the obvious, but he looked at the proof he held in his hand. He was having trouble breathing as images from his past flashed before his eyes. Suddenly, he could clearly picture Kylie at the restaurant on the night of their first anniversary, insisting he go and get the car while she used the ladies' room. He could almost hear the loud splash in the water as they stood on the end of the pier that night on the beach. The same beach where the gun that murdered Joyce washed up on the shore. He could hear her voice insisting that she believed him. Of course, she believed him. She knew all along that he couldn't have been Joyce's killer. She was. She killed Louis Joyce.

Then his mind shifted gears and he thought of Phil. Phil, who had insisted that the killer had to be someone who knew Michael, and knew him well. Someone who was close to him. After all, who could have gotten his gun away from him without him becoming suspicious?

That son-of-a bitch. Phil knew all along it was Kylie. He knew and he never said a word. That's why he was so anxious for Michael to put it all behind him. He understood the consequences of Michael finding out the truth. That was the kind of truth that could kill him if he chose to let it.

Michael sat there lost in his own despair. How could she do this to him? She let him rot in jail for almost two years knowing that he wasn't a killer. Yet, isn't that what she always professed? That she knew he didn't do it? Ha! No wonder her faith was so unshakable.

Eventually 'how could she do it' switched to 'why would she do it.' That was a question that had a much easier answer. Michael quickly understood she did it because she loved him. She loved him and she wanted their lives to be perfect. Louis Joyce was preventing that. He was causing discordance in their world, so she chose to do something about it. And Michael had to admit that since he had been released from prison, their lives were damn near perfect. But still, she killed him. Kylie murdered Joyce.

He had to get out of this room, which had suddenly become too small. He stuck the envelope back in its resting place and went into his bedroom. Kylie would be home soon. What was he going to do? He knew what he should do. He should march right down to the local police station and tell them what he found. He was certain they would reopen the entire investigation, only this time, Kylie would be the focus of their wrath. Then he thought about Kylie, his beautiful wife who had loved him so loyally all these years. His sweet, charming wife, who had blessed him with not only three incredible children, but also who had completely accepted his daughter from a previous marriage. She showed Molly so much love and kindness, did he really want that affection to be taken away from his daughter, who was already struggling so much?

The more he thought about it, the more he realized that Kylie truly was a wonderful wife and an even better mother. She was everything a man could want. And the kids all loved her. As much as he tried, he couldn't develop the bond with their children that she seemed to do so easily.

And what she did, she did for him, for them. She even established a relationship with his parents, something he hadn't been able to do in over forty years. Maybe she had been right to do what she did after all. Maybe she did it for the same reason he initially gave Joyce the money. For Molly. Should he really blame her for doing what any good mother would do? Protecting her child?

Michael grabbed another beer from the small wet bar just outside of their office space. He drank it quickly and then grabbed another. Even though he wasn't usually much of a drinker, the alcohol could not begin to lessen the depth of pain he was feeling. He popped the cap and took another long drink. What was he going to do?

Then it occurred to him that there was one person he could ask for advice. One person he could trust. He picked up his cellphone and dialed Phil's private number. Phil answered immediately.

"Hey, Michael, what can I do you for?"

"You son-of-a-bitch, you knew all along, didn't you?"

"Michael, is that you? You sound funny. I could swear you just called me a son-of-a-bitch."

"You knew it was her and you never said a word."

"Michael, have you been drinking?"

"Damn right, I've been drinking. I've been betrayed by the love of my life and my best friend. You knew."

"Knew what, Michael. What are you talking about?"

"Don't play innocent with me. I know about being innocent better than you can ever imagine. You knew she did it and you let me go to prison anyway. You never gave me a choice."

"Michael, calm down. Listen to me. I didn't know all along. Actually, I thought you did it. I thought you were guilty from the beginning. I didn't figure it out until after you were released. It was only a couple of weeks ago that I put it together. I wasn't sure, but I suspected."

"What do you mean?"

"As you pointed out numerous times, it had to be someone close to you. Someone who had something to gain from Joyce being dead. That really narrowed down the playing field. Basically, that meant it had to be you, one of your parents, your wife, or me. Well, I knew it wasn't me, and that judge's mother proved it wasn't you. That left three. Then, one night during one of our talks, you made some joke about Kylie wanting everything perfect. You said she was trying to make up for a lost childhood. Sounded a bit obsessive, wouldn't you agree?"

"Yes, but…"

"And there was the matter of your gun. You know, the gun that washed up on the same beach where you had been celebrating your anniversary. You said that you hadn't seen the gun for almost a year. You and Kylie had been married for a year. Guns don't just vanish from houses, Michael. It all fit. And neither C. C. nor Cynthia ever went to your house. It had to be her."

"So, if it was so easy to figure out, how come you didn't see it sooner?"

"Look at her, Michael. Kylie is the sweetest, kindest woman I know. Beyond suspicion, don't you think? Isn't that why you never figured it out? Everything points to her, but she was never even a suspect."

"Well, I love her. Love can be blind. But you? Why didn't you say something? Why didn't you turn her in?"

"I'm a lawyer, not an ethicist. Not my job. Anyway, what good would it do? It's not like she's a threat to anyone else. And Joyce was nothing more than scum, anyway, preying on your daughter like that. So, what good would it do? And what about your children? What good could possibly come from taking their mother away from them? They need her. Would you ever forgive me for taking her away from them? Would they?"

"So, she gets away with murder?"

"Didn't you already pay for her? Anyway, I imagine she pays every day in ways neither you nor I will ever understand. By the way, how did you figure it out?"

Although considerably calmer, Michael still took another sip from his beer and explained to Phil about the envelope he found. So lost in conversation was he, that he never saw Kylie's car come down the driveway. He never heard the garage door go up or the back door open. He never even heard her come up the stairs or walk into the bedroom. He jumped at the sound of her voice.

"What are you talking about, Michael? Did I hear you say something about a silver bell necklace that you found? Who are you talking to?" Kylie stood only a few feet away from him, snowflakes glistening on her bright green hat and scarf. Her eyes revealed a look of seriousness and her voice sounded sterner than Michael was accustomed to.

Michael, looking very much like a deer caught in the headlights of a fast-moving semi, looked first at Kylie, then at his cellphone where Phil, too, waited to hear his answer. He fully understood the ramifications of his response and he truly wished that he had not indulged in even one beer, let alone several.

He looked at Kylie. She was the same woman now as

she had been three hours ago. Young, beautiful, kind, loving, sexy, everything he had ever dreamed of, and so much more. She had made a horrible mistake, but as Phil pointed out, who knows in how many ways she was forced to pay for it? And she did make the mistake out of love. Undying, unfaltering love. Was that really such a bad thing? Honestly, was it really even a mistake?

Then Michael glanced back to the cellphone in his hand. He could vocalize his findings right now to Phil. Once they were said aloud in the presence of his wife there would be no going back. Kylie would be taken away. His instinct told him it was the ethical thing to do. The legal thing to do. Certainly, it was the right thing to do.

Michael had to look deep inside himself. What kind of man was he? Was he willing to give up a lifetime of happiness to do the right thing? He could almost hear the clock in his mind ticking, awaiting his decision.

EPILOGUE

Kylie thought back to the night of their anniversary. It was a long time ago. Benji hadn't even been born yet and now he was 24 years old, married, with a son of his own. So much had changed since then, yet that night remained fresh in her mind. She tried to forget about it over the years, but she never really managed to.

Kylie kept watching the clock in the restaurant. She figured Louis Joyce would show up while they were eating dinner as she had planned. She would excuse herself and run to the ladies' room. It would be a simple matter to sneak out to the alley, shoot him with the gun she had taken from Michael's closet so many months earlier, and be back in the restaurant before anyone even knew she was gone. She never dreamed the maître d' would seat them as soon as they arrived, and they would finish early. Michael was never supposed to be involved. Michael didn't even know she knew about Joyce and his blackmailing scheme. Of course, Michael didn't know she knew about Molly, either. Maybe he should have realized she wasn't above calling in sick and snooping through his office to see why he never answered her calls each and every Friday. She found everything on his computer. It wasn't difficult, he used their anniversary date as his password.

When they finished dinner early and it was time for Joyce, she sent Michael to get the vehicle. She didn't expect him to run into Joyce once he was outside. She didn't even realize he had, so she followed through with her plan. She went to the alley, took the picture and the necklace, and reached into her purse. Instead of passing him the key to the post office box with the million dollars in it, she pulled out the gun and shot him. It was easy. She was a good shot. She put the gun back in her purse and quietly slipped back inside the restaurant. By the time Michael returned, she was waiting for him by the front door, ready to go to the beach. Lots of people saw her waiting out front for him. She was sure of that. She struck up a conversation with several different people.

When they had their romantic walk on the beach, she made sure they went to the end of the pier. The water was deep there. It was easy to pull the gun out of her purse and toss it into the swirling water. How it managed to wash ashore still amazed her. She was so thankful she did a good job wiping all the fingerprints off before she dropped it into the water. She only wished she had thought to file off the serial number they used to identify it as Michael's.

In all these years, she never admitted to anyone what she had done. She read once where so many people had to talk about their actions, but she wasn't one of them. Not once did she discuss that night with anyone. Not her husband, not her therapist, not even her clergy. She was very good at keeping a secret.

She was always so sorry for what Michael went through. That was never part of the plan. So many times, she wanted to confess. She didn't want him to suffer for what she had done, but she was sure that Phil would find a way to file an appeal and get him released. Thank God she never told the truth. That was a prayer that passed her lips many times. And then, on that day just a few weeks before Christmas when she came home and realized that Michael had found the necklace, she knew the tables had turned. She saw the Christmas tree lit atop the house as she came up the driveway. Her first thought was how beautiful it looked, the white lights sparkling brightly against the night sky. She ran directly to the bedroom to thank Michael, but she heard him on the telephone. She realized he had found the envelope and he knew what she had done. He was trying to figure out what to do. Michael, the man who loved her, but also the man who had been deceived by her. The man who always did the right thing. The honest, honorable man. Wasn't that one of the things she loved about him? His integrity. Kylie closed her eyes as she remembered how she stared at him, frozen in place. He held her fate in his hands.

****

Michael sat on the vast front porch gently rocking Caleb Matthew Bell. He pulled the soft blue blanket snugly around the baby's tiny body. It was still bright and sunny, but the slightest trace of autumn had snuck into the air and he didn't want the baby to feel a chill. Plus, he had waited a long time to wrap a blue blanket around a baby, and he was determined to make the most of it.

He looked out at the azure ocean as the sun left a golden sheen across it. Even now, after living here for almost twenty years, the ocean brought a sense of joy to him. It calmed his soul like nothing else ever could. Buying this house was the best investment he had ever made. Not a day went by that he didn't take at least a minute or two to gaze out at the Atlantic and whisper a prayer of thanks that he was fortunate enough to live surrounded by such beauty.

This place had proven itself to be not only the perfect location to enjoy a glorious view every day but also the perfect place to raise a family. His children had flourished in this small, seaside town. They made great friends, they received an excellent education, and they grew up healthy and strong. They ran freely in the fields, climbed trees in the surrounding woods, flew kites along the beach, swam in the ocean, and gathered shells and starfish along the shore. It was everything a child could dream of and everything a parent could want for their children.

It also allowed him more time to spend with Molly.

Not only was he able to visit her at the same home she had known since she was three, but Stacy and Francesco were able to bring her to visit him. Benji, Alison, and Alyssa grew up knowing their sister.

Even more amazing, Michael thought, his parents were here to see it all. They spent two or three weeks out of every year staying in the guesthouse in the vast side yard. His children grew up knowing Pop and Nana in a way he never imagined. His parents were gone now, but the children had memories of them that would last a lifetime. Although Michael was never about the money, as the only child of C. C. and Cynthia Bell, he did inherit the family fortune, which was even greater than Michael had imagined. It didn't change his lifestyle at all, he was quite content where he was, but it did bring him some peace knowing that future generations of his family would always be provided with everything they could need.

Michael closed his eyes as he rocked Baby Caleb, remembering clearly when it was his children that were little. He could see Benji running up and down the beach, red hair afire in the July sun as the waves lapped at his sun-tanned toes. How he loved flying kites and collecting seashells and playing tag with the cold ocean waves.

And how many times had he joined Alison and Alyssa with their tea parties, first with their dolls, then with their friends, in the gazebo in the front yard? Ah, he longed for those days now, especially since tea parties in the gazebo had been replaced with Friday night get-togethers in the family room. He was thankful the girls still came over on Friday nights, but how he missed having them all living under the same roof. Everything changed once they became college students.

He closed his eyes as the breeze brought the fragrance of the salty air all around him, filling one more sense with the wonders of oceanfront living. Benji and his wife would be back soon to pick up their son. Funny how Michael had originally thought that Benji and Charlotte getting married and having a baby so soon after college was a bad idea, but now that Caleb was here, he couldn't imagine life without him. Almost as if Caleb could hear his thoughts, he squirmed and opened his big blue eyes. Michael lowered his cheek close to his grandson and kissed the baby's soft forehead. As he did, he couldn't help but notice the patchy red hair that he had so obviously inherited from his grandmother.

He shifted Caleb in his arms and then settled him on his shoulder. Once he was assured of the baby's comfort he leaned back in the chair and closed his eyes. His thoughts immediately turned to Kylie as they had so often over the years. He pictured her standing there before him, just as beautiful today as she was when he met her almost thirty years ago. Sure, her hair may have lost a bit of its red luster, and her trim waistline may have expanded a few inches, but it didn't matter. He loved her today as he did way back then. He thought back to the day when he had to make that life-altering decision about Kylie. Should he turn her in or let her walk away? Funny, once he made up his mind, he knew it was the right thing to do and he never looked back.

A vision of her standing there, snowflakes glistening on her green hat and scarf, came to him and he remembered it like it was yesterday. He hadn't heard her walk into the bedroom and the sound of her voice startled him.

"What are you talking about, Michael? Did I hear you say something about a silver bell necklace you found? Who are you talking to?"

"Kylie, I didn't hear you come in."

Seldom did Kylie enter the house without a smile on her face, but never before had Michael seen the stern, cold look that he saw now. Slowly, with careful enunciation, she repeated her questions. "Who are you talking to, Michael? Did I hear you say something about a silver bell necklace?"

"I'm talking to Phil. And a bell necklace? No, sweetie. A bell. A silver bell. I was telling Phil about the Christmas decorations I was bringing down and I found a silver bell and I was wondering if it goes on top of the Christmas tree. After all, I want this Christmas to be perfect, Kylie. This Christmas and all the Christmases we will share together here, in our home, for the rest of our lives.

ABOUT THE AUTHOR

Other books by this Author:

Nine Lies and a Truth: Ten Tales of Terror
Clementine and the Gold: The Wayward Wabble
Lenny and the Gold

Shary Caya Lavoie was born in Connecticut. She grew up in Lewiston, Maine. Shary graduated with a Bachelor of Arts Degree in Psychology from the University of Maine at Farmington. She is also a registered nurse; recently retired from a long career in clinical research. Shary has a Master of Arts Degree in Human Services with a Focus on Health and Wellness. She is a veteran of the United States Navy. She and her husband, Bert, have a total of six children and eight grandchildren. She currently resides in Southwest Virginia.

Made in the USA
Columbia, SC
15 December 2024

49503309R00174